HIJACKED

A JACK HUNTER NOVEL

HIJACKED
Brookside Publishing

ISBN: 978-0692283103

Printed in the United States of America

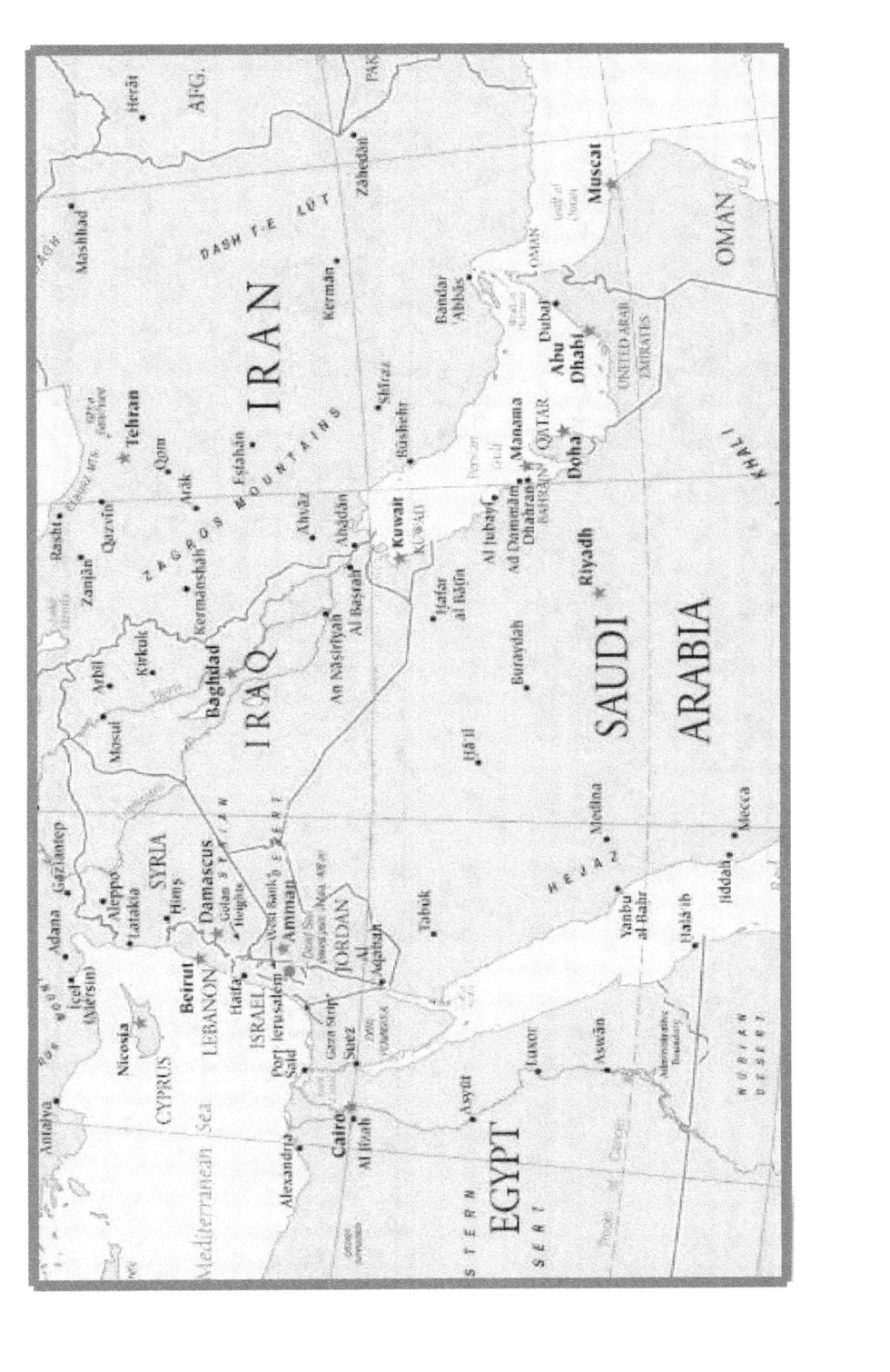

Prologue
November 1914, Cairo Egypt

Addison Devencourt stood on the balcony of his suite at the Gezira Palace Hotel overlooking the evening skyline of Cairo. The suite was elegantly appointed with traditional furniture and included a bedroom, a living room, a dining area and a small kitchenette which made his assignment to Cairo at least tolerable. As Addison surveyed the skyline he decided the fall evenings were still too hot for his liking. Having been born and raised in the British Isles his entire life he has grown accustomed to the harsh winter chill and frequent rains of his English home. From his second floor vantage point the aromas wafting up from the streets below reminded him of the squalor of the old sections of London only worse. It was as if you could smell the age of the city and its inhabitants. Poverty seemed to be everywhere in this flea infested region. The venders below, eager to seek out an existence by selling what little they could from their carts and small shops late into the evening brought to mind the endless struggle to survive in this part of the world. In the distance he could hear what passed for music from the many coffee shops and hookah bars. Never before had he felt so alienated and out of place then he did now compared to his previous assignments given to him as an intern in London by the Foreign Office of Great Britain. As an attaché assigned to the Cairo Embassy and assistant to the British High Commissioner Addison was tasked to seek and to serve the interests of the empire.

During his internship with the Foreign Office Addison enjoyed comfortable assignments in London combined with fine dinner parties, elegant surroundings, lovely ladies and intriguing conversations. Following graduation, his Cambridge classmates all enjoyed the prestige and comfort of posh assignments in London, Paris and America but for his first assignment he was sent to Cairo. He wondered what he had done to deserve this unsung assignment. His orders from director Lord Stephen Talmadge before leaving London were to "seek opportunities and to act in the best interests of the empire" whatever that means. What opportunities were there in this god forsaken land? After all the war effort was thousands of miles away. For a first assignment he felt a little overwhelmed. Addison was sent to Cairo three months ago when England had first declared war with Germany. He tried to discover a reason why he was appointed here rather than a more meaningful location to aid the war. In his youth he was always ready to join a rousing game of rugby and once bloodied the nose of the headmaster's son earning him a reputation as a fearless competitor. At 5 ft. 10 inches and 180 pounds Addison may not have been the biggest student at Cambridge's Government and International Affairs College but he more than made up for it in grit and determination. He reasoned perhaps it was this that won him notice from the chief directorate and his resultant appointment to this forgotten land to which he may yet find a purpose for his presence.

Addison made his way back into his room and poured himself a cup of tea. At least he retained a small measure of culture although the local water did result in a mildly annoying aftertaste. Taking his tea cup with him across the living room he settled comfortably into his leather easy chair and began to think of his young wife Camille whom he left behind already 6 months pregnant that he longed to be with again. They had met his second year at Cambridge. She was the daughter of the local vicar. She indeed was very beautiful and her gentleness, strength of character and Christian witness had a significant impact in changes to his spiritual life. They were together as often as his school schedule and part time job at a local book bindery would allow. They would take turns preparing meals at her father's home and discuss the day's events. Addison looked forward to the time they spent alone in the parlor in the evening. Addison became a devout Christian and valued his relationship with God. He found over time the benefits to his life by being grounded in his faith. They married during his last year at school and looked forward to a life in the diplomatic circles involving travel, dinners and meeting heads of state but this was not to be. Instead he now found himself alone in a forgotten third world nation and yearns for a way to return to England and his wife and soon to be family. The couple agreed that the baby should be born in London where proper medical services were available.

Addison arrives early the next morning at his office in the embassy located at 7 Ahmed Ragheb St, Garden City, in Cairo. The building was in the process of being remodeled which is why Addison had to stay at the Gezira Palace. Hopefully soon residence accommodations would be completed and Camille and the new baby could join him. After settling into his spacious wood paneled office overlooking the open courtyard of the embassy compound and comfortably seating himself behind his oak desk in his padded executive chair he began today like all others by first savoring a fresh cup of tea provided by his secretary Victoria Moore, a pleasant gal from Gloucester whose family has been in service to the crown for two generations. Victoria was pretty and was not an unpleasant distraction for which Addison had to frequently remind himself of Camille and of the work to which he is assigned. This day he begins by reviewing the day's communiques from London along with a briefing of local news and political events prepared by the support staff. Just then Victoria knocks and presents Addison with a message to join Sir Milne Cheetham the British High Commissioner to Egypt in his office at 9:00 AM for a briefing before a later meeting with certain Arab dignitaries. Although not an unusual request Addison made the necessary accommodations to his calendar.

Promptly at 8:55 Addison walks the two doors down the richly appointed and carpeted hallway passed Victoria's reception desk ever mindful to elicit a smile and a nod to her and knocks on the Commissioner's door.

"Come in, come in," bellowed Cheetham as Addison patiently waits outside the door.

"Good morning sir," Addison responds, "how may I assist you today?"

"Addison I'd like to introduce you to Lord Herbert Kitchener. He is the British Military Commander in Chief, sent by the War Department to Egypt to represent Great Britain."

The two men shake hands as Cheetham announces, "Gentlemen, please sit down and make yourselves comfortable." An ornate conference table was centered in the room to which the men availed themselves. Addison always admired Cheetham's corner office. It was decorated with tall windows on two sides, built-in bookcases, paneled walls, wood floors, potted plants and paintings of English sailing ships all designed to remind visiting guests of Britain's wealth and power. Addison made a mental note that someday he too would have an office befitting his station.

"Thank you both for coming. I need to discuss with you a matter that has come to my attention that might be of significant concern to the Empire. As you know this war with Germany will forever change the geo-political structure of the world. Britain must seek and to take advantage of opportunities wherever they present themselves that will insure the health of England and its prosperity and influence in the world far into the future not the least of which is to secure natural resources that will assist in the war effort."

"Are you suggesting there are some untold riches here we are not aware of?" asks Addison.

"That's exactly what I'm suggesting. Now, as you know oil was discovered here in the Middle East in 1905 by an Englishman named William D'Arcy and we are in the process of negotiating trade agreements to secure exploration and production rights but the process is slow. Anything we can do to encourage our Arab friends to work with us in this regard will be of enormous help in winning this war and securing our long term future. In addition I cannot over state our desire to continue to enjoy our access to India for trade and commerce."

"Which is why I believe the foreign office and the war department sent me here to secure these interests" offered Kitchener.

Cheetham continues, "I have received word that a most senior Arab official has requested an audience and I suspect will want to negotiate for military assistance for a campaign to seek their independence from the Turks. As you know the Arab world has been under the thumb of the Ottoman Empire for many years and the Arabs are desperate to throw off the yolk of tyranny and oppression. I believe it may be in our best interests to help them, but we must move cautiously. The Ottoman Empire in Turkey has sided with Germany as you know and if we can get our Arab friends to keep the Turks busy that would free us up to focus on Germany itself. I also firmly believe the foreign office back home will support any agreement or recommendation we make. What do you think Herb?"

"I agree their help in this fight would be welcomed, but can we trust them not to turn those same weapons back on us once they think it is in their best interests? We do not have a long history of dealing with these people and the tenets and customs of their intently religious society may make working with these people a little difficult in the future."

"OK good point. Addison what do you think," queried Cheetham.

"Sir, I agree with you both that we must move cautiously. Let us make them feel we are doing them a favor that way we might avail ourselves to other favorable trading opportunities now and into the future."

"Good idea Addison," said Cheetham.

"Ah sir, do we know any more about the man coming?" asked Addison.

"No I do not know much more other than he is Sharif Hussein bin Ali, king of the Arabs and Emir of Mecca whom I received a telegram from last week announcing his arrival and seeking an audience with us. He is the acknowledged king of numerous tribes and ruler of the Hashemite clan and can claim descent from the family of the prophet Muhammad himself. He is well respected among his people and his word carries a lot of weight in the region. Our intelligence staff has been telling me of this Great Arab Revolt that is building in the region and this is what I suspect is the reason for his visit. He will be here at 11:00 AM. I would like you both to be here to hear what he has to say. We do not have to commit to anything right away."

Cheetham paused to allow further comments from his guests then continued "so, if there is nothing else we will see you both back here at 11:00. Thank you."

Addison slowly walks back to his office, sits at his opulent desk and thinks if this could be the opportunity he was looking for, a chance to orchestrate a significant event to catch the attention of the Foreign Office and warrant a trip back to the real world which he desperately wants. For the rest of the remaining time Addison tries to imagine scenarios of events he could work towards England's favor.

At 10:50 AM Addison walks back down to Cheetham's office and knocks as he gently opens the door.

"Addison. Come on in. We are just getting ready" announces Cheetham.

The three men take neighboring chairs around the table. After a few minutes Victoria knocks, peaks around the door and announces that two guests have arrived. The three men look at each other in surprise.

"By all means show them in Victoria" declares Cheetham.

The two men entered. Both men whore long dark beards and were clothed by the traditional Arab garment of a white thobe robe and keffiyeh head scarf. The tallest and largest man spoke first.

"As-salaam 'alaykum. Sir Milne Cheetham, my name is Abdulla ibn Hussein. I am the eldest son of Sharif Hussein bin Ali who has recently contacted you." Motioning with his right hand "and this is my companion and advisor Muhammad Hamid al-Din."

Cheetham introduces Herb and Addison after which all men warmly shake hands. "Gentlemen, please have a seat. Victoria would you be so kind as to bring our guests some tea and something to eat" Nodding to Abdulla "I am sure they are tired from their long journey"

"Thank you, you are most kind" responded Abdulla.

Once Victoria left and all men were seated Cheetham asks "now, how can the British government be of service to you?"

"Mister Cheetham, thank you for seeing us," began Abdulla, "I know you probably expected my father but hopefully this letter of introduction will satisfy you" as he passes a letter across the table to Cheetham.

The High Commissioner opened the envelope and quietly read the contents.

To Sir Milne Cheetham
The British High Commissioner to Egypt:

Greetings, as-salaam 'alaykum and may God bring blessings upon you and your household. It is most unfortunate that I could not come in person to meet with you as I intended by my telegram last week. Urgent matters prevent me from leaving Mecca at this time. In my stead I have sent my eldest son Abdulla ibn Hussein and my trusted and most senior advisor Muhammad Hamid al-Din. I trust that you would receive them as graciously as you would have myself. I wish through my son to discuss with you matters of grave concern to both our peoples and together it is my prayer that Allah will smile upon us both and grant us victory over our enemies. By this letter I grant full authority to my son Abdulla to enter into any agreement or understanding between us for our mutual benefit. All such agreements will be as binding as if conducted in my presence with you for my son has my blessing and trust. Thank you Sir Milne Cheetham for your trust and support and may Allah watch over you.

The letter was duly signed by Sharif Hussein bin Ali as Emir of Mecca and witnessed by the signature of Abdulla ibn Hussein.

"I am most impressed by your father's confidence in you," begins Cheetham as he passes the letter to Addison, "tell us how we can be of service?"

Abdulla takes a deep breath, straightens his robe, glances at Muhammad and begins. "For many years the Ottoman Empire has oppressed the Arab people. Shortly after 1908 the Ottomans began a policy of Turkish nationalism where non Turkish inhabitants have been overtly discriminated against. Our people have experienced political and cultural persecution. One of the latest intrusions was the construction, in 1908, of a railway from Damascus to al-Medina al-

Munawwara with a planned, although not yet built, extension to Mecca. The supposed purpose of the rail line was to transport pilgrims to Mecca but we see it as a useful tool to transport Ottoman troops and supplies into the Arabian heartland to which we see as a great affront to our people and lands. Commissioner Cheetham, we are a proud and independent people. What we desire is a unified kingdom for the Arab lands and we have come today to seek the support of your country to help us achieve this goal. We are asking for support in the way of arms, supplies and money enough for my father to unite all the Arab clans and tribes to overthrow the Ottomans so we might direct our own future. Will you help us?"

Victoria quietly returns with a tray of fruit and cheese plus a pot of freshly brewed tea and five cups and places the refreshments at the center of the table as she says "Gentlemen please help yourselves."

Cheetham sat for a moment then spoke, "Mister Hussein while your goals are admirable I do not see how this support will be of any benefit to the British Empire."

"Commissioner, we are aware that the Ottoman Empire has aligned itself with Germany and is therefore your enemy also. If we were to aid you by engaging the Turks would this not free your resources to focus on Germany?"

"This is true Mister Hussein but the Turks do not pose much of a threat to England. Our ability to conduct warfare far outpaces theirs. Between our ships, artillery and tanks our war department tells me we could roll through Turkey fairly quickly. Is there another reason we would want to help you obtain this unified kingdom of Arab lands you speak of? And, how do we know this army you will raise up with our help will not turn against us once you get what you want?"

Abdulla responded, "It is true the power and might of England is great but, we can offer you a trade route from the Mediterranean across our lands to the Persian Gulf greatly reducing your travel time to India with which you enjoy a lucrative commerce do you not? In addition as you know oil was discovered in Persia. There are many who believe there is more to be found throughout this region which you may have use for both in your war effort and in the years to come. We would be agreeable to entering discussions for further exploration and production by you on Arab lands. Commissioner, we are a simple people who have lived here in the desert for hundreds of years. We do not have aspirations of a world power. We wish to be left alone to honor the Quran in our everyday lives and be at peace with all. I assure you if we treat each other fairly any agreement we arrive at we have no intension of breaking."

"Mister Hussein, just how much aid and equipment are we talking about" asked Cheetham.

"My father intends to gather together an army made up of all willing men from the tribes and clans from the Arabian Peninsula, Syria and Iraq. We are estimating, if successful, to have a total of 25,000 men, more if we add Ottoman deserters and any assistance we can obtain from Egypt through you. We may not be trained infantry soldiers but we have intimate knowledge of the desert and we fight for our land and way of life. May Allah be praised."

"Mister Kitchener," asked Cheetham using his formal name for the benefit of their gusts, "do we have sufficient resources we might avail to our Arab friends?"

"I believe we do have arms in reserve of sufficient number that might be acquired. We will be looking at rifles, smokeless powder ammunition, artillery, food, medical supplies plus money for the troops.

The five men went on to discuss other minor details of resources, regional participation members and battle tactics after which Cheetham declared "OK, I think that covers it, thank you for your candor Mister Hussein, we have much to consider and discuss among ourselves. I will also need to confer any final decision with our Foreign Office back in London you understand. Will you be available here in Cairo for a few more days so that we may conclude any agreement between our peoples?"

"My father wishes for us to return in two days to begin to assist in convincing the tribes to unite as one in our quest but, we are willing to stay a few days longer if this means securing a favorable agreement."

"Excellent, then we will send word to you when we have prepared our official response to your request. I assume you are staying at the Gezira Palace Hotel as is some of our staff?"

"Yes, we will await your call. Until then. Good day and may Allah be with you." answered Abdulla.

As the two men left the room the three remaining Englishmen sat quietly for a few moments to ensure their guests have clearly departed. Cheetham was the first to speak.

"Well gentlemen, what do you think?"

Lord Kitchener began. "I believe an opportunity has presented itself that could offer long reaching benefits for the empire. For a relatively small amount of resources we could equip the local clans to occupy the Turks and hopefully defeat them while we concentrate on Germany itself. It's a win-win plus the good will of the people we obtain plus the political capitol we attain with the ruling class will only aid us in the future."

"I agree," echoes Addison "but we have not dealt with these people very long. As Abdulla said they just want to be left alone to practice their faith. What if they see us as an intrusion upon their faith at some point? Our relationship has never been really tested. Can we trust them to not turn on us in the future? Perhaps we should be looking for some type of assurances from them now. Other than the promises they made we have nothing of substance while we are giving significant money and supplies for their benefit."

Commissioner Cheetham sat for a moment contemplating the comments from his staff before speaking. "You both have expressed noteworthy opinions and I find value in each. These are indeed changing times that could impact events far into the future. So much so that I believe the risk is worth it. I will contact London to share these latest developments and recommend we proceed. I believe they will concur with our decision as they have in the past relying upon our judgment in local matters. Addison if you believe a recompense of some type is reasonable at this point perhaps you could put some ideas together tonight. Let us meet back here tomorrow to finalize our response. Gentlemen, thank you that will be all."

Addison walks back to his office and for the rest of the afternoon tries to imagine a suitable means of compensation for the empire, one readily affordable by the Arabs yet not egregious enough to cancel the deal or leave the empire in a position of anything other than a benefactor to the Arab people.

Addison decides to have dinner in his room, later that night, rather than suffer the congestion and noise prevalent in the hotel's main dining hall as he had much to think about. Frequently he would share diner with Milne Cheetham or other members of the embassy staff to maintain relationships or to gather information of any kind. Some men spoke of the rich and colorful nightlife in Cairo or of interesting persons they met, others spoke of missed loved ones left behind in England. As Addison was reviewing war reports from London, following his late dinner, he begins to think more of the days meeting with their two Arab guests. The agreement discussed seemed very favorable to both parties. For a few thousand guns and supplies the Arabs could keep the Turks busy while England focused on Germany, plus by creating allies in the region inroads into other matters of national concern could be made at a later date. While pondering the implications of the day's events Addison peers out his bedroom window which overlooks the garden courtyard. Being as he was only on the second floor he could clearly see a man nervously pacing about below. Though dressed in the traditional Arab garb Addison is able to recognize him as Muhammad Hamid al-Din whom he had met earlier that day. As he curiously watched the man Addison could clearly tell that Muhammad was seriously troubled by something. His pacing was short and crisp as he shook his head from side to side. Addison watched for some time before finally deciding to go down and approach the man to inquire of his welfare.

Addison left his room, descended the hotel staircase, exited the courtyard doors and quietly approached the man. "Good evening Muhammad what brings you out this late in the evening? Is everything alright?"

As Addison approached the man stopped and stared at him. "I do not wish to burden you with my troubles Mister Devencourt."

"Please, call me Addison. How can I be of assistance to you?"

"I am afraid Allah has found me unworthy in some manner and has begun me on a path I do not wish to take."

"Now, now Muhammad things cannot be as bad as all that. Tell you what, come upstairs to my room and have some tea with me and I'm sure we can sort this all out. After all we are now partners of a sort and partners help each other. Do they not? We both desire our agreement discussed today to be successful and if that means making adjustments or even attending to matters unrelated we wish to be of help if we can. Please come upstairs."

"You are most kind but I do not know what you can do to help. I will come."

The two men quietly walked through the lobby and up the stairs to Addison's room. After entering the living room Addison led the man to a sofa and soon returned from the small kitchen area with a fresh pot of tea. After pouring two cups and seating himself across from the man Addison began.

"So, please tell me what is troubling you. Speak freely you are among friends."

After taking a long drink of tea the man began. "This is a matter that brings shame to not only my house but brings dishonor to Sharif Hussein bin Ali himself. It troubles me to even speak of it."

"Muhammad, if I am to help you must trust me and tell me everything."

"Very well, this is a problem for which I see no resolution. Earlier this evening after my evening meal with Abdulla where we discussed plans on uniting the tribes Abdulla decided to remain in his room to pray and be with his thoughts. I decided to visit a nearby hookah lounge to enjoy the evening's entertainment over a cup of coffee. I have been told the women who dance here are the most captivating and alluring in all the Middle East. As I watched one woman in particular caught my eye and I hers. On more than one occasion she would dance before me at my table. I asked her to join me at my table for coffee to which she readily agreed. One thing led to another and agreed to accompany me back to my room for a more private visit.

Once there she soon demanded money. I told her I do not have money for this. She became angry and hit me. I pushed her away she fell and hit her head on the corner of a small table. She bled heavily and I could not wake her. I think she is dead. She is still there and I do not know what to do. A scandal such as this would be disastrous to Sharif's plans."

"But why is this so disastrous? It was an accident although a serious one. Will not the truth prevail?"

"You do not understand Addison. The woman was Sunni. Sharif will not prevail in his goal if he does not have the support of all tribes especially the Sunni. They will not listen to the truth, they will see only the murder of one of their own at the hands of the Hashemite Family. If Sharif is unsuccessful in his plan we will forever be under the thumb of the Turks. For this heinous act of mine I also fear for my life which I would gladly forfeit if I could right this wrong. There is only one course I can take and that is to tell Abdulla everything and see if we may yet convince the tribes. Perhaps their desire for unity and freedom exceeds their desire for honor and retribution or perhaps I can offer my life as payment for their continued support."

Addison thought quickly for alternatives that may yet prove a winning outcome for all sides including England. "Allow me to offer an alternative that will prove beneficial in solving the problem at hand and yet may save the day. You must trust me when I say we have a very talented staff in these matters and I trust their abilities implicitly. First off, the women is dead and we can do nothing to help her but I will send our people to your room to remove the body without anyone seeing them then have them clean the room of all traces of the women's presence and accident. I will have them dispose of the body where it will never be found. Many saw the two of you leave together from the bar and my people will say they saw her leave your room alone shortly thereafter. You therefore cannot be tied to her disappearance. Your mission will go on as if this unpleasant business never happened. How does this sound to you?"

Muhammad looked directly into Addison's eyes for a few moments then responded, "You can truly do this?"

Addison quickly thought that this could be the opportunity he had hoped for. A twist of fate had presented itself that would propel him back to stellar graces with the Foreign Office and a trip back to England but he must obtain something of value to England from the Arabs. To do this he must play upon the fears and insecurities of the other man and the notion that the only thing that mattered was the success of the mission of the two Arabs. The man was in a vulnerable state of mind and cared more for his king's plan for all Arabs than for his own life. Addison realized Muhammad could be easily manipulated if he could guarantee success in the man's mission to Cairo but he must put something in place quickly while the man was in turmoil and not thinking clearly. "Yes we can do this but we must move quickly. You must stay here for now. I will alert my people of what they must do immediately and return shortly."

Addison left a hopeful Muhammad and went to his bedroom to call the embassy's chief of intelligence and related the story with directions to secretly dispose of the body immediately far out into the Mediterranean and to sterilize the room.

When this was done Addison returned to his living room where he found a worried Muhammad staring into space. He sat down next to the man and placed his hand on the man's shoulder to comfort him. After a moment of quietly consoling the man he said "do not be worried my friend, all will be as we planned. You will get your arms and supplies, you will unite the tribes and you will be victorious over the Turks, you will be a hero to your people and this nasty business will all be forgotten in a short time. Your life will not be forfeit nor your family disgraced."

Muhammad sat still for a short time in thought and finally said "yes, I must look at the greater good for all Arabs. I am still very much troubled and am unsure of the correct path to take but I agree the greater mission must go forward and if Allah so wishes it then it will succeed. Let it be as you say."

"Very good" returned Addison "now there is one remaining thing you must do to complete our plan and safeguard the future of your people."

"And what would that be?" queried Muhammad.

Addison new the man was preoccupied with the ramifications of the nights events and was not thinking clearly and was relying upon this fact to convince the man that this next step was the right thing to do. This was the opportunity he was waiting for.

"It is a small matter really but one which will protect your people and provide security for mine along with a legal means for England to provide for and protect your people into the future. I will prepare a document that will convey all rights and interests of the Arabian Peninsula to England so that it will become as a protectorate of England. England has no intention of taking over your land and this is just a temporary understanding I assure you. Think of this as insurance such that if, however unlikely, you do not prevail against the Turks they will not be able to drive you from your land as England will then have the right to challenge their victory over you and as we said earlier today we can easily defeat the Turks so that you will maintain a homeland forever more in a united kingdom. We will have fortified our relationship with your people and have provided for a long term access to India again as we discussed earlier today. We both win. I will prepare the document and you will need to have Abdulla sign it tonight. Will you be able to do this?"

Muhammad began to see Addison as a trusted friend, one that has saved the mission entrusted to him that was severely marred by his thoughtless indiscretion. Yes I will convince Abdulla tonight.

"Excellent," began Addison, "I will go now to prepare the document that will protect all our futures" you may relax here and rejoice in knowing that Allah's mercy is still upon you."

With Muhammad finally relaxed Addison went to his bedroom desk to retrieve some official embassy stationary and began to create the deed transferring the Arabian Peninsula from king Sharif Hussein bin Ali by way of Abdulla ibn Hussein to Great Britain. Returning a short time later to Muhammad Addison handed him the document and said "go quickly and convince Abdulla to sign this for the good of your mission and of a unified kingdom of Arab lands. My people have begun cleaning your room and tomorrow I will convince our leadership to support your cause in full."

Late that evening Muhammad returned with the signed document. Addison told him to go and rest, all will be taken care of and we will meet tomorrow to finalize our aide agreement to your people. Addison felt great relief and pride in his accomplishment and sat for some time enjoying the moment and began to entertain thoughts of his new life once again in England. After a while however feelings of betrayal and deceit began to seep into his heart. As he pondering the events and his actions this evening he penned a heartfelt letter to his wife:

> *My dearest Camille, a day does not go by when I do not think of you and how much I miss not being with you. The thought of not seeing you and our new child or seeing him take his first steps fills me with great despair. So it is with both excitement and regret that I write to you and tell of the latest developments in my service to the crown here in Cairo. I believe I have found a way to not only return to England very soon but to do so by also bringing great honor to myself and our family and much strategic advantage to the empire. An opportunity has presented itself whereby I have convinced the King of the Arabs to transfer all rights to the Arabian Peninsula to England in return for our offering our protection to his people from the Turks. This welcome achievement is not without a misgiving that lies heavily upon my heart. I fear the lost days we have spent apart has at times clouded my judgment and I have placed my selfish desire to be with you once again ahead of the tenants of our faith. For it is by less than honest means that I was able to have these men agree to this transaction which comprises the essence of my sin and sorrow in this matter. Tomorrow I will begin the journey back to England with the deed and letter of authenticity. Perhaps yet all things will work together for good and this deed will not become the instrument of my destruction nor a thorn*

between our peoples but an instrument of peace. Please pray for me.

Your Loving Husband

Addison
May God have mercy

Addison prepares the letter to be mailed the next day and prepares a second note to Sir Milne Cheetham the British High Commissioner to offer his apology for his urgent return to London for personal reasons and again relates his total support for the Arab cause and recommends England's support as discussed earlier. Next he places the signed deed and authorization letter passed to him earlier by Cheetham in a sealed leather pouch to which he will secure to his torso beneath his shirt with a strap.

Addison rose early the next day and begins to pack a few belongings. The conflict within him, as explained in the letter to his wife, is beginning to take its toll as he begins to question his actions and his own moral character. Addison knew that what he was doing was wrong. Never before had he had to shoulder the dire consequences of the results of his actions of this magnitude. He tells himself that this was war and actions taken for the good of the empire were all that mattered and was this not why he was sent to Egypt, to support the interests of the empire? But what weighed heaviest on his mind and caused him the most pain was thoughts of what Camille would think of his actions. He knew that she would feel disappointment in the choices he now made and for not adhering to the tenants of their faith and of not being a righteous and honorable man, still the die has been cast he had to see it through. But these arguments did little to quell the turmoil within and he was determined to resolve this conflict in his mind and heart before reaching England. He prayed that it would work out for the best.

Descending the grand stair case to the lobby he approached the front desk and gave the letter he wrote for Cheetham to the manager with directions to deliver it to the embassy as soon as possible and to mail the letter to his wife and then to order him a cab. There was little traffic at this hour which enabled him to run quickly to the embassy. Entering the embassy Addison showed his security I.D. to the marine guard and entered the building. On the lower level in the east wing was the legal department where Addison was able to convince the sole clerk to notarize the signed document without actually witnessing the signatures, another infraction he prayed would not haunt him. Placing the now legally approved documents in his leather pouch he raced back to the hotel just in time to catch his cab and directed the driver to take him to the harbor and to the nearest passenger steam ship line.

By mid-morning the Cairo port was a bustling conglomerate of activity and humanity. Venders, merchants, travelers and dock workers scurrying about seeking out a living or conducting their private affairs all oblivious to the maelstrom of war soon to cover the region. As Addison watched them he envied them in that none experienced the pangs and burden of responsibility he now felt. Part of him wished to trade places with the least of them just to relieve himself of the weight of his conscience. The cab driver stopped at the passenger terminal and directed Addison to the ticket window. Fortunately a liner was scheduled to leave within the hour and he was able to purchase one of the last remaining tickets to Naples. Addison planned to sail to Naples, as Italy had not yet joined the war, then travel by train to Paris and then on to the coast and finally a short ferry across the channel to home. He reasoned a train across the continent was quicker than to sail around the coast to England.

At the appointed time the liners whistle blew signaling the boarding process where he joined the hoard of travelers and ascended the gangway. Clutching his belongings tightly against himself he navigates his way through the bustling crowd and quickly found his cabin avoiding eye contact and interaction with crewmen and passengers as much as possible. He purposely did not purchase first class accommodations as he wanted this trip to be as unassuming as possible. Addison took most of his meals in his cabin and rarely ventured out on deck so as to maintain his anonymity not to mention his preoccupation of safeguarding the two documents he now held close to his bosom. His evenings were spent in further contemplation of his deed and thoughts of his wife. The two realities warred constantly in his mind. He was a man torn between serving his country fully with no reservations and being the man of principal his wife looked up to and fell in love with. It was a struggle of immense proportion in his mind that began to affect his hold on reality. Periodically during his infrequent forays on deck, for much needed air, men of Arab decent would make eye contact with him. As feelings of guilt welled up and consumed his mind he imagined them passing judgment of betrayal upon him further heightening his anxiety. Each time Addison would return to his cabin in a cold sweat.

Arriving in Naples Addison gathered his bag ever remembering to touch the leather pouch fixed to his body to insure its presence and leaves his cabin. Embarking quickly and hailing a cab to take him to the train station he begins to feel more at ease the closer he gets to England. Addison purchased a first class single sleeping berth in the first car behind the locomotive as he felt the sooner he got to Paris the better as if its position in the train had any real impact on travel time. As the train left Naples on its way through the Alps Addison spent most of his time alone in his room again safeguarding the documents and admiring the country side through the large viewing window. He felt a greater relief just knowing he was back in Europe. The uphill journey was relatively slow but relaxing. Addison watched the lush countryside roll by mile after mile and he began to allow his thoughts to turn to Camille and of their soon to be reunion back in London. This allowed a measure of peace and long awaited sleep to finally wash over him.

Early the next evening he could feel the grade increase on the tracks and new they were approaching the final climb into the Alps. Snow now covered the ground and the boughs of the trees. The air was noticeably colder the higher the train progressed into the Alps. Addison began to hear excited chatter in the aisle outside his door. Passengers were racing to and fro, anxious voices filled the air. Addison gently opened his door and stopped a conductor attempting to calm the excited throng and asked the reason for the disturbance. The conductor informed him that German troops have crossed over into Northern Italy in an attempt to flank French forces protecting their boarder with Germany. He was told not to worry the train would be through the Alps by morning. A new flood of anxiety began to fill Addison's mind. He began to worry if the train is stopped or attacked what will happen to him and his documents.

The train rolls on gradually ascending the grade into the Alps. Addison decides not to retire to bed this night but to remain dressed and be ready to respond in all likelihood of a German attack on the train. He continues to clutch the pouch beneath his shirt as he strains to look out the window of his berth for signs of troops but sees only the now snow covered forested mountains. Mile after mile the train chugs on and his anxiety once again builds with each mile. His troubled mind once consumed with thoughts of betrayal returns but now also is consumed with fears for his life. His fate was now out of his hands. Addison prays "please dear lord take this cup from me so I may once again see my wife and child but not my will but yours be done." Addison sat still looking out the window of his darkened birth having left the light off to aide his vision of the countryside and what lies ahead.

Late that evening, still ascending deeper into the mountains, he could see the train about to pass over a bridge spanning a gorge and instinctively tightened his grip on the arms of his cabin's sofa. He emits a slight sigh of relief as the locomotive and his car pass the upper bridge abutment when a large explosion rocks the entire train and jolts him from his seat. He can hear passengers screaming, glass breaking and brakes squealing as the train shudders to a halt. Addison quickly lowers his window and looks out to find the center section of the bridge and train missing, plummeting downward to the rocky gorge below erupting in a ball of fire. The car directly behind his has its rear wheels already out in space being pulled into the void by the car still attached behind it. The two cars being dragged into the abyss begin to pull his car and the locomotive back with them further and further toward the yawning chasm. Addison races from his berth leaving all but his precious documents behind. As he reaches the landing between his car and the locomotive a second explosion erupts and collapses the remaining section of bridge holding the train. The explosion causes Addison to be hurled away from the train onto the rocky upper slope of the gorge as he watches the remaining cars and locomotive fall away in a fiery explosion of twisted steal and hot steam. In the distance he can hear the voices of German soldiers and the firing of rifles at survivors below. Addison now bruised and bloodied from flying glass and being tossed upon the rocky terrain knows he must hide and find shelter quickly to survive the night. Taking a quick inventory that no bones are broken but does notice the lacerations to his face and arms he begins to climb out of the rocky gorge to seek temporary shelter in the trees. Dragging himself up the final few yards of rocky terrain and nearing the tree line shots ring out and he is hit in the right rear shoulder with an 8.2mm spitzer round from a German Gewehr 88 which felt like being hit with a sledge hammer. The impact spun him around and he falls to the ground. Though not a fatal wound he quickly rises and forces himself to stagger into the trees. He can feel the sticky wetness running down his arm and realizes he must do something to stem the loss of blood or all is lost. Addison staggers further into the woods attempting to put as much distance as he can between himself and the Germans. His physical conditioning playing sports in school becomes an aide and enables him to advance a few kilometers from the attach site. He decides to trek to a lower elevation as walking uphill would consume too much precious energy and besides the higher he walks the colder it would get. Trying to maintain as much body warmth as possible but becoming weak from the loss of blood he notices a monastery in a clearing. Approaching the monastery he first sees the chapel and decides to rest there to warm up as best he can and to attend to his wound. He enters the church and locks quickly for anyone that might come to his aide. Finding no one he sits near the front and rips his shirt to make a tourniquet in an attempt to bind the wound and stop the bleeding. As Addison ponders his fate he comes to realize his life has come full circle. Those few years ago when through Camille his faith began followed by his time spent striving toward earthly gains only to find him at the end sitting once again in God's house. Addison finally comes to realize that his true course is to trust in God. Just as Muhammad Hamid al-Din left his actions in God's hands just a few days ago so too does Addison.

Leaving the pouch "in God's hands" he makes his way out of the church staggering through the falling snow as he hears the voices of the German soldiers getting ever closer. Now very week from the loss of blood and with each step seeming to be his last he looks desperately to find someone to help him hide and care for his wounds. But his plans were not to be. Traveling only a short distance he hears the voice of a German soldier "aufhalten." Addison tries to get away but receives another 8.2mm round to his right thigh. Addison's legs collapse beneath him no longer possessing the strength to carry him. As Addison lays face down upon the cold snowy ground he hears the approach of the German soldier. He says a final prayer to God asking for forgiveness of his sin of pride and blind ambition and prays that his selfish deed may yet be used for good. He prays for his wife that she may find comfort and peace in life. The soldier raises his rifle and all goes black.

Chapter 1
Arabian Sea, Today

The morning sea was calm. Before the sun had a chance to heat the air and begin the daily breezes that caused the swells to grow, the early hours gave a placid appearance to the surface of the water. Early morning was his favorite time of day to be on deck. Well, actually standing on the wing outside the bridge with the beginnings of the day's breeze in his hair, the new morning sun on his face and a hot cup of coffee in his hand. Captain Benjamin Hitchcock was pure Navy, a graduate of Annapolis now serving his third tour of duty and his first command. An officer who took his duties seriously with a keen eye for detail and a thorough knowledge of the ship's systems and who was respected and liked by his crew. He had lobbied hard with the Navy brass for this assignment and was committed to its success.

Captain Hitchcock was also a devout family man. Leaving his wife and young daughter behind in Norfolk for nine months was the hardest thing he had to do. But being a Navy family they realized this was his job and they must support each other. The last six months before sea trials began was one of the happiest times in their lives. They spent each day together. Little Jamie loved to help her daddy barbecue hot dogs and hamburgers in the back yard. "Daddy I want the one with the tiger stripes" six year old Jamie would say noticing the burn marks the grill would leave on the hotdogs.

Summertime was spent listening to the free evening concerts on the Virginia Beach boardwalk. Ben would carry his young daughter home at night amazed at how heavy she seemed when she was asleep only to start the next day wide awake. "Where are we going today daddy?" His loving wife June would only smile and shake her head. "You two." was all she would say knowing full well that the love they shared together was a bond that could not be broken. Ben and his wife and family would make the most of each day knowing he would soon have to leave. Finally the day came for deployment with shared mixed emotions. Ben was excited for taking his first command but sorry to be leaving his family behind. He knew he would be missing out on the joys of being a part of his young daughter's life on a daily basis. Times he knew he would never see again. But until his tour was over he took some measure of solace in knowing they could still communicate by video conferencing every other day from his ship. The last day in port was especially trying for the Hitchcocks. As June and Jamie left Ben off at the gate of the ship yard Jamie gave him a big hug and with tears in her eyes said "come home to us daddy we love you."

Although not the biggest ship in America's inventory, the *USS Nathanael Greene* was, at this stage of America's war on terror, an integral part of the intelligence gathering function for potential threats to the nation. Following the curtailing of NSA electronic listening activities on US soil over the outrage by American citizens the US Navy brass along with members of congress assigned to the House Armed Services Committee were able to secure funding, a few years ago, for the design and construction of a ship to serve a unique and special purpose. As a result, the *USS Nathanael Greene* was built as an Aegis class destroyer equipped with both ELINT and SIGINT capabilities. Never again would the US Navy repeat an incident like the seizure of the *USS Pueblo* in 1968 by North Korea. For this reason it was decided that electronic and signal intelligence gathering ships off foreign shores were to be more than adequate of defending themselves. With its powerful 6 megawatt AN/SPY-1 radar and MK 99 Fire Control System the *Nathanael Greene* was more than capable to defend itself utilizing various missile systems and Phalanx guns against any threat from land, sea or air.

The current mission for this unique and powerful ship was to monitor all Middle East phone, internet, satellite uplink, radio or video signal communications over a broad band of frequencies. The digital world made eavesdropping all the more viable method of gathering intel foreign or domestic. Powerful and sophisticated computer systems would translate and decode signals and look for preselected names, phrases and words that might denote a potential threat and thus warrant concern and further investigation. Once these intercepts denoting a potential threat were discovered and verified by highly trained operators the information was encoded and sent directly to Navy Intelligence before being sent on to NSA/CSS for concurrence and further threat analysis. The National Security Agency and Central Security Service combined this new information with information received from field agents and other strategically based intelligence organizations to make the final determination of threat level and magnitude of the threat.

One last deep breath of clear sea air and a sip of his coffee Captain Hitchcock stepped onto the bridge and stood next to his XO Lieutenant Commander James Toliver. As Commanding Officer, Ben was able to hand pick his Executive Officer and chose "Jim" having served together on previous deployments where the two nurtured a mutual trust and respect that sometimes allowed for lax informality.

"Jim, what have we got"?

"Helmsman report."

"Sir, course and speed is 084^0 at 24 knots, we are approximately 150 nautical miles off the south coast of Yemen.

"Captain all systems report normal operation and no aircraft within 100 nautical mile radius. Surface radar reports one commercial fishing vessel 10 nautical miles off our port bow."

"Steady as she goes Jim."

"Aye, sir"

The *USS Nathanael Greene* has two nerve centers tasked with conducting the two main functions of the ship. The combat information center or CIC is located directly behind the bridge and one deck below. It controls all the Aegis offense and defensive weapon systems and is basically the sharp stick that shouts do not mess with us. Directly behind the CIC is the main AN/SPY-1 radar. The second and larger operations section serves the electronic intelligence gathering function located aft of the main radar and is comprised itself of two sections. The first section contains the crew tasked with monitoring and recording all signal transmissions and the second houses the highly sophisticated computer systems necessary to listen and decode land, sea or air based transmissions. The unique and advanced antenna system necessary to support this function was located directly above both sections.

The mess hall aboard the *Nathanael Greene* was always a hotbed of activity. Crew members either coming off a shift or starting a shift were always sure to take advantage of the commitment the Navy made to feed their members well. The mess hall was a place all crew members could come at any time day or night for something to eat or drink. The origins of the word "mess" comes from an Old French word "mes" which means "food portion" which itself comes from the Latin word "mittere" which means "to put" and "to send" combining the two to form the meaning "to put food on the table". In the 13th century "mess" was used to refer to liquid or cooked dishes. By about the 15th century the word evolved to describe any groups of people who dinned together. The military establishment which prides itself on tradition has kept the word as part of their standard vocabulary referring to a "mess hall."

Bobby Silas made his way into the mess hall in anticipation of starting his day as senior signal analyst. "Hey Darin, what's happening?"

Darin Cooper, the radar intercept operator assigned to the CIC was already seated and enjoying his tray of pancakes, bacon, eggs and a big glass of milk. Darin hailed from the mid-west and was raised on big breakfasts. "Most important meal of the day" he would always say.

Bobby Silas grew up in Atlanta in a large working class family. He had two sisters and one brother. The three siblings liked to tease each other every chance they got growing up but never forgot the love and respect each had for the other caringly taught to them by their mother's tender example.

Both men met at the US Navy basic training class at Foss Park North of Chicago and became instant friends sharing similar interests in sports, hunting and music. Time off together during basic training usually meant site seeing and sharing a beer. Following basic training the two separated for further training in their respective chosen fields. Darin chose weapons systems training and became the Aegis Weapon

System radar operator while Bobby chose information warfare training and became senior signal analyst aboard the *Nathanael Greene*. Both men had worked their way up to the rank of Petty Officer, Second Class. It was just by chance that both men were assigned to the same ship and were happy to renew their friendship.

"Hey Bobby, not much, come on over".

Bobby got his tray of chow and worked his way over to Darin's table. "Did you see the game last night on the TV?" he said.

"Yeah did I, made 10 bucks off seaman Atwood."

Both men chuckled.

"Hey Bobbie, you being a good southern boy and all, I'll give your Falcons ten points against my Broncos next Sunday. Whatdaya say?"

"I'll think about it. I'm trying to save some money each month to send home to my mom. She's having a hard time making ends meet. After my dad passed away my younger brother is the only man in the family but he's only 16. My older sister has a part-time job and my mom still works check out at the grocery but it's not enough. My youngest sister is only 10. They need me."

"I hear ya man. Say remember my uncle Jim I told you about the one with the trucking business in Reynolds Town just east of downtown Atlanta? He's always looking for good help. How about I put a good word in for your sister? can't hurt."

"Thanks man I appreciate it. Send me his name and address and stuff. I'll forward it to my sister to follow up. Thanks again."

"No problem. What are friends for?"

"So Darin, how have things been going up in the guns and ammo department?"

"All's quiet on the western front man. But on the news last night they were talking about some al-Qaeda cells stirring up the mobs in Cairo with their normal death to America chants. It seems this whole place is going down the tubes fast. Anything can happen. How are things up in the sneak and peak department? Did I ever tell you you could get arrested back in the states for being a peeping tom listening in on others phone calls?"

The two men lived to razz each other as a way of showing friendship and as a way to reduce workplace tension. Bobby responded "yeah but at least I don't make bad jokes about the size of my missile like you guys up in the CIC."

"Ugh, you got me. On that note it's time to take my leave. My shipmates await my dazzling talents to once again save the world."

"Don't trip over your cape on the way out. By the way you want to catch dinner tonight before the movie?"

"See you there cowboy."

Darin left the mess and headed up to his station in the CIC eager to start the day's shift. Bobby left a few minutes later and headed up to the "spook territory" to begin his day. For the past two weeks Bobby had been cataloging increased email and phone traffic of sufficient nature to suggest a major terrorist operation is in the planning stages and for which he has been sending copies including reports back to the ONI or Office of Naval Intelligence in Suitland Maryland. He was eager to see what had transpired since his last shift. Upon logging in to his station Bobby reviewed the ELINT traffic recorded the previous night.

Previously the NSA, on American soil, was only permitted to record the phone numbers, time and length of calls between parties and required a court order to review the actual conversation after proving probable cause to a federal judge. This activity was terminated by the American people when abuses were discovered hence the creation of the *Nathanial Greene* operating in foreign waters.

The engineers at Systems Dynamics who built and programmed the computer system, nicknamed ESRAD for Enhanced Signal Recognition and Decoding, did a masterful job at creating a system that can monitor simultaneously thousands of transmissions. Through its database of known terrorist names and aliases plus a listing of selected code words and phrases the system can compile in real time an ongoing potential threat analysis all while translating the voice or data from its original language into English. In addition the system is designed such that if a selected phrase or suspects name is identified and recorded for analysis Bobby has the opportunity to review each selected data segment where he can then request the computer to play for him the entire message so as to verify the context of the message to determine the threat level before passing it on to ONI.

As Bobby begins to read the listing of intercepts from the previous night recorded by the system he notices a phone conversation between a man identified as Utep, which the system identifies as an alias of Azzir Kelil, a known terrorist found complicit in numerous previous attacks on American interests in the region, and another man discussing plans to destroy America. He calls up the original complete recording to determine the full conversation. While alarmed at his discovery and studying his screen the officer of the watch, lieutenant Somers, approaches.

"Petty Officer Silas, what do you have?"

"Lieutenant, sir we have a significant and verified finding of a serious threat. I have a cell phone recording from a known terrorist discussing an impending operation. As you know for the past few weeks we have been hearing disturbing language suggesting something was in the works, now we have confirmation."

"Let's hear it." Bobby replays the entire message for the lieutenant before he says "good job Petty Officer, wrap it up and send it on."

"Aye, Sir."

Up in the CIC Darin is manning his radar screen looking for threats. Since putting to sea three months ago he has not seen one unidentified contact. Jokingly he wishes to himself that he sees something to bring some excitement to an otherwise uneventful mission.

Not far away Bobby continues to monitor the selected voice and signal data collected by the computer and begins to notice an unusual high frequency data signal. The strength of the signal suggests its origin is quite close, as close as ten miles. The computer identifies the signal as telemetry data.

"Ah lieutenant, I've got a strange signal coming in. Computer shows it to be a telemetry signal for some vehicle but I've not been briefed on any flights in the area."

The officer walks over and stands behind Bobby to look at the raw data and the computers interpretation of the signal. "I agree it does look suspicious. Call up to the CIC and see if they have picked up any strange bogies."

"Aye sir." Bobby picks up his phone to call Darin. "Hey Darin I need your help with a little problem."

"Hey buddy you got some bugs talking to you through that fancy computer system?"

"No not exactly but I would like you to check on something for me. I'm receiving a telemetry signal from a fairly close source but I'm not aware of any scheduled flights in the area. What are you showing on your radar for contacts?"

"Hold on let me recheck my air search radar. No, no contacts showing up. Let me check the surface search radar. Sorry Bobby I got nothing showing up in the air and I'm still only seeing what seems to be a small fishing trawler, which I reported to the bridge last hour, approximately 10 nautical miles out bearing 015^0."

"Darin this is really strange. Keep a look out this should not be happening. Bobby out."

Back on the bridge the Captain and the XO continue to scan the horizon with binoculars as Seaman First Class Eric Dobler mans the helm.

A few minutes later Darin observes a brief blip on his air search radar of a contact but it disappears as quickly as it appeared. Darin calls over the lieutenant. "Lieutenant, for just an instant I showed a contact but it quickly disappeared." As the two men stared at the screen..."look there it is again. And now it's gone."

The lieutenant thought for a moment before responding. "See if you can adjust the gain on your signal and reduce your sweep angle to focus in on that area to try to reestablish contact in the meantime report intermittent contact to the bridge."

"Aye sir."

As the XO hangs up the phone he turns to the Captain. "Captain, CIC says we have an intermittent unidentified contact bearing 350^0 on an intercept course range 60 nautical miles."

Both men turn their glasses to port and begin to scan the sky. Finding nothing the Captain orders "XO, have CIC use the fire control radar to see if they can get a better read on that contact."

"Aye sir." A few moments he reports back. "No luck Sir. Air space is showing clear. Perhaps it was just a glitch."

"Perhaps you're right. Everyone keep a sharp look out."

As the minutes ebb no new information was forthcoming until the helmsman announces "ah Captain what is that dark object on the port side headed this way."

Both officers instantly turn their glasses to view the possible threat. Captain Hitchcock grabs for the phone and keys the CIC. "I got a visual on a bogie coming in hot on our port side. Launch SAMs and activate Phalanx guns."

Lieutenant Somers answers back "sir our screens are blank. We show no aircraft in the area. There is nothing the MK Fire Control System can lock weapons onto. All systems require a radar lock to control firing response. Even the self-contained targeting system on the Phalanx Gatling guns show no target and cannot be operated manually."

It took ten additional seconds for the weapon to reach the *USS Nathanael Greene.* Contact was made amidship five feet above the deck directly below the main AN/SPY-1 radar antenna. The resulting explosion from the ten pounds of semtex contained in the war head resulted in the complete destruction of both the CIC and the ELINT and SIGINT command centers. The resulting fires quickly spread and upon reaching the liquid missile propellant produced a secondary explosion which destroyed the remainder of the ships armament. It took the remaining crew five hours to get the fire under control. A number of crew members were trapped below decks as a result of the initial explosion and subsequent fires. The final report filed days later listed 53 men perished, 42 more required hospitalization and 5 were listed unaccounted for. The Captain transmitted an urgent may day following the initial explosion before subsequent explosions and fire consumed the bridge and its complement of officers and crew. Help arrived as soon as possible and the injured were air lifted out to the nearest ship 250 miles away. The remaining crew managed to help the Nathanael Greene limp back to its port in Aden.

Chapter 2
The White House

At 1:00 AM the phone rings at the President's bedside table. President Gordon Hatch turns in bed and answers softly not wishing to wake his wife. Due to the rigors of his position he regularly retires late into the evening and rises early each morning yet still attempts to get as much rest as he can in the few hours available each night. Annoyed by the interruption he manages to answer the phone professionally.

"What is it?"

"Mr. President it's Bob Hammond. I'm sorry to awaken you but one of our ships was just attacked in the Arabian Sea."

Bob Hammond was the Secretary of Defense and the President's first choice for the job. Hammond served on the House Armed Services Committee as a Congressman for six years when the President was a senior Senator from Wyoming. The two collaborated on numerous defense bills and became close friends.

"Wait a moment Bob let me get this in the other room." The President quickly dons his robe and exits his bedroom headed for his desk in the private sitting room next door. "OK Bob what do we know?"

"All we know right now is one hour ago one of our ships the *USS Nathanial Greene* operating in International Waters off the coast of Yemen was attacked. No report yet on the number of casualties but the ship was heavily damaged."

"Are they still under attack?"

"No sir by all accounts so far it was a single attack."

"Bob, I want all the aide we can muster sent to those men. I want a full report at our morning briefing. I want to know who was behind this and our options for response."

"Yes sir."

The President was swept into office on a groundswell of emotion by a populous tired of being the targets of terrorists bent on the destruction of America. Whether it was street bombings or embassy attacks the American people wanted it to stop. Gordon Hatch campaigned on the promise of rooting out terrorist and preventing attacks by taking a proactive approach to dealing with America's enemies. The President always led from the front, not afraid to make the tuff decisions. His policies of dealing with aggressive nations and factions were not always shared by his opponents in both houses of congress. Some said he lacked diplomacy, unwilling to talk and barter to resolve conflicts. Others felt his aggressive stance only fanned the flames of hatred and discontent. Either way he was a deeply committed man who took his oath seriously to defend this nation and the constitution unlike some of his predecessors.

The President returns to bed but is unable to get much rest the remainder of the night. His mind is consumed with discerning the rippling effect of any action either perpetrated against America or any outward response by America. The world was no longer a simple place where nations are isolated from each other. The world economy has forever linked all nations such that actions in one corner affected markets and events in another. Air travel, the internet, international shipping, stock markets, advances in technology all played a role in shrinking the planet. Now more than ever everyone needed to play by the same rules if some resemblance of order was to be maintained where business, economies and peoples could flourish.

Rising early from bed the President dresses and heads downstairs from the family residence area of the White House for his morning breakfast. He is greeted there by the days Secret Service Duty Commander who hands him the morning wire service's leading headlines and story summaries.

"Good morning Mr. President."

"Good morning Mat. How's that little girl of yours?"

"She's just fine sir. Having just a light breakfast today?"

"Yeah, got to get to work early today circle the wagons and all."

"Good luck sir."

"Thanks Mat."

Scanning the news briefs as he walks down the hallway toward the Oval Office grateful not to find reference to the attack Bob Hammond spoke about last night. He was glad they were able to keep a lid on it until he had a chance to deal with it.

Arriving at the oval office, anxious to hear of the latest developments promised by Bob Hammond the night before the President peruses legislative documents, opinions and briefs that have begun to consume the majority of his desk top.

In an effort to keep himself apprised of what is happening worldwide the President has ordered a daily briefing at 8:00 AM each morning with his National Security Council. In attendance is Vice President Ryan Granger, Secretary of State Anthony Lomax, Secretary of Defense Robert Hammond and at special request of the President Admiral Douglas McMillan Chairman of the Joint Chiefs-of-Staff. The Chairman is not normally a member of the National Security Council but due to a general feeling of unrest in the Middle East the President has sought the advice from time to time of an experienced military professional.

The Presidents Chief of Staff knocks briefly at his door and announces the assembly of men to the President. As the four men enter the President steps out from behind his desk to great them.

"Tony, good morning how was that dinner at the French Embassy last night"?

"Just fine Mr. President. I've been to enough of them to find they all start to taste alike. The French seem to take great pride in their culinary skills but give me a slab of prime rib medium well any day. On another note, when you have time sir, I wish to share with you concerns the French have regarding a trade imbalance. You know how they are."

"Indeed I do. See me later on that. Good morning gentlemen, Ryan, Bob, Doug, gentlemen take a seat let's get down to it."

The four men take their places on two opposing sofas as the President takes a seat in his favorite wingback chair at the head of the two sofas positioned so he may see his team. The chair was presented to the President as a welcoming gift, at his inauguration, from the Prime Minister of Great Britain after a stellar career in the senate championing policies aimed to strengthen both America and Great Britain.

Robert Hammond raises his hand slightly and begins "ah Mr. President, if I may I would like to begin concerning a recent significant event I mentioned to you last night. Approximately eight hours ago one of our intelligence gathering listening ships the *USS Nathanael Greene* an Aegis Class destroyer operating in the Arabian Sea off the Yemen coast was attacked by person or persons unknown. Survivors have been air lifted to the nearest ship for emergency care before being taken to the nearest base hospital. The remaining crew is piloting the ship back to port under limited power. Final numbers are not yet in but dozens of crewmen have been either killed or wounded. Included in the casualties are most of the technical leadership as well as the senior bridge officers. I witness accounts by survivors a few moments before impact suggest the weapon resembled a stealth drone possibly reengineered from the one lost over Iran in 2011. The weapon was unobserved by our tactical systems and as a result the ship was unable to defend itself."

The President interrupts "Bob do they really have our stealth technology?"

The Secretary continues "Mr. President stealth capabilities are 80% shape and 20% material, so if they model the shape from the one we lost with whatever material remained from the crash then yes they can do it. I'm going to guess that multiple targets are planned because that is the way of most terrorist groups. Although no one has claimed responsibility for the attack I can only conclude that we are dealing with a very deadly and serious threat. As to additional attacks, since they were successful on their first attempt, I anticipate the crafts will be smaller than ours but potentially very deadly. In addition NCIS forensic consultants will be working with the FBI crime lab to analyze the explosive residue to determine the type used."

"What will that tell us?" the Vice President asks.

Secretary Hammond responds "The type of explosive will tell us of the sophistication of their weapons supply and how much damage they can inflict. It may also give us an indication of who they are doing business with whereby we may be able to interrupt their supply chain."

Vice President Ryan Granger interrupts the Secretary of Defense before addressing the President, "excuse me Bob but what do we want to tell the press Gordon?" The VP is the only one who addresses the President by his first name due to their long association in the senate and close friendship.

"Well Ryan, we tell the truth of course. My administration will not begin lying to the American people. Our recent history as a nation is replete with bad intelligence, misinformation and downright incompetence. We have an attack by person or persons unknown and we are investigating the crime to our fullest ability. These are the facts as they stand right now. You can work out the language for my Press Corp briefing. Go on Bob what were you saying?"

"Yes sir, on another matter" continues Hammond "As you recall from a previous meeting we have been picking up increased chatter from our friends in the Middle East again suggesting something new was in the works. Yesterday the *USS Nathanael Greene*, the surveillance ship that was attacked, picked up a conversation between a known terrorist and another man discussing an upcoming attack they were planning."

"Just a moment Bob" interrupts the Secretary of State "is this a serious threat or are two guys talking big in some show of bravado? Do we have any supporting confirmation?"

"Mr. Secretary" responds Hammond "this is information we must take as a serious threat. The man's voice print identified him as Azzir Kelil. Azzir has been on our watch list for some time. He has been active in numerous al-Qaida attacks over the years including ambushes on our troops during the Iraq war and more recently the attack on our embassies in Afghanistan and Libya. Recent intelligence information suggests he has become well-funded and has even been considered contracting his services to those willing to pay."

The President stops him "Bob, what do we know about this guy?"

Hammond continues "The CIA has assembled a dossier on this fellow that reads something like a who's who in Islamic Terrorism. We think he graduate from Tehran University with a degree in economics and a minor in mid-east studies, a longtime follower of Ayatollah Ruhollah Khomeini who helped cultivate his hatred for all things Western.

"Do you think this guy had anything to do with the attack you just spoke of?" asked the President.

"We don't know yet for sure but it does sound like the type of operation he would engage in. Between the intercepted communiques and the suspiciously timed attack on our ship I would say he is a likely perpetrator." Hammond continues "He has no great devotion to Allah only great hatred for the West. He has been active in both Iraq and Afghanistan as I mentioned, received his training at the tutelage of seasoned mullahs, is well respected among al-Qaida's senior leadership, blends in well in all Middle East regions and speaks Arabic and Farsi as well as English. The down side is that no pictures of him exist. He has shown to be quite effective in operating off the grid so to speak so formal identification has been problematic. The voice print we have is from communiques recorded over the years where his name was given. We have also matched his voice print to other aliases he has used."

The Vice President interrupts "so how do we find and stop him?"

"Just a moment Ryan" interrupts the President "gentlemen you all know that preventing Iran from developing a nuclear capability is job one for this administration and our allies. These other matters are an unwelcome distraction yet cannot be overlooked. We need to keep our eyes on the big picture. Gentlemen discuss this among yourselves for a while I need a moment to digest all this."

The President turns in his chair and gazes toward the window deep in thought feeling the weight of the office on his shoulders and allows the issues and his thoughts to run free in his mind. President hatch was elected 16 months ago with the promise to reduce tensions in the region and safeguard America while not starting expensive wars the country can no longer afford. He wrestles with the notion of demonstrating a willingness to talk and seek common ground with a people that hate the US and seek its demise at the tip of a sword and now he is also faced with stealth drone attacks plus perhaps other unknown threats. In addition to all this there is great political pressure from US allies to deny Iran a nuclear capability. Further terrorist actions are turning the world's attention away from the greater nuclear issue. In addition his political opponents will say he is soft on Iran by not wishing to deal with the issue while being preoccupied by terrorist attacks and threats. If the US were to respond with any significant military action it will only serve to heighten western/Islamic tensions and result in a new major war. It's a no win scenario. If he focuses on Iran the terrorists become unchecked and if he focuses on the terrorists he loses points with his political opponents for being soft on Iran. *Yet the buck stops here.*

The President turns back in his chair and takes a deep breath "Ok what else have you got?" he asks.

Hammond broke in "Mister Vice President you asked earlier how can we stop Azzir. There may be a way. If we can covertly locate Azzir and take out his organization you Mister President will be free to focus on the Iranian nuclear issue and not appear week on terrorists as they are silently eliminated."

"Bob, do you have the intelligence information necessary to find and stop this guy?" asked the President.

"Yes sir I believe we do. The hard part is done. We know who we are looking for. We have the people and the resources to find him and stop him."

"I think one of my predecessors was told something similar prior to 911" the President says sullenly.

The President stood and turned from his chair and walked silently to the window and stared out, lost in thought, trying to imagine a more peaceful age where lives of men, women and children were not caught in the balance and blind hate did not control the affairs of men. *So be it. Doing nothing at this point was worse than doing something.* He owed it to the families of the fallen crewmen to bring to justice those responsible for their death. The President turned and approached the Chairman of the Joint Chiefs.

"Doug can you recommend someone to head a team to covertly look into and eliminate this stealth drone threat and possible impending attack?"

"Yes sir I think I have just the man for the job. It just so happens my senior aide Brigadier General Bishop Kincaid is out in the hallway right now. General Kincaid has commanded covert troops in Somalia, Afghanistan and was the go-to guy for early reconnaissance activities prior to Desert Storm. I think he would be perfect for the job."

"Bring him in here will you Doug."

The Admiral steps out into the hallway and waves to the General. "General, come on in for a moment the President wants a few words with you."

"Yes Sir."

The Admiral returns to the Oval office followed by the General. The Marine General wore his service "A" uniform stood 6 foot tall with a barrel chest and short graying hair. Bishop was a twenty year man but still in his prime, a man who had earned the been there done it tee shirt many times over and cut from the old school can do attitude keenly devoted to his oath to defend his country.

"Mister President, I'd like to introduce you to Brigadier General Bishop Kincaid."

The two shook hands warmly yet firmly. "General, please come sit I have a situation that the good Admiral has volunteered you for."

The Admiral and the General enjoy a warm close working relationship having served together for many years. Bishop gave the Admiral a quick glance with a surprised expression on his face.

"Yes sir I'll remember to thank the Chairman for singing my praises."

The President smiles and sits opposite the General and proceeds to fill Bishop in on all that was previously discussed prior to his arrival. "Well, what do you think? Do you want the job?"

"Yes sir, I would be honored."

"Before you commit" begins the President "I need to give you the fine print. This must be off the books. The Iranian nuclear issue is job one for this country and its allies. If this sordid mess leads back to Iran and I target their people it will only serve to heighten mid-east tensions and may further obstruct our diplomatic and economic efforts to eliminate their nuclear capabilities. My political opponents will have a field day if I announce a sanctioned military action on Iranian assets. The Iraq and Afghanistan wars are one thing but a surgical military strike on Iran is something else. I promised no new unnecessary wars to the American people during my campaign so if I launch a military strike it sure looks like I may have one. This terrorist thing is an unwelcome distraction from our true objective. I need you to make it go away completely and quietly. It never happened. Your people do not exist. I do not want terrorists arrested in front of cameras and shipped off to Gitmo. I do not want cable news covering fire fights involving American military personnel I want the world's attention focused on the Iranian nuclear issue only. You report back to me. Cost is no object I will get you the funds you need, any questions?"

"No sir. I will get right on it."

The president turns to the rest of his cabinet team "does anyone have anything else to add?"

"No sir" was the collective response.

"Make it happen General."

The Chairman and the General leave the President's office and West Wing together to their chauffeured vehicle awaiting them on West Executive Ave NW and head back to the Pentagon.

"Well General it looks like you got your work cut out for you. If anyone can pull this off I know it will be you."

"Thanks for the vote of confidence Admiral."

"You know Bishop if what Secretary Hammond was saying is true and Azzir is to the point of constructing working test drones he could be very close to launching his planned attack. I'll be sure Secretary Hammond has the FBI step up their watch on our ports and internal activities but the rest will be up to you."

"I know and I think I know just how to do it."

For the remaining trip back to the Pentagon both men sit silently as the General begins to formulate in his mind the unique qualities in team members he is looking for. As he reviews in his mind the hundreds of men he either commanded or served with he remembers one man that stood out above all the rest.

"Yes, he will do just fine."

Chapter 3
Wickenburg, Arizona

The morning was bright and clear much like every other day in Arizona. He knew that the temperature would be rising soon which dictated his morning regiment of a 4 mile run before 7:00 A.M. His 6'– 2" 200 lb. frame glistened with sweat as he returned to the house. His breathing was heavy but not labored. Standing on his back porch he wiped the sweat from his face and short blond hair. His piercing blue eyes surveyed the expanse of his realm just as an African lion scans the Serengeti secure in his mastery over his domain. Time permitting he would spend another 30 minutes at the bench press followed by 100 sit-ups on his converted back porch/workout gym. His workout also included 50 deep squat lifts while holding a 100 lb. barbell. A regiment he designed to strengthen his legs to aide his stamina. The daily workout was a welcome habit developed from his time spent in the Marines and looked forward to it each day as a means to keep himself active and fit.

Jack Hunter finally found contentment in his life. Following two tours of duty as a Marine in both Iraq and Afghanistan completing his service as a Captain and disillusioned by the military establishment he terminated his service in favor of civilian life. The family ranch he lived on was first homesteaded by his great grandfather at the turn of the century. Great grandfather Hyrum Hunter homesteaded 640 acres just North of Wickenburg against the Weaver Mountains raising cattle and horses and built the house Jack now lives in. Hyrum also purchased and worked 960 acres west of the Town of Buckeye to raise cotton. When Jack was a small boy his father added a few more rooms to the house for the new family to grow into. But, the large family was not to be. Jack was an only child but did not want for the love, support and attention of both parents. At a young age Jack learned to ride, shoot and track with the best. These skills proved to serve him well more than once both on and off his rural central Arizona ranch. Jack graduated Arizona State University with a degree in Civil Engineering just before his mom passed away when Jack decided he needed something more and joined the Marines. Jack's father finally retired about this time and is living the easy life in a Scottsdale condo. Jack no longer ranches or farms the land but rents it out to others to work. Jack keeps a percentage of the proceeds. He is not rich but is content with the simple things in life.

Today Jack owns and operates a small consulting engineering business providing infrastructure design improvements to cities and towns throughout Arizona. The job keeps him on the road frequently which he does not mind as this gives him time to relax and enjoy the outdoors.

Following his morning workout Jack enters his modest yet comfortable ranch house, decorated years ago by his parents yet still possesses some items to denote his personal space. Jack manages to collect items from his travels. From his military time spent in the Middle East Jack has added a collection of the curved janbiya and khanjar knives carried by Muslim men. Also adorning his study are a series of photographs of the men he served with which will always reside in a special place in his heart. The bond shared by men forged in battle as you trust your life to the one beside you is a bond like no other.

Jack takes a quick shower, dons a clean pare of Levi's, a Wrangler western shirt and a pair of Toni Lama western work boots, downs a quick cup of coffee and heads to the barn and his 1972 Ford Bronco. He recently had the Bronco modified to include a 6 inch lift kit, 36 inch tires and a full role cage to protect and enhance his much enjoyed forays into the rouged desert and mountains.

Eager to complete a proposal for new work Jack heads off to his office in downtown Wickenburg. He enjoys a strong sense of independence which operating his own business gives him and relishes the time spent out of doors. Long ago he realized an office job behind a desk would be a near death sentence for him. After a short 20 min trip down US 93 he pulls into the parking lot of his office. One of the luxuries he allowed himself was a covered parking space with his name stenciled on a plaque above the stall.

Entering the modest one story building Jack greets Sherry his loyal secretary who hands him the day's mail. He quickly thumbs through it – bills and advertisements – hands it back to Sherry and tells her to take care of it to which she gently smiles and shakes her head in quiet surrender. Sherry became Jack's secretary when he opened the business three years ago after opting out his third tour for the marines and has been his secretary and office assistant ever since. Sherry was a high school cheer leader who completed two years at the local community college before joining Jack.

"Jack, do you have that proposal completed yet for Lake Havasu?" she asks.

"When I do you will be the first to know" he answers. "Where's Raul?"

"I think he's in the back"

Jack heads to his office. As President of his company he has designed his office to be simple but tastefully appointed, large glass windows front his office so he may see clients entering into the reception area. Jack bangs out the last few pages of the proposal on his computer, transmits it to Sherry and asks her to make it pretty before printing the final copies to be mailed off to the city.

Jack heads off to the back room "Hey Raul you back here?"

Raul de Martinez lost his family many years ago in a deadly accident. He joined the Marines to obtain some stability in his life. Service to his country brought meaning once again to a life void of significance. His military haircut long gone Raul now wears his jet black hair combed straight back. If asked he would say the military version cramped his style. Blue jeans, work boots and a plaid sheet buttoned up to the collar complete his daily ensemble. Although four inches shorter and 20 pounds lighter, Raul is every much the combat veteran Jack is and has never backed down from a fight. Jack and Raul have been friends for many years. They meet in Afghanistan where Raul was assigned, as a gunnery sergeant, to Jack's team. Jack and Raul saved each other's life more times than each man can remember which cemented a bond that has lasted since then. A year following his separation from the Marine Corps Raul showed up at Jacks office. One thing led to another and an old friendship was rekindled but to each man the bond never really ended. Today Raul performs odd jobs around the office and is slowly learning the business from Jack. Ever since they met Raul has hinted that someday he would open his own Mexican restaurant. "To follow in his roots" he would say.

"I am here boss. What's up?"

"Can you go over to Cave Creek today and pick up those concrete cylinders from that paving job and take them to the lab for testing?"

"Sure can. Where are you going?"

"Into Phoenix I need to talk to the planning department. I'll meet you back here later today."

Jack turns and sniffs the air. "Raul, what's that smell?"

"Oh that. I'm trying out a new recipe for green sauce in the break room. Smells good huh?"

Jack allows a great deal of latitude to his friend's activities because of their close friendship. Jack shakes his head. "Just don't burn the place down."

"You got it boss."

Jack grabs his briefcase from his office gives Sherry a nod and heads to his car for the trip downtown. Jack enjoys the challenges of his business. His new life is a welcome change from what he experienced in the Middle East although the corps did teach him skills he would not have learned anywhere else. Skills that few people here, besides Raul, new he possessed. Skills he wondered if he would ever need again in his new life.

US 60 is a relatively direct route from Wickenburg to down town Phoenix. A trip he has taken many times before both for business and pleasure. The mindless drive allows him to think about growing his business and the people now in his life. He was gradually growing accustomed to his new life and friends but some higher purpose still pulls at the far corners of his mind. He begins to wonder that his true calling was one not yet discovered. It was in one of these far off moments as he approaches the SR 303L interchange that Jack notices a black SUV approaching him from behind at a high rate of speed. Moments before impact the SUV swerves left barely missing Jack's rear bumper. Just ahead of Jack in the left lane a flatbed truck loaded with landscape supplies slows to enter the left turn lane. The SUV driver unable to slow in time to avoid the truck jerks his wheel back to the right in front of Jack. The overcorrection causes the SUV to slide sideways and as its front tire succumbs to a pothole the entire vehicle begins to roll over and over on the pavement before coming to rest on its side on the graded shoulder of the roadway.

Jack immediately locks his brakes to avoid contacting the careening SUV. Pulling his own car to a stop on the shoulder ahead of the damaged SUV he quickly runs to offer aide to the stricken driver. "Someone call 911" he yells to other motorists now parked and attempting further assistance.

Upon reaching the vehicle Jack could see through the windshield an unconscious driver with a bad scalp laceration with blood running down his face. At the same moment his senses alert him to first the smell then sight of gasoline leaking from a damaged fuel line beneath the vehicle. Fearing an impending explosive and fire Jack kicks in then pulls out the damaged windshield to enter the cab. Jack, disturbed that the driver was not wearing his seatbelt, examines the man as best he can for broken bones and holding his head and neck as straight as he can begins to pull the man from the wreckage just as the vehicle catches fire. Easing the man to the ground and cradling the man's head and neck in his hands a safe distance from the burning vehicle he awaits the EMTs. A news crew in the area covering a house fire was the first to arrive followed by police and fire personnel. The news crew was poised enough to capture a touching photo of Jack holding the injured driver for a human interest piece the paper regularly runs. The medical team soon arrives and takes over. Jack gives his name and a report to the police and gives his name to the news crew but refused a further interview by them before resuming his drive to Phoenix.

Chapter 4
Tehran, Iran

The Ministry of Intelligence and National Security of the Islamic Republic is in a sprawling campus of parks and offices located south and west of the Hemmat and Sayyad Shirazi Highway Interchange in Mehran, Tehran. The organization more commonly known as VEVAK or Vezarat-e Ettala'at va Amniyat-e Keshvar was created following the over-throw of the Shaw and is tasked with securing and promoting the affairs of state. In recent years this has meant supporting regimes sympathetic to the dictates of Tehran, suppressing internal opposition to the state and expanding the influence and dominance of Islam in the region. The Iranian government is not opposed to the support of terrorist organizations in the region for the advancement of their goals of regional domination and the destruction of Israel and the West but only does so through third parties to maintain an air of plausible deniability.

As Minister of VEVAK, Sayid Kamal, takes great pride in his position and the influence he commands. He controls a network of field operatives both in state and throughout the Middle East and provides regular reports to the President. He has served the Republic for many years and now provides to the President and Council intelligence information on dissidents, opposition party members and foreign governments all for the purpose of maintaining control by the current administration. The average Iranian does not share the vision of regional dominance and the destruction of Israel and the West as the administration enjoys but they quickly realized the futility of any objections they may voice as evidenced during the last presidential election where many dissenters were arrested or killed with the help of Sayid's Department. This long running devotion to the service of the state does have its benefits. Sayid has become a trusted member of the senior government leadership and is able to control the Ministry of Intelligence and conduct operations with little to no oversight.

Some years earlier Sayid made the acquaintance of another Iranian man by the name of Azzir Kelil. Azzir had been working with and training with al-Qaida in Iraq and Afghanistan. Reports by Sayid's field operatives reported the talents and skills of this new man. After many discussions on ideology and Islam's place in the world Sayid offered Azzir an opportunity to engage in grander operations for the good of Islam and for the shared goal of Western destruction. Together the men planned and carried out numerous embassy bombings, convoy strikes, assassinations and assorted terrorist strikes. Their efforts have largely been successful in maintaining a heightened tension over the region and have prevented the progress of any lasting peace talks among opposing parties. Embolden by their successes, brought about by Sayid's leadership and Azzir's operational skills, the two have gradually increased the magnitude and effectiveness of their attacks. Feeling unstoppable Sayid takes great pride as the self-proclaimed architect of Islam's advancement in the world and the inevitable defeat of the West while Azzir has succumbed to the pleasures of wanton destruction itself just as an addict relishes that next fix of the drug that offers that inner fulfillment and satisfaction. His drug of choice is supplying death and destruction on an ever grander scale.

One year previously a US drone attack in the Northwest province of Pakistan resulted in the unfortunate death of a Pakistani scientist's wife and two children who were visiting her parents in the area. Hearing the horrible news of the death of his family the scientist vowed to avenge their deaths. Learning of his hatred of the West through his field agents Sayid secretly met with Raheem Shirani at his home in Islamabad and convinced him to work for him participating in a grand plan to attack America.

"Raheem," Sayid began, "do you recall back in 2011 when we acquired an American surveillance drone? We told the world that we shot it down but in truth it somehow lost contact with whoever was flying it and it simply landed itself in our desert per its base programming. We have an intact American stealth drone. I need you to copy the design and build more, and then we will send them into the heart of America and let them know the fist of Allah first hand such that the streets will run red with their blood."

"This is an answer to my prayers that I would welcome with open arms my friend. Praise Allah" answered Raheem, "and I know of others who will lend their technical assistance and would give their lives for this noble cause, but as you may know this will be an expensive undertaking. Very special systems will need to be designed and constructed such as guidance systems, avionics, electronic flight controls plus others. It will be expensive. Do you have the necessary funds to complete this grand attack?"

"I do and I will secure any additional funds necessary. I have acquired the drone under authority of the Intelligence Ministry and am holding it in a secure location. You and your men will come to begin your work."

Raheem and his men began designing the new drones at a secrete site inside Iran but soon Sayid decided to relocate the final construction to a warehouse in Damascus for fear the discovery of the operation inside Iran would result in great international condemnation of the Iranian leadership, something he needed to avoid at all costs. To accomplish the move Sayid introduced Azzir to Raheem. Azzir was placed in charge of the operation and facilitated the relocation by crating the work completed to date and airlifting them to Damascus under diplomatic privilege through Sayid's Ministry.

Azzir arrives as requested to Sayid's office for a briefing on the progress of their operation against the West. Sayid had arranged some time ago for Azzir to be given a standard issue security badge so entrance into the Ministries facilities would not draw question.

"How is Raheem progressing with the construction of our drones Azzir?"

"All is going as planned. We have purchased much of the necessary materials and manufacturing machines necessary to construct the airframes but the design and construction of the propulsion system and avionics necessary to fly the drones will take time and we must be careful in our purchases not to alert the Americans. Your counterpart in the Syrian government is being helpful by facilitating the acquisition of certain parts from the Russian Federation. We constructed a working prototype on a smaller scale recently just to test our design. The guidance system was somewhat primitive which required on scene visual inputs to control the drone's flight. You may have heard of our successful attack on an American ship off the coast of Yemen recently in the news.

"Yes, good, good when do you think it will all be complete?"

"Let me get back to you on that. Let me first acquire the guidance systems and other electronic items for the final version and I can then better tell of a completion date."

"Very well, anything else to report?"

"Yes there is." Azzir passes over a copy of a recent local Phoenix newspaper showing a photo of a man assisting another man injured in a traffic accident.

"What is this?" asks Sayid.

"That is Mohammed Sharf one of our agents in this operation who died in a foolish traffic accident. The man attending to him is our old friend Jack Hunter."

"What! How can this be? I thought we were through with his meddling three years ago when he left military service. Do you know how much time and money we had invested into that Afghanistan operation only to see it all crumble do to this Jack's interference? If you remember we turned that Afghani captain and paid him very well to work for us aiding the assassinations of key US military officers from inside their own ranks only to have the plot discovered by this Jack Hunter before our man could carry it out. Luckily Jack killed him before the trail led the Americans to us."

"I agree Sayid, Jack has been a most worthy opponent. I was a part of that very operation where Jack and I traded fire across a compound when our eyes met for the first time after he killed our man. In a way I wish he was still around so I may repay him for prying into our affairs."

"This Jack has a habit of sticking his nose into things he should not. There is no telling what Mohammed may have told him before he died. Before he has a chance to interfere you should have the rest of your team remove him before it is too late. We have too much invested to leave things to chance. Make it happen as soon as possible the sooner the better."

"Very well" says Azzir "I will tell my team today and let you know when it is done."

Chapter 5
Phoenix, Arizona

The building Jack purchased three years ago when he started his business was something less than new. Repairs and sprucing up were needed but the price was right and Jack new he could get around to improvements as the business grew when he could afford the upgrades. The agent who sold Jack the property said the building had been constructed in the 1950's as a veterinary clinic whose owner recently passed away which is why the building was in a state of disrepair. With his small savings and doing most of the work himself Jack was able to remove many of the walls which functioned as the examination rooms, repaint the walls and concrete floor. But there was much more that needed to be done to make the place truly attractive. It was Sherry who took it upon herself to bring in paint swatches, floor covering samples and furniture catalogs on a regular basis for Jack's review.

"Jack did you look at those design sketches and sample furniture photos I gave you the other day?"

"No not yet I've had a few other things on my mind."

"When Tim Riley from the Maricopa County Flood Control Dept. was he last week he stood outside for a while talking on his phone. It looked like he really didn't want to come inside."

"OK, OK you win" concedes Jack "I'll do it." He knew that improvements were a necessary expense for the image of his business. He was growing successful and conceded that his establishment needed to reflect that image. Fortunately for him Jack met Jennifer White a few months ago. They had met at a local nursery where he was looking to replace a few desert bushes in his front yard and she was looking for house plants for a home she was renovating as part of her interior design business. A conversation was struck which grew in time into a warm friendship built on a natural attraction. Jack enjoyed

Jennifer's company and looked forward to their time together. Jennifer was instantly attracted to Jack's strong masculine persona that still contained a hint of boyish charm. The charm, though real, masked the stern confidence of a man who was not afraid to take command of a situation and bend it to his will and a man who has seen the worst of mankind and survived. She found herself frequently wondering to herself if this could be the one.

"For your information I have arranged to have lunch today with Jennifer. She has agreed to work up some plans for the renovation of the office, outside, inside, floors, walls and furniture for a complete makeover. I'll even let you help with the final color selections. OK."

"I knew you could do it" answered Sherry grinning "when are you leaving?"

"Good grief right away if that's all right with you" he playfully chides.

Jack left and headed for his bronco, he wondered if he was just using this as an excuse to see Jennifer but realized he did not need an excuse for that. The drive into Phoenix went quickly. Jack tried to formulate design schemes in his mind in anticipation of what Jennifer might have prepared but then decided to rely upon her skills and professionalism to create the final product, with Sherry's input.

Navigating the downtown traffic Jack eventually located a parking place not far from where they were to have lunch. Charley's was a downtown hot spot the lunchtime business crowd liked to frequent. Named after a retired Phoenix Suns player it featured outside dining in two rows along the front sidewalk plus inside accommodations as well. Jack arrived a few minutes before Jennifer and secured a table outside set back from the sidewalk against the building. When he saw her approaching he waved her over. Jack enjoyed the way her face lit up whenever they got together.

"Hey sailor new in town?" she exclaimed as she made her way over to his table.

Not to be outdone "ah a woman after my mother's own heart" he quipped. Jennifer's sense of humor was one of the things that attracted her to him.

The two hugged and shared a brief kiss then sat. A waitress appeared and announced the daily specials from a previously well-rehearsed presentation. Jack ordered the chili and corn bread while Jennifer ordered the chicken Caesar salad. The two enjoyed the warm sun, fresh air and coveted the time they spent together away from their busy schedules.

Previously Azzir's three agents in the US on tourist visas decide to stakeout Jack's home and business in an attempt to locate him to carry out their assignment. The two men watching Jack's business see him leaving in his bronco and follow. They place a call to the third member their location and direct him to follow. Soon all three cars are heading down US 60 towards Phoenix. Not wishing to be seen by Jack the two trailing cars hang back.

The leader tells the others "we will wait until he is stopped at his destination so we can be sure not to miss."

The Phoenix traffic proves problematic for the agents who lose sight of Jack's car. The three agents join up in one car and begin to look for Jack. Deciding that searching the many parking garages in the downtown area would be too time consuming and probably result in only finding Jack's car they decide to peruse the downtown streets in hopes to locate him walking.

"If this does not work we will hit him tonight at his home" instructed the lead agent.

After combing the downtown area they finally find him seated with Jennifer at a restaurant.

"We will circle around the block and then get him as we pass by. Get ready."

As Jack and Jennifer discuss the sketches she made of his office Jack's finely tuned combat senses go on high alert. From out the corner of his eye he sees a vehicle slow down far less than the speed of normal traffic passing the restaurant and its right side windows are rolled down. His subconscious calls to memory similar tactics by insurgents in Iraq prior to an attack. As Jack turns his head to look he sees two AK-47 gun barrels extend from the windows. Jack instinctively lunges toward Jennifer carrying her to the ground cushioning her fall as best he can just as the 7.62mm rounds begin shredding the restaurant. The first row of tables are shattered and overturned, their occupants are mercilessly cut down. Glass fragments from water pitchers and table tops rain down upon everyone as the unceasing barrage of high velocity bullets tear through the restaurant. As Jack's table erupts he covers her body with his own for protection as their table crashes down upon them its corner gashing her scalp. A waitress carrying a large tray of food just exiting the front door is cut down as more glass rains down upon the crowd of helpless patrons. The large plate glass window behind Jack's table explodes from the onslaught of automatic fire and showers down a torrent of deadly shards upon them. Customers inside the restaurant are not spared from the assault as some are either cut down by the deadly ammunition or lacerated by flying glass. The attack ended as quickly as it began, their supply of ammunition expended the agents race off, before the authorities arrive, leaving in their wake the dead and injured.

Jack slowly raises himself up on both knees and reaches down for Jennifer and notices the gash on her head and lacerations on her face arms and legs. "Jennifer, are you all right?"

"Oh Jack what happened? Are you OK? My head hurts."

Noticing her injuries were not life threatening though there was quite a bit of blood running down her face he said "lie still help is on the way, you're going to be alright I promise." Jack held her in his arms and wiped away the blood as best he could and waited for the EMTs. He did not notice nor care that his face and hands contained the same lacerations. As he waited he could sense the anger begin to rise within him rekindling sordid memories of fellow solders he comforted on the battle field. *This is not supposed to happen here* he thought as he held Jennifer and waited for help.

It took 20 to 30 minutes for sufficient medical help to arrive to treat or stabilize everyone who needed medical care. By this time Jack had Jennifer sitting up in a chair applying a cold wet compress to her scalp wound after washing her cuts and scratches as best he could. His long sleeve shirt and Levi pants protected him from the falling glass far more than the sleeveless blouse and short skirt Jennifer wore.

Jennifer looked at Jack "stop fussing over me I'll be fine, look at yourself. You look like you could use some help also."

"I'll be fine I care more what happened to you" he answers.

As she smiles up at him the EMTs approach having got the more seriously injured patrons sent off to the local hospital. "Mam that cut looks like it will require some attention can we take you next?" one medic asks.

As the medics bring a gurney for Jennifer they take a look at Jack. "I'll be OK just look after her."

As they load her into the ambulance Jack takes her hand "I'll meet you at the hospital. Trust me you'll be alright."

As they start to drive away Jack heads back to his car anger and disbelief fill his mind.

Chapter 6
Phoenix, Arizona

Jack drives the short distance to the hospital. He relives the events of the past hour or so in his mind over and over looking for something that might shed some light as to why or who. Finding none he locates a space in the visitors parking garage and walks over the pedestrian bridge and down one flight of stairs to the emergency room. The charge nurse at the counter was an elderly woman with a quick smile and a kind face, just what Jack needed after the events of this afternoon. As Jack approached he wondered how someone could endure being a part of the trauma and anguish she must see on a daily basis year after year. Thank God there were people like her in the world whose work was to ease the pain and suffering of others.

"May I help you?" she asks.

"Yes please, I am looking for Jennifer White. She was brought in a little while ago."

"Are you a family member?"

"No I'm sorry I'm not."

"I believe the doctor is just finishing with her. Please have a seat I'll let you know when you can see her."

Jack took a seat on one of the hard fiberglass institutional chairs in the waiting room convinced they were designed for the expressed purpose of inflicting discomfort to all who attempted to employ their use. Looking around the room he saw what he assumed to be family members and friends of the victims in tears or consumed by the shock and grief of this senseless tragedy still so fresh in everyone's mind.

Rerunning the events through his mind again and again he finally realizes there was nothing he could have done to prevent the attack and feels that he and Jennifer are just lucky to be alive.

After a few minutes that seemed liked hours to him the charge nurse catches his eye. "She's in the third stall on the right. You can go back now."

"Thank you. By the way" he asks "what was the final total number of people hurt if I may ask?"

The nurse, looking him over slowly and noticing the same cuts and abrasions over his face and hands as all the other patients admitted the past hour and concludes he was probably one of the lucky ones.

"There were six that did not make it and ten will be spending the night maybe longer."

Jack lowers his head in silent respect for the fallen and says "thank you mam." He walks the short distance down the sterile antiseptic smelling hospital floor to Jennifer's stall passing other stalls whose curtains are drawn and hears the weeping of loved ones inside. He stands still for a moment to gather himself then parts the curtain, smiles as he enters and says "the things you'll do to get out of having lunch with me."

Her face beams at seeing Jack once again. "That's OK I didn't like the special of the day anyhow." They both laugh. She winces from the pain of the stitches in her scalp.

Jack takes her hand, "I am so sorry this happened I'm glad you were not hurt worse."

"That makes two of us besides it's not your fault Jack. I'm glad you were there for me though. Thank you."

Their eyes met and each feels the warm connection that has been growing over time. Jack reaches in to give Jennifer a hug and warm kiss. "They told me the doc was done with you, at least let me take you home."

"Oh no that's all right I can call a friend" She says.

"Did I tell you I am working on my next merit badge and have to assist three damsels in distress this week? You would be my first. You wouldn't want to see an over aged Boy Scout out done by some young kids now would you?"

"No I guess not."

"Good my car is just outside. Since we missed lunch I will make you dinner. No strings, I promise."

"You're on."

Jennifer gathers up her belongings and signs the hospital release papers presented by the nurse as they leave. Jennifer is placed in the obligatory wheelchair by the helpful staff and wheeled out the hospital.

Jack drives his Bronco up to the emergency room doors and helps Jennifer in then heads off down 15th Avenue to her home in the historic Encanto district of Phoenix.

As Jack pulls up he gazes at her house "did I ever tell you what a wonderful job you did restoring this house?"

"Why thank you. It is a classic bungalow style built in the 1930's. When I found it I could not resist the charm of its architecture. Besides, being an interior designer it's a good investment for my business. I've had many complements on it."

"I can see why."

"Come on in Jack, I'll make us some tea."

Jack follows Jennifer into the kitchen, leans against the cherry wood cabinets and quartz counter tops and once again admires her talents. "So tell me what do you do when you're not fixing up old houses or getting raked by gunfire at outdoor cafes with handsome men?"

She turns smiles at him and says "well if you must know I just picked up a new hobby. I'm discovering my roots so to speak. My father, Louis White passed away a few years ago and I recently had to place my mother in a senior care facility and in cleaning out her home I found boxes and boxes of papers and correspondence of family members going all the way back to my great grandfather. My mother's name was Elizabeth Devencourt. Her father was Jonathan Devencourt and his father was Addison Devencourt who evidently was with the diplomatic corps of England during the First World War. My mother does not remember too much about the family other than she remembers her father telling her that his mother Camille loved her husband Addison very much and after he died in the war she never remarried. My mother was quite close to her parents so after they died she moved to America to marry my father and brought with her many of their personal belongings including all the letters and documents she collected through the years. I'm hoping that all these will help fill in the details about my family. Come let me show you."

Jennifer takes Jack into her dining room where boxes fill the table. "I've managed to separate the boxes into generations. These on the table are from my mother and father's time and these are from my grandmother and grandfathers time. Those on the floor I have not looked at yet. Those I think are all my great grandfather's papers."

Jack bends down to pick up a handful of old letters. One of the letters falls from his hand. As he bends to retrieve it he becomes intrigued by the postage stamp and embassy seal on the envelope. "This looks like one of your great grandfather's letters. The postmark is from Cairo and dated 1914. Was he stationed in Cairo in 1914?"

"I do not know all mom ever told me was he worked with the diplomatic corps for the foreign office. Let me open it I'm curious now."

Jennifer begins to read the letter written long ago by a man caught up in the turmoil of his time conflicted by the desire to serve his country and vexed by the weight of his own conscious concerning the things he did. The letter revealed a man of honor and principal embroiled in the horrors of war as it unfolds and realizing the very survival of his country hinged and what he may or may not do.

Jack, reading over her shoulder, is also moved by the magnitude of the implications revealed in the letter. "Do you know when your great grandfather died? Was it before or after he returned to England with the deeds?"

"I do not know. Mother never spoke of any deeds or documents that great grandfather speaks of in this letter and I have not found anything resembling a deed. Do you think it has any significance?"

"An event of this magnitude could not have been overlooked by the British Government if it existed. History makes no mention of this transfer ever taking place but does record Great Britain supplying military aide to the Arab people seeking independence from the Ottoman Empire during this time frame. I can only conclude the documents were either destroyed or lost or in any event never made their way back to England. You see events were orchestrated not in the best interests of the Arab people from the beginning. The Arabs were successful against the Turks and at the end of the war controlled all of modern Jordan, and most of the Arabian Peninsula including much of southern Syria and thought to finally realize their objective of a Unified Arab State from Syria to Yemen. But these aspirations were dashed by the British due to conflicting promises. This came about through a series of letters by Britain's High Commissioner in Egypt when speaking for Great Britain pledged to support Arab Independence if forces of Sharif Hussein bin Ali, the Arab's leader, revolted against the Turks. This pledge identified three areas to be excluded from Arab sovereignty: the Ottoman provinces of Basra and Bagdad, the Turkish districts of Alexandretta and Mersin, and finally "portions of Syria lying to the west of the district of Damascus. This last district proved to be the most contentious of the three. The British claimed that Palestine was meant to be excluded from the area of Arab rule while the Arabs interpreted the poorly worded document to read that the exclusion included Lebanon not Palestine as it is west of Damascus. In either event the European powers prevailed over the promises made to the Arabs. The next nail in the coffin was that while Arab independence was acknowledged in the High Commissioner's Correspondence the Sykes-Picot Agreement signed by Britain, France and Russia in 1916 further divided the area into zones of European influence. The agreement afforded French influence in Greater Syria and Northern Iraq and British influence covered a region from the Mediterranean to the Persian Gulf to protect its trade routes with India. The agreement also specified that most of Palestine was to be controlled by an international administration. This agreement clearly contradicted the promises made to Sharif Hussein bin Ali back in 1914. The final nail in the coffin came in the form of the Balfour Declaration when in 1917 the British Foreign Secretary, James Balfour, sent a letter to a prominent British Jew promising Britain's commitment for a permanent Jewish home in Palestine. This resulted in mass immigration of Jews from around the world which displaced many of the Palestinian people. Clearly the colonial powers simply redrew national boundaries irrespective of the indigenous peoples a practice common throughout history mirrored again in the settling of our own American West. Now today add Islamic extremism to the mix and I think you can see the reason for the unrest and turmoil that plagues the region."

"That's fascinating" she admits "how do you know so much about the Middle East?"

"Hey I'm not just a pretty face" he says "besides I have somewhat of an intimate knowledge of the place from passed experiences."

"Care to elaborate on that?"

Not wanting to frighten her regarding the atrocities he's seen or the chilling battles he fought he sidesteps the question for the moment "Maybe another time." Thinking more of the issue at hand and the potential significance the documents hold if they can be found he asks "can you do me a favor and find out all you can about your great grandfather? When where and how he died and oh yeah can I have a copy of his letter? I may have a few ideas."

"Sure," she says, "I'll send it to your office. You know after all this excitement I am feeling a little tired from the pain medication they gave me at the hospital can I have a rain check on diner?

"No problem I understand. I'll call you again soon. OK?"

Chapter 7
Phoenix, Arizona

Jack waves good bye gets into his Bronco and heads back to his office. The drive from Jennifer's allows him time to think about the day's events. It did not make sense. Of what value was it to shoot up a cafe and kill a half dozen people? He could understand a large scale attack like the World Trade Center where many died in the name of some misplaced jihad based upon the lies and deceit of some crazed Imam, or the Fort Hood shootings where identified combatants were targeted in some warped attempted at revenge, but a small cafe in the heart of a western city made no sense. From a military tactical perspective the resources you would lose greatly exceeded the benefit gained from achieving such an objective. That is assuming you knew the perpetrators would eventually be caught by the authorities. Still losing three to get six was a poor return when considering the six held no significant rank or importance in the struggle compared to the cost to put the three in place to carry out the assignment. But wait, suppose there was someone at the scene that was significant enough to warrant expending these assets. As try as he may he could not remember anyone at the cafe of significant political or military interest. He decided to wait and see what the authorities and media came up with in the days ahead.

Jack thankfully arrives back at his office by late afternoon. A standard green government sedan is parked in the visitors slot near the front door. The letters DOD are clearly stenciled on the side of the vehicle.

"Good grief now what" he says to himself as he heads to the door.

Inside the reception area beside Sherry's desk he finds Raul standing next to a tall stocky man with short gray hair wearing what is called a service "B" uniform. Jack quickly notices the single Silver Star on the man's collar denoting the rank of Brigadier General and instantly becomes suspicious of the man's presence.

The man turns to face Jack. "Captain Jack Hunter I presume?"

"You presume correctly but you can leave the captain off its just plan Jack Hunter now. And whom may I ask are you?"

Raul chimes in "Jack this is General Bishop Kincaid, he's been telling me a lot of things about what's been going on. I think you should hear what he has to say."

"Oh really? Gentlemen I've had a most trying day and I would really like to just go home and get some rest."

"Bishop reaches out his hand to greet Jack "it's a pleasure to meet you Mister Hunter, how are you? I trust you were not hurt in the attempt on your life today."

Jack stops and stares at him "What? Why do you say that? Who are you anyway?"

"Allow me to explain" begins the General "I've read your file, very impressive. Jack, may I call you Jack?"

Jack does not answer.

Bishop continues. "Anyhow, we think Azzir Kelil is planning a major attack on US interests but we do not know whether the target or targets are home or abroad. Our listening posts have recorded significant chatter to this effect and his name and voice were detected discussing the event but no details were given. He tried to kill you today and will try again because he does not want you to interfere with whatever he has planned like you did before in Afghanistan."

"Whoa, whoa, slow down. First off I'm off the radar doing my own thing he doesn't know where I am and two, I'm not involved with hunting bad guys for the US military anymore."

"But Jack you are already involved. When you helped that guy in the car accident recently your pictures was plastered all over the newspaper and guess what? That guy was identified as Mohammed Sharif who was in the country on a visa with forged papers identifying him as Akeem Salib. We're doing further checking to see if he pops up on a watch list but as you know where one is more are sure to exist. We believe that possibly others in the cell are the ones who tried to take you out."

"Jack, one more thing you are not aware of" the general continues. "A few days ago one of our Aegis cruisers was attacked in the Arabian Sea. An undetected stealth drone impacted the ship. Fifty three men died. We do not know yet if Azzir was connected to this but the clock is ticking."

"Why are you telling to me with this? Surely you have teams of people you can assign to this."

"Jack, you are the only one who knows what Azzir looks like. You've crossed swords with him before. You can I.D. him and follow him to find out what he has planned and stop him."

"Not my problem. Do you know why I got out when my tour was up? I'll tell you. It's because of sanctimonious career officers more intent on covering their butts than serving the mission. That assassination squad in Afghanistan I discovered and took down resulted in more finger pointing and ass covering than a Texas prison. All they cared about was keeping their records clean so they could get that next promotion. The same thing happened in Iraq at the Abu Ghraib prison. Senior commanders new and approved what was going on but nothing happened to them. Only the guys at the lower end of the food chain took the full weight of that screw up. And do you know how many of our guys died needlessly because when they were pinned down in a fire fight you guys would not send in air support to get them out because there MIGHT be civilians in the area? The rules of engagement you guys dictated had the deck stacked against us like one arm tied around our back. Am I upset? You bet I am. The integrity, duty and honor in the military is lacking. I guess I should not be surprised though since the rest of the country does the same thing, from Wall Street to Main Street the watch words seem to be do what's best for you and if you can get away with it then go for it. Progressive liberalism and political correctness have infected too many areas of our government and society. Yeah I'm upset and like I said I've had a bad day and need to get some rest. So if you don't mind. Besides I have a life and commitments here now. Why would I want to get back up on that horse?"

"Jack what do I have to say to convince you that you're the perfect man for the job? Being a civilian you can fly under the radar, you know the lay of the land, you have what it takes and your country needs you.

"No thanks not interested. My country has made it clear that it can make decisions quite well without me. Granted poor decisions but none the less decisions with which it has to live."

"Then that's all the more reason for you to get back in the game. You can do what they can't and show them their ways are wrong."

Jack thought for a moment. "No."

"How about if I was to tell you that we feel fairly certain that after you rotated out Azzir masterminded a revenge attack on the rest of your team and killed them all in an ambush? The only reason Raul survived was because he was on leave at the time."

Jack hung his head in silent memory of good men he left behind that day when his tour ended. "Sorry, I can't. I'm needed here now."

Bishop lowers his head hoping he would not have to play his trump card but after reading Jack's file and fitness reports he knows where Jack's heart lies. Bishop recalls the account that resulted in awarding Jack the Navy Cross and Captains bars when he carried out of harm's way two solders injured from an errant shelling attack by allied troops then returned to the scene, while under heavy enemy fire, and single handedly rescued an Iraqi woman and her two children from her village trapped by the onslaught. "Jack, innocent women and children could be at risk here, American women and children. I know what you did for that family in Fallujah. I know how much you detest the taking of innocent life. We don't know what he has planned but we have to believe entire sections of our population could be at risk. You know this guy and what he is capable of. We need to stop him at all costs."

Jack freezes for a moment and stares at Bishop. He thinks of Jennifer and Sherry and what could happen to them. Jack squints his eyes "You son-of-a-bitch you know what buttons to push don't you?"

"Jack, it's important we need you."

Jack looks over at Raul for some sign either yes or no. Raul smiles and gives a quick thumbs up signal to Jack.

Jack takes a deep breath and lets it out. "OK you got me. What happens next?"

Bishop smiles and says "now let me give you the fine print. The President cannot risk raising further the tensions in the Middle East therefore a direct military engagement is out. This needs to be handled quietly. The operation can in no way be connected to the US Government. In other words you are on your own; no one will be coming to your rescue. That could be a good thing considering how you feel about the bureaucracy of the military establishment. You still want in?"

"Yeah I'll do it but only under certain conditions: 1) I do it my way, I'm in control, 2) You supply everything I need and ask for, 3) I get a get out of jail free card from the President just in case, and 4) you pay my standard consulting fee while I'm away from the office."

Bishop smiles, "done. Meet me tomorrow morning at 0700 at the airport. You can meet the rest of the team and oh by the way I'll leave the incident report file on the attack on our cruiser for your review."

Bishop turns and nods to a slack jawed Sherry as he leaves.

Jack turns and looks at Raul "what have you got me mixed up with this time?"

"Hey Jack I've always had your back. Just like old times eh-kimosabe."

Jack lifts his head and rolls his eyes.

Chapter 8
Medina, Saudi Arabia

Ammar was the youngest of three children. His older brother and sister having left home a few years ago to begin their own careers finds Ammar living with his mother, father and grandmother in their spacious central Medina home. His father is an assistant to the governor and enjoys a certain respect in the community. Their home has been in the family for three generations. Ammar is an active but typical 17 year old attending his third and final year of secondary education at the local public school. For a recent school assignment each student was asked to prepare a report researching the history of his family. They were asked to prepare a family tree and find out as much as they can about each family member. Ammar excited for the opportunity to discover the accomplishments of his proud family rushes home to begin quizzing his mother and father. Entering the kitchen he finds his mother and grandmother preparing the evening meal and shares his desire to learn about his family.

"Mother, Grandmother can you tell me anything about grandfather and great grandfather. It's for a class project. I need to find out when and where they lived and what they did. Can you help? Do we have any pictures, awards or souvenirs left that belonged to them? Huh do we?"

"Slow down Ammar" his mother cautioned "go wash-up for dinner. We can talk all about it over dinner when your father gets home. He will know more than I do anyhow."

Ammar does as he was asked and begins his other homework struggling as he always does with his math homework." Ugh how I hate it" he would say to himself. Finally his mother called everyone to the table. Father sat at the head of the table and as the second oldest male of the household he sat to the right of his father.

As the bread, humus, fruit and lamb was passed around the table Ammar eager to begin his assignment asks "Father I was telling mother earlier that for a school project we need to make a family tree identifying as much information as we can as far back as we can. Can you tell me anything of grandfather and great grandfather and what they did?"

His father always eager to encourage his son in academic pursuits responds "Well now let's see, you know pretty much about me and what I do. Remember that day I took you to work with me. You saw where I work and you saw the governor's office. Your grandfather was on the council of elders in our district back before we had a governor. I'm sure we can find some old photos of him. I do not know much about your great grandfather except that he must have been well respected for his son to become a council elder. I do recall that there are a number of old boxes in the attic perhaps they may contain some additional insight into our family. Tomorrow after school when there is more light why don't you go up and have a look around.

The next day after school, anxious to begin his search, Ammar races home and climbs a ladder through an access panel at the end of the second floor hallway to reach the attic. It was dark and very dusty. He could see why anyone rarely comes up here. Opening up the vents in the gables he was able to let in more light to begin his quest. Against both side walls he finds assorted boxes of old clothes and broken furniture. Digging deeper he finds a few picture frames but lacking any acknowledgement he could not tell of who the people in the pictures were. Was one of these rugged men dressed in their long thobe garments and keffiyeh head scarfs brandishing rifles his great grandfather he asked himself? Looking behind an old trunk he caught the glimmer of something metal. Reaching back behind it Ammar pulls forward an old scimitar sword. Excited about the find he examines it closely then begins swinging and thrusting it about in mock battles with imagined foes. Proud of his find he lays it aside and digs deeper. Noticing again the old trunk he previously passed up in favor of the sword he detects the tarnished corner caps and lid latches and decides it must be very old and wonders could this have belonged to his great grandfather. Removing the clutter from atop the trunk he gently opens the lid and peers inside. Sifting passed the old clothes, bottles, reading glasses and assorted trinkets Ammar discovers what appears to be a book rapped in brown paper tied by a string. Because of the care used in packing this item he realized it must be of some importance. Gently untying the string and removing the paper covering he holds a 7" by 4" hard covered book with the name Muhammad Hamid al-Din embossed on the cover. Realizing that this probably belonged to his great grandfather he quietly sits and gently opens the book and begins to read the handwritten script. Finding each page labeled by a date he reads of his great grandfather's early years of being chosen, because of his loyalty and gallantry in battle, to become an advisor to an Arab king. Reading further he learns his great grandfather was sent to accompany the king's son on a secret mission to Cairo to seek aide from the British in their fight against the Turks. Becoming more and more excited with each page Ammar soon finds a chilling account of that fateful trip to Cairo those many years ago.

Mecca, May 1915

It has been six months since we embarked upon the trip to Cairo. Our efforts have proven successful. The aide we sought from the British has come and we have begun our campaign against our enemy the oppressive Turks much to the joy of our king who has bestowed much admiration upon us. My fear which travels constantly within me and at times weighs heavy upon my spirit is in the knowledge of the price I paid to achieve this advantage we so desperately needed. I fear also that if the reality of my transgression comes to light it may prove devastating to all Arab peoples and bring great shame to my family and most certainly death to me. Abdulla whom I trustfully served and traveled with to Cairo has kept our secret and shares the same pain as I, for it is with his signature the ownership of the Arabian Peninsula has become the property of the British Empire. The blame for this misdeed rests upon my shoulders alone as it was because of my weakness in a time of great confusion and despair that I was deceitfully guided into this ill-conceived transfer of our land so as to preserve my name and insure the success of our mission.

*Since that fateful night I have tried in vain to contact
Addison Devencourt, the English attaché assigned to the
embassy, to retrieve or modify the deed he so masterfully
crafted playing upon my weakened emotions. It is as if he has
vanished along with the deed and I am left holding my breath
awaiting its appearance. Because of this my daily prayer to
Allah is that the deed and its author become lost or destroyed
never reaching the light of day so that my shame stays hidden
and the good name of my master Abdulla remains whole for
the good of our people for all time.*

May Allah be with us and watch over us.

Ammar sat and read the diary three times before finally closing the
cover and carries it downstairs along with the photos to see if anyone
in his family could recognize his great grandfather. All through dinner
that evening Ammar sat silently listening to his father share current
news of the district all the while thinking of the significance of the
entry into the diary. He knew that Saudi Arabia was an independent
nation not owned by the British so what was the meaning of the
notation in the diary? Was the document real or not? Later that night
he showed the diary to his father and asked his opinion.

"I do not know son. I have not heard of this before. If it was real
we would have either heard about it or seen some evidence of its
enactment."

Still the young man lacked satisfaction not knowing that his
inquisitive mind would somehow bring the world to the brink of war
when he sought the advice of a visiting Imam at his local mosque.

Following school Friday Ammar attends a young men's Islamic
teaching class at the local mosque as he does every Sabbath intending
to ground young men into the tenants of the faith. On this day the
local Imam introduces a guest teacher who speaks to the group of
teenage young men of Islam's place as the true religion of the world
and for all Muslims to stand firm for their faith willing to destroy any

that chose to oppose it. He tells of the current struggles with the West and of their ongoing attempts to limit intrusions by the West into political and social issues. This made Ammar think once again of his great grandfather's diary and the disturbing words within. After class he approaches the new teacher.

"Excuse me sir may I speak with you briefly?"

"Why of course young man, come please sit here." the radical Imam says as he motions to two empty chairs.

Ammar begins "in doing research for a class project on family genealogy I came across my great grandfather's diary. In it he talks about a deed that was executed on behalf of the Arabic king back in 1914 giving our land to England. Do you know of such a transaction?"

The man stops and stares at Ammar alarmed at the significance of such a transferal. Many years ago he heard wild tales of just such an event but being only rumors they were quickly discarded as myths and legend. Now he hears of a documented containing collaborative proof that may lend evidence to the 100 year old legend.

"Tell me young man do you have the diary with you? May I see it?"

Ammar removes the diary from his backpack and hands it to the Imam who studies the passage for several minutes. "This is most interesting" he says "may I make a copy of this. I have some friends more learned than myself that may be able to shed more light on the accuracy of the events depicted in this text."

The young man gives his permission to the old Imam who uses his cell phone to take pictures of the pertinent pages.

"Thank you Ammar you are progressing well in your studies. I will get back to you if I learn any more of this text."

The Imam bids goodbye to his local counterpart thanking him for his permission to address the young men and says goodbye to the young men as he walks outside to his car where he has time to think in private. The significance of this document, if it truly exists, has unprecedented importance to Islam and to all Arab peoples. For the infidels to own and control Islam's holiest sites is blasphemous requiring the most egregious response. He decides this is too important to leave to chance. Someone needs to begin a search for this document. He removes his cell phone and calls a preprogrammed number.

"Hello Jamal, I have much to report."

****

The International Association for the Advancement of Islam is a quasi-secret society currently headquartered on the penthouse floor of the Aladdin Hotel Casino & Resort in Macau China. Middle-East oil money built the casino and proceeds from the casino fund the operation of the IAAI along with a continued influx of oil revenue. All oil producing Middle East countries have as a line item in their annual budgets the obligation to send a small percentage of their gross revenue to the IAAI as dictated by the ruling Imams or Ayatollahs of their country as a spiritual obligation for the advancement of Islam. Outwardly the organization portrays itself as a humanitarian organization but their true mission, cloaked in secrecy, is to wipe out or convert all non-believers to the true faith of Islam. A vast network of Imams, ambassadors, emissaries, finance ministers and correspondence crews worldwide report back to the IAAI any opportunity they see to exploit a perceived weakness in the social or political sphere of Western culture. Al-Qaeda, an independent militant offshoot focused purely on terrorist attacks, is secondary to IAAI in their influence and resources to conduct successful campaigns against the West.

Omar Al Asiri was born the son of a Saudi businessman, intently schooled by radicle Imams of the superiority of Muslims over all peoples. He was taught that to deny Islam as the true religion and Allah the true god with Muhammad his prophet was a sin punishable by death. Over time, under the guidance of like-minded Imams, he embarked upon a personal crusade to destroy all nonbelievers and institutions of their making. As the son of a respected businessman as well as being spoken for very highly by influential Imams he was permitted an audience with ruling members of all Muslim OPEC nations. Meeting with each secretly he convinced them in 1973 to stage an embargo of oil sales to western countries. He persuaded the 3 key nations of Saudi Arabia, Iraq and Iran to enact the embargo initially because of America's support of Israel during the Yom Kippur war but later convinced them that their resources could be used as economic leverage against the west and their single greatest enemy Israel. He argued that America's strength was in its wealth therefore to deny them the oil they need to operate their economy and war machine was a logical step in promoting their downfall and thus deny Israel its coveted protection by the west.

Embolden by his initial success against western interests Omar next recruited a group of radical Palestinians along with members of a militant German leftist group in June 1976 to hijack an Air France jet and had them take it to the Entebbe Airport near Kampala in Uganda. The plot to kill over 100 Israeli citizens was foiled at the last moment by Israeli Defense Forces who mounted a daring raid killing all the terrorists. Omar vowed never again to take lightly his opponents and to plan future operations more carefully and more deadly to insure success.

As the years passed Omar continued to develop his craft. In 1978 he assembled a small group of radical Palestinians to hijack a bus near Haifa where they killed 38 Israelis and wounded 71 others. Following this in 1980 he assembled a group of Palestinian followers to bomb the Jewish owned Norfolk Hotel in Nairobi, Kenya killing 15 and wounding 85 and again in 1982 his followers utilizing a car bomb drove the vehicle into the Israeli Military Headquarters in Tyre killing 75 Israelis. His recruiting activities culminated in 1983 with the truck bombing of the US Marine barracks in Lebanon killing 241 American Soldiers. His lust for killing westerners and Israelis was insatiable, a quest which proved all consuming.

Through the years he learned quickly that no target was safe from attack when the attack is well planned. He also developed a network of informants who became his eyes and ears throughout the world and at the same time improved his recruiting skills which broadened his burgeoning organization worldwide. Ever careful to recruit others to carry out his plans while he remained in the background undetected to guard his identity he was able to build a reputation as a global strategist in radical Islam's war against the West. Only a small number of people now know of his name and accomplishments. Because of this he was able to convince the radical yet respected Muslim religious leaders of each OPEC nation to meet secretly with the heads of those nations and convince them to financially back his goal of Islamic dominance in the world by building his new headquarters in Macau. It was at this time that Omar met Tarique Hassan a dedicated and committed follower who shared the ideals and goals of his new found friend and mentor who more than once proved to be a valuable ally in Omar's quest.

Omar Al Asiri and his associate Tarique Hassan comprise the ruling members of the joint council of IAAI and act with total autonomy in the affairs of the organization answering to no one. Each man has a large office on opposite ends of the penthouse with a large conference room between them. On the opposite side of the main hallway beside the elevator is a receptionist surrounded by a series of smaller offices for finance and accounting staff and operation coordinators who are tasked with carrying out the directives of the IAAI. Regularly the two men meet to review ongoing operations and discuss new areas of opportunity.

There is a brief knock on Omar's door one morning and Tarique peeks around the corner "Omar, do you have a few minutes?"

"Certainly my brother come in come in."

Tarique enters and takes a seat facing Omar on the opposite side of his desk and stares out the large picture window for a moment enjoying the view of the harbor. "I never get tired of the sight of the morning sun rising over the harbor. Allah has truly blessed us in his work."

"Yes he has" answers Omar "a blessing I am most thankful for but tell me what have you heard of our newest operation to construct the stealth drones."

"The bureaucrat Sayid Kamal seems to be up for the task. He has selected people to do the actual work which is best I would not trust him with field work of any kind. We chose him only because he possessed the American stealth drone in the first place to be used as a template for building more. The initial payment to begin the work has been made."

"Do we see any problem on the horizon implementing our plan?"

"Not so far. All is proceeding well. They have even conducted a test flight of an early model which proved effective on an American war ship."

There is a knock at the door. An impeccably dressed young man steps in. "Excuse me sirs but I just received a message from one of our operatives that you are going to want to hear about."

"By all means Jamal come in" announces Omar "you are always welcome. Tell us, what is so important."

Jamal enters and stands at Omar's desk so as to face both men. "Late yesterday afternoon I received a call from one of our Imams in Saudi Arabia telling me of a 100 year old diary one of his students brought him. What sparked his interest and mine is one of the entries he photographed and sent to me. I think everything will be explained when you read the passage."

Omar and Tarique look at each other questionably as Omar reaches for the copied script. He reclines in his chair and reads the text many times over before passing it to Tarique. "Do you think this is real?" he asks.

"The timing is correct and it is historically accurate" the agent concludes "the Arab king did send emissaries to Cairo seeking British aide but as to the rest I cannot say."

Tarique lowers the note he has been reading and stares again out the window for a moment lost in thought. "There are legends alluding to this but few believe the truth in them. This is the first documented evidence that the deed may truly exist. The reason it has not been exercised by Britain might be that it is lost, destroyed or they may not know they have it. Never the less Omar can we take the chance and ignore this?"

"You are right Tarique the implications are too great. The thought of the great Satans of the West controlling much less owning our most holy sites is an abomination to all Arabs not to mention displacing our people and taking over the oil. I recommend we begin an all-out effort to track down this deed and let nothing stand in our way."

"I agree brother we must lend our full resources to destroying this deed and anyone standing in our way. We must gather our best team."

Chapter 9
Phoenix, Arizona

Jack and Raul arrive at the executive terminal beside the North runway at Sky Harbor International Airport at 7:00 AM. The terminal serviced aircraft either corporate or privately owned. The building had a simple painted slump block exterior and inside consisted of a moderately sized lounge area with seating plus a service counter to file flight plans and pay for fuel. One room to the rear serves as the manager's office for files and communication equipment. The two men enter the lobby and find Bishop quietly seated reading a newspaper. As the two men approach the general looks up.

"Hi Jack, Hi Raul glad you made it. Jack you're a pretty popular guy lately. You made the newspapers twice this month."

"Yeah that's me mister popular" he retorts.

As the three men shake hands the general waves his hand toward the door leading outside to the tarmac "Come on outside there is someone I want you to meet."

The three men exit the small terminal and walk a short distance to the first row of parked aircraft to find a short wiry man standing next to a sleek new corporate jet. "Gentlemen I'd like to introduce you to Mitch McAdams pilot of the Gulfstream" announces Bishop "Mitch can fly just about anything made and he and the plane will be available to you 24/7 for the duration of the operation." The three men shake hands as Jack and Raul introduce themselves.

"Well, what do you think of her" says Mitch as he waves his arm toward the plane.

"Sure beats riding Humvees and APCs across the desert" quips Raul.

Mitch continues, "The Gulfstream G650 has a max range of 7000 nautical miles and a max speed of Mach .925. She normally seats eight with a crew of four but we cut that down to six and no crew to make room for other things."

"Gentlemen, come on inside so we can begin" says Bishop.

The four men mount the retractable stairs and head inside to take their seats. Mitch takes his seat in the cockpit and begins his preflight check. The interior of the jet is plush and well-appointed without being garish. Six padded leather seats adjoin the windows in two neat rows. A refreshment cabinet including an ice maker abuts the rear bulkhead.

"Say General, what are those cabinets in the back for?" asks Jack.

"That's the armory and equipment lockers. You may want to notice we added a rear door through the aft bulkhead which exits beneath the plane's tail somewhat similar to the rear door on a C-130 cargo plane. This is to allow egress from the aircraft while in flight."

Jack and Raul look at each other "O......K."

Bishop takes the center seat on the starboard side of the aircraft. The work station surrounding him consists of a computer and docking port and a raised cabinet behind a desk. Bishop types a command into the computer and a 40 inch flat screen monitor rises from the cabinet in front of him. He then punches a separate key pad which activates the screen displaying the image of a very studious looking young man with glasses wearing a Batman tee shirt.

"Good morning General" he says.

"Good morning Jason. I thought it would be helpful for all of us to meet. Jack, Raul I would like you to meet Jason Hightower. He is our resident computer expert and was tasked with assembling the state of the art computer system we will be using complete with satellite hookup that will rival most any government agency. I managed to spirit Jason away from the NSA where he was adept at monitoring worldwide cell phone and email traffic and other ELINT and SIGINT and who is near criminally proficient at breaking into most any computer system worldwide. Presently Jason is residing in a nondescript vacant GAO building I found between Washington DC and Andrews Air Force Base."

"Jack, Raul good morning I've heard a lot of good things about you two" says Jason.

"Ah thank you Jason we look forward to working with you too" responds Jack.

"General, have you given Jack and Raul the items I prepared for them?"

"No I was just getting to that." Bishop hands to both men a cell phone and ear piece and to Jack a flash drive.

"What's all this?" Jack asks.

Jason chimes in "the cell phone is a special little number I made up where you two will be able to talk to each other or to me in the field hands free. The flash drive will download the contents of any computer you insert it into automatically then by inserting it into the special USB port on the phone you can transmit the files to me. I thought it might be a useful tool at times to aid your investigation. In addition I can also activate anyone's GPS signal on their phone and provide to you their constant location. Good for finding people if you know their cell phone number."

Bishop breaks back in "thanks Jason is Chester nearby?"

A short nearly bald middle aged man built like a fire plug wearing a plaid shirt open at the collar appears "I'm here general."

"Jack, Raul this is Chester Grawboski. He is in charge of armament. He is a retired master gunnery sergeant who can get for you anything you may need."

"Jack, Raul always nice to meet a fellow grunt."

"Thanks Chester" says Jack "by the way since we'll be starting this op right away I do feel a little exposed if you know what I mean."

"I'm way ahead of you Jack. Go to the rear of the plane, top drawer first cabinet on the left you'll find two Glock-17's with two standard clips and three 30 round extended clips each plus belt holsters and combat vests for storage. I've also included enough ammunition to keep you happy. This should get you started."

"Thanks Chester" says Jack as he settles back into his seat facing Bishop and the screen "I'd like to talk to all of you now about where we go from here."

"I was hoping you would have some ideas as I'm stymied" admits the General. "My contacts with the CIA have nothing. Any informants they have over in the Middle East aren't talking. Even the NSA has nothing more than the original heads up they got last week which got this ball rolling."

"Well General fortunately I do" responds Jack. "Jason I'd like you to provide the address and all background information you can about this Mohammed Sharif aka Akeem Salib who died in the accident. General if you can acquire the dead man's cell phone somehow and have Jason download and identify the call list I would appreciate it. Raul and I will check out Mohammed's place to see what we can find. Jason let me know when you get that call list and Mohammed's address. Does anyone have anything to add?

"Why pick on some strange guy who died in some self-inflicted accident and what do you intend to do with the information" inquires the General?

"Since I don't believe in coincidences and if someone really was after me like you said the only way they would know about me was my picture in the paper from the accident site and like you told me at my office he had forged papers. That's a good enough reason to start with him. We need to start somewhere and hopefully he can lead us to someone or somewhere else. Anyone have anything else"?

No one offers any further comment. "OK then let's get going" announces Jack.

Bishop signs off from the team in Washington and closes down the view screen.

"Oh General I have one more thing. I've been seeing a woman lately, Jennifer, who showed me a letter from her great grandfather who worked for the British consulate in Cairo during the First World War. The letter made reference to a deed he had granting ownership of the Arabian Peninsula to Great Britain. It might be worth checking into."

"I don't know Jack it sounds a little far-fetched to me. Let's take care of the immediate threat first. I'll mention it to the President."

Jack and Raul exit the plane as Mitch begins spooling up the two big Rolls-Royce BR725A1-12 engines for the trip back to Washington.

The two men head back to Jack's Bronco for the drive back home agreeing to start fresh tomorrow as soon as they receive the dead man's address from Jason. As they drive Raul asks "Jack, our country has been engaged in armed combat with those people over there for some time but I never really understood why they hate us so."

Jack thought for a moment, "Raul it's like this. The people I met in the villages of Iraq and Afghanistan were good caring people. They loved and cared for each other just as you or I. But poverty and oppression sometimes does strange things to people. When a people draw their identity and self-worth from their culture and their religion they tend to get hostile if one or both are threatened. Arabs have always existed as a tribal society more or less wanting only to be left alone to worship god through the Quran in peace. But some have seen the rise of western influence since the turn of the century as an affront or threat to their way of life and identity hence strike out, but instead of entering a discourse to arrive at a harmonious state ignorance, resentment and hatred stoked by the lies of crazed Imams have guided their actions. In addition radicals have asserted the superiority of Islam over other religions justifying the use of force as a means to cleanse the world of all nonbelievers opposed to the teachings of Muhammad and the Quran. Over the last 40 years or so this religion has been hijacked and distorted by those wishing to adhere to a strict narrow self-serving interpretation of the Quran until all the world comes under their banner. The radicals have created a repressive religion removing what we consider as basic human rights and freedoms so they can maintain their influence and power. The majority of Muslims recognize that the extremists are a cancer that needs to be eradicated because they tarnish the image of the whole whereby the world becomes suspicious of all Muslims. Today even many of the more peaceful Muslims of these Middle East countries are afraid themselves to speak out for fear of receiving the ire of their wayward brethren. Most all of the Muslims who have immigrated to America have embraced the American spirit and have found an ever increasing sense of freedom and peace. True Islam does not support the actions of al-Qaida the Taliban or any other faction. The terrorists are an affront against Islam and god.

"So what's the answer" asks Raul.

"I'm not sure. I think it would be a good idea for the Muslims of America who know freedom and peace to take a more active role working with moderates of their home land to help recreate the American Muslim experience. Right now two opposing narratives are playing out. One group portrays Muslims as being victimized both here and abroad. The victim narrative, propagated by Muslim leaders, has served to justify the actions of terrorists. They have advanced the Islamist grievance narrative toward a point of dominating the Muslim consciousness.

The counter narrative is not getting as much attention as it should. This narrative that Muslims love American liberty and law more so than the political climate of Muslim nations is there but is not getting traction it needs to be effective. Free Muslims need to take ownership of the problem and no longer stay silent where America could begin to see them as an asset in combating the problem. The war of narratives must give Muslim youth an alternative to help them embrace their American identity while also maintaining their faith and utterly reject the ever enticing draw that is political Islam. Muslims need to play a greater role in this struggle and not allow the victimization narrative to consume the identity of its youth. True non-Islamist Muslims need to be heard in a loud voice proclaim that they are proud of the unity which is America and wish to live nowhere else or no other way."

Raul sits silently in thought staring out the windshield.

"Let's get home Raul we've got a big day tomorrow."

Chapter 10
Tehran, Iran

To the casual observer Tehran appears like any western city. There are parks, freeways, wide paved streets, cars, traffic and buses. But looking closer at the architecture and people you begin to see the Persian influence. Hundreds of coffee shops have sprouted up in recent years and now dot the landscape such that they have become a part of society offering a private setting for meeting or a place to just escape life's pace for a while. Married and unmarried couples, friends, businessmen or single people all enjoy the private retreat and atmosphere the shops offer. Many shops offer free Wi-Fi for convenience of their customers who consist mainly of young people that comprise the largest segment of Iranian society. It is here that Azzir usually goes to meet and call contacts or to view his email. He maintains a vast network of suppliers and contacts assembled from years of work listening and talking to others at mosques and in small groups in cities and rural communities who share his view of disdain for the west. Azzir would say the harvest is ripe for rising up loyal jihadists willing to martyr themselves for the sake of Islam and Allah. From this fertile ground he has raised up many who have tasted battle with the West across the entire Middle East. Azzir would chuckle to himself inwardly each time a new recruit eagerly accepted a new assignment to conduct an attack. He knew the recruit was motivated by visions of endearing service to fulfill the will of Allah, views which he did not share or believe. His only motivation was hatred for the West and if appealing to the misguided religious beliefs of others helped achieve success for his crusade so be it. Azzir possessed no lofty ideals for his crusade of death nor did he offer any heart felt allegiance to any one group be they al Qaida, the Taliban or Sayid Kamal. He was not immune to offering his services to anyone willing to pay.

Azzir is seated quietly at the rear of the shop typing emails to an associate he was mentoring that sought advice for the best way to infiltrate an American sponsored police station in Afghanistan. Attacks such as these have proved effective since American forces were far superior at fighting long distance with aircraft, missiles and snipers. Getting close to the enemy increased the success of the attack and instilled an element of fear he actively sought whenever possible. Besides he knew he lacked the numbers necessary for an outright frontal attack therefore reasoned deception and trickery were his only option to inflict death and destruction with minimal resources. He maintained numerous email accounts and aliases with various groups and contacts which helped to secure his identity.

Sitting across the table from him is Jasim Halabi who has accompanied Azzir on many attacks and has become a trusted associate whom he has relied upon on a regular basis. Jasim, just like Azzir, began as an al Qaida fighter who quickly developed a taste for killing all things Western. Though he lacked the organizational and planning skills he was quick to recognize these skills in Azzir and sought to join his quest. There is nothing the two men will not do in the course of their war with the West. No attack too atrocious no group immune to their reign of terror. In Iraq on more than one occasion they assembled car bombs that exploded in market places killing men, women and children all designed to instill fear and hatred in the local populace against the West. His taste for the macabre started at the beginning of the Iraq war where he witnessed the beheading of an American business man. It was from here the fuse was lit that burned hot in his heart for the destruction of the West.

"Jasim, it appears one of our friends in Kabul is following in our footsteps seeking to get close to the traitors in the local police force."

"That is good my friend. If no one will join the American occupiers there is less we have to fight."

Azzir's phone begins to ring and motions to his protégé he will only be a moment. He recognizes the caller to be the leader of the advance team in America previously tasked with eliminating Jack.

"Report."

"I am most sorry to report that we were unsuccessful in carrying out your last assignment."

"Explain."

"The jackal must have nine lives. We emptied all our rounds into the restaurant where he was and still he lives."

"You failed to kill an unarmed man with all the weapons you were given. How is this possible? I am beginning to believe I sent the wrong men. You are incompetent and not worthy to be called to Allah's army and fight our enemy in his name."

Azzir was not reluctant to invoke the name of Allah in an attempt to question the worthiness of men to serve in his name knowing that their motivation stemmed from their duty and service to Allah above all else but it held no special importance to him.

"I will give you one last chance. You will kill this Jack Hunter now or you will not return at all. Reclaim your worthiness to Allah. Do you understand?"

"Yes we understand. With Allah's help it will be done."

Azzir hung up and sat for a moment staring at his phone wondering to himself if he was seeing another failed operation like the last one Jack became involved with. Was it fate? No, he did not believe in such nonsense. He looked up at Jasim.

"The team in America failed?"

"Yes, keep in touch with these men and let me know what happens."

Chapter 11
Phoenix, Arizona

Raul arrives at Jack's house early eager to get started checking out Mohammed's residence. He takes a seat on one of the padded bench seats of the breakfast nook in the kitchen where Jack offers him a cup of coffee.

As Jack pours a cup he says "Help yourself to a bagel. I got an email this morning from Jason giving us Mohammed's address. Hopefully we won't be seen but what I want to look for is evidence of what he has been up to plus signs of other players. If we can identify their names so much the better, we can have the FBI round them up while we go after Azzir. I don't know what to expect today but after my last episode with these guys I'd rather be safe than sorry" confides Jack.

"I agree but what if we are jumped? All we have is these little 9mm side arms. I'd feel a lot safer with a full auto and a few fragmentation grenades."

"Whoa easy Raul remember we are home not halfway around the world dodging camels and Taliban. We won't be looking for trouble and if we find it we'll try to avoid it. We don't want innocent people hurt. Not here."

Following breakfast the two men strap on the Glocks given by Chester and store the additional magazines in the webbing of their combat vests. "I still say these light hand guns are OK for chasing petty thieves but for real bad guys I feel a little exposed if you know what I mean" says Raul.

"They should be fine for the time being" responds Jack. He hands Raul a jacket. "I realize its Arizona but you may want to put on this light jacket anyhow to conceal the guns and magazines better.

They then head out to the barn and Jack's Bronco. "If we meet the same guys that tried to make a hit on me the other day than we have to expect they have some measure of training and they are desperate now to redeem themselves. This means if they come at us they will come hard. We need to stay alert and evade them as much as possible."

The men head out down US 60 toward Glendale, a Phoenix suburb, and the address given by Jason. "I'm somewhat familiar with the area we're going to it has a high ethnic population that may be good or bad" Jack explains.

"Does that mean there may be a network of sympathetic neighbors who will be watching and alert the hit squad of our presence?" queries Raul.

"I think the strength of their local network is a function of how long they've been here. If they have been here long enough to develop close relationships with their neighbors and if there is a sense of comradery or similar social views then yes we may have a problem. But according to Jason Mohammed has been in the country only a short while so I can safely assume the others, if they exist, have not been here long either" explains Jack.

Jack cruises around the neighborhood for a few minutes to get a sense of the culture and social fabric. Satisfied that the area is predominantly Hispanic not Muslim the two men feel they are less likely to be announced prematurely to any of Mohammed's potential associates.

As they get closer to Mohammed's apartment in Glendale Raul asks "I think it may be a good idea to just recon the place first no sense walking into any ambush besides Mrs. de Martinez didn't raise any fools."

"Good idea I'll park a block away we can pretend we're missionaries trolling for converts. We'll watch the place for a while to see if anyone is home."

Jack parks the car a block away and they both slowly walk up towards the apartment complex. Not wishing to attract attention they stop periodically and pretend to talk acting like they belong there. They managed to find a location where they could watch the apartment front door and yet not be readily visible to anyone looking out.

Raul asks "do you see the car they used when they attacked you the other day?"

"No, Bishop told me the police found it abandoned later that day, wiped clean no finger prints. It turned out to be stolen anyhow."

A couple of children are in the enclosed play area of the complex their mothers are nearby talking among themselves. Two men dressed in what appears to be their work uniform leave separately in their cars. The area appears normal in every respect.

The men watched for about 20 minutes for signs of movement within the apartment. Finding none and not wishing to draw attention to themselves by standing around any longer than necessary decide to advance on the apartment. Using high end lock picks Jack begins working the lock.

Raul, looking over his shoulder and asks "where did you get those?"

"Would you believe remnants from a misspent youth? No? Alright I had Chester send them to me after Jason sent me this address. There I got it."

The two men look around once more before entering the apartment guns drawn. As they step inside and quietly close the door behind them Raul asks "hey Jack do we need a warrant to do this?"

Jack turns grins and says in his best Mexican accent. "Warrant? We don't need no stinking warrant." They both laugh. "Besides we are not really here are we? You look in the living room I'll go check out the bed room."

A few minutes later Raul calls out "hey Jack I think I found something."

Jack comes back in "what have you got?"

"I found his lap top on the end table under a Sports Illustrated magazine. I'm thinking it may have something important on it."

"Good job. Let me stick this flash drive into it that Jason gave me. While it's down loading go get the car. I want to get out of here as soon as possible. While in the back I found evidence of five men living here. One would be the dead man from the traffic accident plus four more. I don't want to be around when they come back."

While Raul walks quickly back to retrieve the car Jack completes the down load and transmits the files to Jason.

"Jason, how does it look" asks Jack.

"It's all protected by an encryption code. It will take me a while to break it. I'll get back to you."

Jack does one last look around the place trying his best to leave everything just as they found it. He exits and locks the door behind him and walks over to Raul and the Bronco.

Slowly turning the corner up the street the three terrorists notice Jack's Bronco in front of their apartment complex. "Well, well Allah be praised. Muhammad does not have to go to the mountain the mountain has come to him. Look, is that not the same car we chased yesterday with this Jack Hunter in it? And there he is getting into the car now. This time we will not miss. Ready yourselves" the leader announces.

Jack pulls away from the curb as the SUV follows. Jack turns the corner and heads down the street. Raul takes a quick look over his shoulder and sees a suspicious black SUV. "I don't want to alarm you but I think we are being followed."

Jack peeks into the side mirror "I think you're right."

Jack reaches 43rd Ave just as the light turns yellow and slides the Bronco through a sweeping left turn. The SUV not wanting to be left behind careens through the signal now turned red narrowly missing the through traffic just receiving the green light and accelerates after the Bronco. Jack watches the advancing SUV in his rear view mirror with concern.

"I don't think my straight six can outrun his V8" he adds.

Jack sprints ahead and slides in front of a moving van which blocks the sight of his vehicle from the SUV. As Jack nears Glendale Ave he makes a hard right his tires protesting on the asphalt. The SUV not seeing Jack make the turn while blocked by the van lock their brakes to keep from missing Jack's turn. The SUV slides through the intersection, backs up much to the protests of the surrounding vehicles who voice their displeasure with blaring horns, turns and accelerates after its prey. Jack races ahead down the street and gains a few precious seconds. The SUV unleashes its full power and quickly narrows the gap with the smaller Bronco.

Jack attempts changing lanes frequently keeping other cars between his and the menacing SUV but to no avail as his assailants match him move for move. Up ahead he notices two delivery trucks traveling side by side blocking further advancement. In a daring attempt he swerves into oncoming lanes just missing head on traffic and swerves back in front of the delivery trucks thus hoping the trucks can block further advancement of the threatening SUV.

The SUV not wanting to be denied its quarry swerves also into oncoming lanes sideswiping an elderly couple from Sun City causing them to spin out of control coming to rest unhurt but pointed in the opposite direction. The SUV resumes its pursuit of the Bronco.

"This is getting out of hand Raul I'm just about out of tricks. Got any ideas?"

"Where's a cop when you need one" laments Raul.

Jack weaves the Bronco in and out of traffic trying in vain to keep distance between the two vehicles. Both vehicles race down the street. As the big SUV nears the Bronco Jack sees two 9mm Uzi's extend from both the right and left side of the vehicle and hollers "Raul get down."

A hail of 9mm rounds shower the smaller vehicle blasting out the rear window. Both men hunch themselves down below the tops of their seats. Jack tries weaving the Bronco from lane to lane to throw off the aim of their deranged assailants. "Raul, see if you can return the favor."

Raul turns around in his seat and with his left hand out the side window fires his Glock. His rounds pepper the front windshield of the SUV diminishing temporarily the rate of fire from the Uzi's. Raul's single shot Glock is no match for the fusillade of rounds coming from the automatic weapons now blasting out the side windows and front windshield of the Bronco. Raul changes magazines and continues his beleaguered assault on the SUV as the assassins continue to shred the smaller vehicle. With the body of his car now replete with holes the two men are amazed and thankful they themselves are still in one piece. Three of Jack's tires finally succumb to the onslaught of fire power from the trailing vehicle. As the Bronco begins to swerve erratically now due to the deflated tires Raul remarks "I think it's time to find cover more suitable to our safety and wellbeing. Your car has more holes than a role of Swiss cheese."

With 3 flat tires and all window glass shattered Jack pulls a hard left. The increased ground clearance of the Bronco enables Jack to jump the curb and the parking lot bumpers before swinging around into the alley behind a Big 10 Sporting Goods store. The SUV, having less ground clearance than the modified Bronco, is unable to clear the curbs and must travel a short distance further to the driveway entrance of the shopping center to continue the chase. The two men quickly exit the shattered car and head toward the rear door of the store. Jack takes aim at the door and blasts the lock and dead bolt off with his Glock. "Any port in a storm I always say" announces Jack as the men enter the building.

As the SUV rounds the corner of the alley a hail of 9mm rounds shred the door just behind the two men. Jack and Raul grateful that the store does not open until 11:00 AM this day, not placing innocent civilians in harm's way, take up positions behind shelves of camping supplies. The three assailants enter the store under a barrage of automatic weapons fire. Both teams effectively utilize the available features of the store for concealment as the fire fight continues. Jack sprints behind a display of free weights for cover as he targets the supports of an overhead shelf releasing a deluge of tents and camping stoves upon his pursuers eliciting cries in a language he thankfully does not understand. The rate of fire from the Uzi's cause Jack and Raul to keep their heads down more than they would have liked relying upon movement and quick bursts of fire to keep their assailants at bay. Jack and Raul split up to prevent the terrorist from flanking their position but the overwhelming fire power of the Uzi's cause the two men to slowly retreat further and further into the store finally reaching the front of the store where ATV's are arrayed behind the front window next to a section displaying tennis racquets. The men take up positions behind a half wall and the off road machines. Here the two teams trade fire unable to achieve any significant advantage over the other. The front window of the store becoming a series of holes and spidery cracks from the onslaught of 9mm rounds from the terrorist. Cornered and running low on ammunition Jack looks around for a means of escape. He looks over at one of the ATV's. "Do you think you can get one of these things started?"

"Good idea let me try" answers Raul.

"It appears our new friends do not have our best interests at heart" says Jack.

"I agree. Perhaps it was something we said. Do you think if we asked them nicely they will stop trying to ventilate our new clothes with bullets?" responds Raul.

"No, and I think they are about to raise the ante on our demise. How are you coming with the ATV?"

"If you can hold them off for a few more minutes I think I can get this thing started"

"Pass me one of those tennis rackets, I've got an idea" says jack.

Realizing their fusillade of 9mm ammo was not having its intended effect the terrorists decide to release a barrage of soviet RGD-5 Blast & Fragmentation Grenades into the enclosed space protecting the two men. Jack, watching each terrorist rise up to arc their supply of deadly ordinance times his response perfectly. Recalling his high school days playing varsity tennis, Jack deftly utilizes the racket to volley a return of each grenade with dazzling accuracy of forehand and backhand strokes effectively returning the lethal dose of 110g of TNT back where they came. The resulting explosions decimate what was left of the sporting goods store and the three terrorists.

"Let's get out of here before any more help arrives" exclaims jack.

"I couldn't agree more." Raul hits the starter on the ATV one more time as the big engine comes to life. Both men jumped on the powerful machine, with Jack hanging on the rear, and take off through what is left of the front window leaving three dead terrorists behind.

With shattered glass cascading down around them they race off down the street. Raul leans over his shoulder and says "Next time you ask me to go shopping with you remind me to bring my big gun and bullet proof vest"

Jack responds "It's a deal but next time I get to drive."

Chapter 12
Phoenix, Arizona

Jack and Raul ditch the ATV behind a 7-Eleven a few blocks away from the sporting goods store and call Sherry to pick them up on the next corner. Sherry arrives in her Jeep Cherokee an hour later. Two disheveled men enter the car. "What happened to you two and where is your car Jack?"

"You don't want to know but we must be getting warm" Jack responds.

"There are fire trucks and police cars all over the area. Tell me you're not responsible for this" she complains.

"OK I won't"

"I told you we should have brought more fire power" grumbles Raul.

"Raul, now don't get Sherry all upset we're fine although it looks like Bishop owes me a new car. Speaking of Bishop I better call him."

"You two guys are going to be the death of me yet" she laments.

Jack hits the speed dial number for Bishop on the cell phone Jason gave him. Bishop answers and Jack begins to tell him of the mornings events. "I need you to do me a favor. Work your magic and see if you can identify the three dead men and all you can about them. Also obtain their cell phones then have Jason go through the call lists to look for any recurring numbers either local or overseas and I.D. the numbers to find who they belong to. Oh, one more thing my car was left at the scene. Do what you can to smooth things over with the local P.D."

"Jack, you're asking for an awful lot" complains Bishop.

"Then put in a stolen vehicle report for me your call. I'm making progress. You want me to keep going or not, tic tic remember?"

"Okay, Okay you win. I'll do something. By the way Jason has nothing yet on the lap top he's still trying to break the encryption" says Bishop.

****

The next day Raul arrives early again at Jack's house. "Where are we going today" he asks.

"These guys were not ghosts. Someone has to know something about who they were or what they were doing. Let's go back to their apartment and ask around" suggests Jack.

Having had destroyed Jack's car the previous day the two men head out in Raul's F-150 pick-up toward Glendale once again. Jack asks "So how do you like your new truck?"

"I like it fine. We've always had a truck in my family. When I was little my mother and father would take my brother and sister, me and my nanna and poppa to the drive in movies. We'd all sit in back eat my mom's tacos, homemade salsa and chips and watch the movie. It was a good time. Many good memories were had by all. How about you Jack, any good childhood memories?"

"Yeah, I used to go hunting with my father. Good memories. We'd barbeque a lot out back of the ranch invite neighbors or friends over."

"Ever wonder why good memories in most people's lives surround time spent eating? I guess that's why I always wanted my own restaurant" says Raul.

"I hear you there buddy."

The two men pull up to the apartment complex and park, no longer having any reason to hide down the street. They enter through the gate and notice the same two women watching their children in the play area. "Excuse me ladies" as Jack points behind him and to the left asks "do either of you know the gentlemen living in apartment 108?"

The two women stop and look at Jack and Raul in an appraising manner suspicious of who they may be realizing the two men are new to the area. "Who are you?" one asks.

"We are friends of Akeem" Jack responds not wishing to heighten the suspicion of the two women "can you tell me where he or his roommates may be they have not been home for some time I need to speak with him?"

"No" one responds "they keep to themselves pretty much but I do know they spend a lot of time at that mosque a few blocks over."

"Thank you. We'll try over there" responds Jack.

The duo get back into the truck and head over to the mosque with help from the directions given by the women and soon find a newly constructed domed shape building with four tall minarets one in each corner of the square structure. The property also consisted of a moderately sized parking lot on the front and side of the structure. As they approach the front door they see a caretaker sweeping the steps.

"Good morning sir" Jack says "is there someone in charge we may speak with?"

The older gentleman appraises the two young men and concludes they are not of his faith. "What is this in regard" the old man asks.

"We are trying to locate some friends of ours. We were told they frequent this mosque on a regular basis."

"I do not know everyone who worships here but you can ask our Imam Abdul-Al-Malik he leads our salahs each day.

"Thank you. Where can we find him?" asks Jack.

"At this hour he is probably in his office behind the musalla or main prayer room. If you wish to speak to him please remove your shoes before you go in."

"Thank you." The two men enter, remove their shoes, and notice the beautiful rugs that line the hallways and floor. Stepping into the main prayer hall beneath the dome they notice the tall walls and a row of windows directly below and surrounding the dome to let in sunlight during much of the day. They manage to find the Imam's office as directed by the old man down a far hallway from the main prayer hall. Jack knocks on the open door "excuse me are you Abdul-Al-Malik?"

"Yes, yes I am please, please come in. How may I help you?"

Jack and Raul each introduce themselves. Finally Jack begins "Mr. Malik do you know a gentleman by the name of Mohammed Sharif or Akeem Salib that may have belonged to your mosque?"

"Why yes I do but unfortunately he died recently in a most unfortunate traffic accident. Did you know him?"

"I did but very briefly sir. Do you know the men he was sharing an apartment with?"

"Yes, they were all good young men. They were faithful in their prayers and helped out around the mosque as much as they could. Someone told me that these young men also died yesterday but the details of how or why I was not given, a most tragic loss for our community. Why may I ask are you seeking these men?"

Before Jack could answer another man enters the room. He is close to Raul's size but much younger with the beginnings of what will someday become a beard about his face but most notable to Jack was the IPod in his shirt pocket with ear buds attached to each side of his head and the apparent obliviousness to his surroundings as most young people are today he concludes.

"Oh, allow me to introduce to you my assistant" begins the Imam. "Faruq Nassar. He has been with me for some time."

The young man removes one bud and displays a questioning look upon his face, "did someone call me" he asks.

Before any could answer Jack interrupts "your Imam was just telling us that you know Akeem Salib and the men he was sharing an apartment with is that right?"

"Yes I have seen them a few times here at the mosque but I do not know them well. I am sorry I could not be of more help."

"Mr. Malik" begins Jack again "can you tell us anything about the men and what they did away from the mosque?"

The Imam thought for a moment then said "no, but they did leave a package with me containing some personal affects or so they told me. It seemed a bit strange at the time but they insisted I keep it for them. I have not looked at the items out of respect for their wishes.

"May we see the package Mr. Malik?" asks Jack.

"Certainly, I cannot see how it would hurt now that they are gone." The Imam went to his desk and retrieved a 8" x 10" manila envelope and handed it to Jack.

Jack looked at Raul and spilled the contents onto the Imam's desk. Inside was a two-year day planner and magazine clippings containing photos of New Year's celebration in Times Square New York, the

Super Bowl and the New York Stock Exchange. Jack looks at the Imam and asks "is this all?"

"That is everything they gave me" the man replied.

Jack and Raul thank the Imam for his help and walk back out to retrieve their shoes. When they get back to the truck Jack asks Raul "where is the next Super Bowl being played?"

"I believe it is at the Giants new indoor stadium in East Rutherford, New Jersey. Why."

"Do you see a pattern? New Year's Eve celebration Times Square approx. 750,000 people, the Super Bowl in the first week of February approx. 100,000 people, and the New York Stock Exchange although not encompassing a great number of people it does represent a cornerstone of our financial strength. I think we are looking at possible targets.

As the two men ponder this new revelation Jack notices Faruq leaving the parking lot in his van the ear buds still connected and other odd looking antennas on the roof.

Jack shakes his head and mumbles to himself "kids and their stereos."

Chapter 13
Macau, China

"Show him into my office as soon as he arrives" directs Omar to the attractive burka clad receptionist as he turns and walks back toward his office. As he nears his office he notices Tarique down the hall talking to an aide. "Tarique come down when you have a chance, we can get started before he gets here."

Omar enters his office and takes his place behind his desk. Tarique follows a few moments later and closes the door behind him.

Seating himself opposite Omar he begins "do you approve of my selection of Jericho for this most important quest?"

"I do. This task will require all of his talents in cunning and resourcefulness. He will need all the help our affiliates at the local level can offer along with any government officials that reside under our banner. I will give him the necessary authorization credentials to elicit their help as he directs."

Just then the young receptionist knocks on the door and announces the arrival of Jericho.

"Show him in please."

A young man enters the room. "Come in please" requests Omar "take a seat. I trust your accommodations are to your liking?"

The young man strides into the room dressed casually yet professionally in a sport coat, dress shirt, slacks and polished shoes. His movements are that of a fine tuned athlete yet does not portray the bulk of an overly muscular physique. His eyes are sharp and display an unmistakable confidence in his character. "Yes very well thank you" he returns.

"Let us begin. Tarique informs me he has shared with you a copy of the diary and he has already apprised you of the nature of the task set before you."

"He has and I will do everything in my power to recover the document."

"We know, that is why you were selected. To that end, if needed, our network of worldwide personnel will safeguard your activities. They can smuggle you out of any country before the local authorities can apprehend you if it should come to that. You will be given free rein to act as you see fit and authorized by the IAAI to request local help as needed from any of our followers. The full resources of this organization are at your disposal. You must succeed and let nothing or no one stop you. Do you understand?"

"I do, but I have a question. Why do we think this deed even exists? Surely if it did they would have exercised it by now. Logic dictates it is lost and they do not have it either or if they do have it they do not know they have it or it never existed. Either way the status quo remains. Why even call attention to it?"

"Because the implications if found are too extreme to even imagine" responds Omar "we cannot take the chance of it being found by the West. We must assure ourselves that either it does not exist or we must recover it and destroy it."

"I understand" responds the young man "how do you wish to proceed?"

"Tarique and I have decided the best place to start is to backtrack this Englishman Addison Devencourt mentioned in the diary. First go to Cairo to see if they have the deed. If it exists it will probably be hidden in their archives without their knowing. Use whatever disguise or subterfuge you wish. We can supply you with identification documents for any alias. If this proves unsuccessful go to Great Britain and make a similar search at their Foreign Office inquire about correspondence between their Cairo office and London in 1914. If this does not work research the existing relatives of Addison Devencourt for correspondence between family members."

"But if they had the deed again surely they would have given it to the government by now" responds the young man.

"Perhaps they do not know they have it" answers Omar. "We must proceed cautiously we do not want anyone to know what we are looking for so that we will be the only ones looking. If no one else believes the document exists so much the better. Keep me informed."

Chapter 14
Tehran, Iran

Azzir arrives early to the Ministry of Intelligence and National Security gaining access by way of the I.D. badge given to him by Sayid some time ago. His frequent visits to the director's office enable him to move with little to no suspicion throughout the ministry. He is pleased at how easy it has been to gain the trust of many of the employees due to his relationship with Sayid. A relationship he intends to exploit to its fullest in pursuit of his own agenda.

The Surveillance and Intelligence Records Section is located on the second floor down the hall from Sayid's office. An office Azzir has passed by many times. On each of his visits he made a point to greet the attractive young woman who manages the front counter and who is responsible to maintain the cataloging system for all intelligence records. On more than one occasion he has initiated lengthy conversations with the woman and has purposely shown a personal interest in her. The woman now believing a handsome suitor is vying for her affection allows her judgment to lax.

"Nadereh how good it is to see you today. Look I brought you some of those cookies you like from the bake shop down the street."

"Thank you Azzir but you did not have to do that."

"But I like doing things for you. I see you just received some new surveillance records. Let me help you carry them back to the sorting room. They look heavy."

"Okay, but you really should not be back here."

"But Nadereh are we not all on the same side? If it will make you feel better I will not look I promise."

She buzzes him through the security door. He lifts the two boxes and follows her back to the sorting room where documents are categorized for filing purposes.

****

The previous week Azzir visited the Fordow Fuel Enrichment Plant located 17 miles North East of the city of Qom. Here he waited patiently as workers left the facility at the end of the shift. A short time after joining the Ministry and receiving his I.D. badge from Sayid, Azzir had one of his contacts produce a duplicate under the name Farrokh Milani to hide his identity. Approaching one of the workers he shows his false Ministry of Intelligence credentials and asks the man to identify someone who works in the enrichment processing department. The man not wishing to antagonize an agent of the Ministry points out one of the engineers from that group. Azzir follows the engineer home, introduces himself as an agent and after displaying his false credentials yet again asks if he may come inside the man's home to discuss issues of national security. The man, startled by the reference, agrees to meet with Azzir.

"Mr. Hamidi it has come to our attention that there may be a person or persons within your department who are passing classified government information in the form of nuclear enrichment progress totals to the International Atomic Energy Commission. As you know this puppet of America wants nothing more than to curtail our nation from achieving our right to safe nuclear power so they may further show their arrogance and dominance over us. I need your help by giving me the names of all the scientists who work with the centrifuges and have access to the enriched uranium."

"But surely you do not need my help for this" answered the man "why not simply go to Fordow's personnel department for any or all the names of those that work there?"

"Mr. Hamidi I am sure you can appreciate the sensitive nature of this enquiry. I am also sure you can understand the need to limit the number of people who are aware of this investigation. I therefore request that you not only share the information with me but I also request your discretion in this matter and tell no one of my investigation. If I am successful in locating and apprehending the offending party or parties I will personally recommend you for an accommodation for your help in this matter. Will you help me?"

Not wishing to offend the agent or jeopardize his career by obstructing an investigation by the Ministry of Intelligence the man accedes to the request and supplies the list.

****

After placing the boxes on the table the two begin to empty them arranging the items in piles according to content. While emptying the boxes Nadereh hears someone at the front desk and excuses herself.

"Azzir stay back here out of sight so no one will see you."

When the woman leaves Azzir removes the list of names from his pocket of the nuclear scientists he received last week and quietly strolls over to the file section containing the records of government protesters active in the last presidential election. Leafing through the file of photos, names and dossiers he finds a match he was looking for.

Azzir was not sure if a match could be found but it was worth a try. Thousands of citizens in Tehran took part in the protests during the last election claiming fraud for the election of a hard line Islamic president when clearly the masses where leaning more moderate with an emphasis toward greater personal freedoms. The scientists themselves either were a product of the local university or were attached to a government agency requiring their expertise thus also their presence in Tehran so the likelihood of a son involved in the protests while also being a son of one of the scientist though not high was worth pursuing. Azzir lucked out and found a match. One of the protesters arrested but later released after the election and after the disturbances subsided was a son of a scientist on his list.

Azzir quickly concealed the photo and dossier beneath his shirt and quietly made his way back to the sorting room without being seen.

Nadereh returns to the room just then and takes Azzir's hand "come quickly you must leave before you are seen."

As she opens the security door to allow Azzir to exit the section Sayid is just entering his office. He turns to see Azzir leave from the secure facility and wonders why he would be in the Surveillance and Intelligence Records Section. The attack plan Sayid gave him for New

York did not require information contained in this section. He made a mental note to ask Azzir the next time they meet but did not see it a major concern as his trust for the man was implicit.

Azzir now armed with the evidence and documentation he needed to carry out his plan makes the 80 mile trip from Tehran to Qom in a borrowed Ministry Mercedes. In his mind he did not have a conflict between wanting the destruction of the west while yet enjoying the trappings of their technology and manufacturing prowess. Under the tutelage of Ayatollah Ruhollah Khomeini the seeds of hatred were planted and watered by the achievement of many successful attacks on western targets and personnel. The violent assaults became an obsession for him almost an addiction no longer relishing any ambitious political statement but rather delighting in the death and destruction itself. He became a man consumed by his addiction a single mindedness that could only be satisfied by ever bigger acts of violence and destruction. It was to this end that guided his journey to Qom.

Azzir located the scientist's house from the address given by the local phone directory. He realizes he must meet alone with the scientist to secure his help and so arrives by late afternoon. The dossier reveals the scientist is not married therefore he will not have to contend with a wife. Azzir breaks the glass in a basement window to gain entry into the house secure in knowing no one in this working class neighborhood will hear his entry as they are all at work. He climbs his way up to the first floor and makes himself comfortable in the living room and waits for the scientist.

The scientist arrives precisely at dinner time following his shift at the plant. He enters his house and throws his coat over the nearest chair wanting nothing more than to relax before making dinner thankful the day is over. He stops in the kitchen to pour himself a glass of ice tea from the refrigerator before entering the living room to relax in his favorite chair. As he enters the room he is startled to see a stern faced man seated on his sofa.

"Mr. Amiri I presume, please come in do not be frightened."

"Who are you what do you want?"

"Allow me to introduce myself" begins Azzir as he displays his false I.D. "my name is Milani. I work for the Ministry of Intelligence and National Security. There is a very serious matter I have come to discuss with you.

"Go on."

"As you recall your son Teymour was arrested during the last presidential election. We have records containing photos of him actively participating in anti-government protests and voice recordings of him insighting others to riot."

"He did not riot. It was a peaceful demonstration expressing his views through free speech" replied the boy's father."

"Ah there-in lies the rub. We at the Ministry interpret all acts of opposition against the government to be acts of treason and thus punishable by imprisonment for a duration as established by the Ayatollah."

"Wait" the now frightened man began "my son was released from custody and cleared of these charges."

"Released yes but not cleared. I think you can appreciate that we could not hold all the people arrested at one time. Our local detention facilities were only so big. It has taken us time to process each case separately. These are serious charges as you well know. We already have an arrest warrant and are now ready to proceed with the apprehension, trial and incarceration of your son for crimes of sedition against the government for which we have ample proof."

"Wait, this is all happening too fast. My son is only 20 years of age his whole life is ahead of him. This will destroy his life. Surely there is something we can do. I love my son I will do anything for him."

This act of desperation is what Azzir was waiting for. "I do have the authority to exercise a certain amount of discretion in these matters if we can come to a mutual understanding."

"What do you mean?"

"It is a small matter really a show of good faith on your part, an exchange of favors if you will. You do something for me and I will do something for you."

"Go on, what can I do for you to save my son?"

"Is it true Mr. Amiri that you work in the fuel enrichment section of Fordow near the centrifuges that enrich the uranium?"

"Yes but what does that have to do with my son?"

"Mr. Amiri I need you to secure ten pounds of enriched uranium. I need you to divide it up equally into four lead lined canisters. After you give to me the four canisters I will destroy the file we have on your son. He will be free to live out the rest of his life as he wishes assuming he does not repeat his transgressions. Is it a deal Mr. Amiri?"

"Are you mad? I cannot do this."

"I'm sure you can find a way. Perhaps a simple accounting error in the production levels can be made. You do have access to the production records do you not? Either way I will leave this to you. Hide the canisters in one of the outgoing delivery trucks. Call me and tell me which one has the shipment and I will do the rest. Remember your son is counting on you."

"I will do what I can."

Azzir leaves and drives back to Tehran. On the way back he calls Jasim and tells him his plan to secure the uranium is in play. He asks him to take a few men with him and to intercept the truck at a time and place he will supply soon.

One week later Azzir receives a call from Amiri. "It is done. Tomorrow at 10:00 A.M. a commercial laundry truck will arrive to drop off fresh lab coats and clean room smocks. I will conceal the four canisters in one of the soiled returning bags of clothes. The truck should leave the facility at approximately 10:45 A.M. and you will destroy my son's file. Are we clear Mr. Milani?"

"We are Mr. Amiri. If it will ease your mind you have performed a great service to the Government and your son's life is back in his hands."

Azzir calls Jasim to relay the message and his plan for the theft.

At exactly 10:46 A.M. the following day a delivery van with the name Behzadi Uniform Supply Company exits passed the guard shack at the entrance of the Fordow Fuel Enrichment Plant turns and heads back toward Qom. A few minutes later it is stopped by a large black

SUV. Three men in ski masks approach the delivery truck their H&K MP5 machine guns clearly shown.

"Please get down from the vehicle one of the gunmen urges. Open the rear door. If you do as we ask no harm will come to you."

"What is the meaning of this" the man protests "I have no money."

The driver is pushed toward the rear of the truck and opens the vertical door. "It is not your money we want." Jasim calls to one of his men "get in the back and find the canisters."

The man does so and soon locates the bag of dirty laundry containing the lead lined canisters. "I've found it" the man announces. "Let's go."

All three men jump back into the SUV turn around and head toward Tehran leaving the laundry driver confused as to what just happened. The three remove their masks and laugh together at how smoothly the theft was to conduct. The men have all worked and fought beside Azzir previously and after today have renewed respect for Azzir and his ability to plan an operation. Jasim calls Azzir on his phone.

"We have them, all went well."

"Excellent Jasim, go to the airport and wait. Do not let them out of your sight. I will arrange transport and call you back."

Azzir relaxing at a nearby coffee shop calls Sayid and makes an appointment to speak with the man telling him he has further developments to share regarding their operation. Arriving at the Ministry Headquarters a few minutes later Sayid's secretary allows his admittance to the Director's office.

"What do you have for me Azzir?" asks Sayid.

"As you know any operation of this magnitude is not without its unexpected problems. Although I sincerely intend to minimize any likelihood of disturbances I must plan for contingencies just the same."

"I agree" says the Minister "what do you need?"

"I am gathering a small team of a dozen men to act as security personnel and to offer resistance against those who would challenge the success of this mission. What I would need from you would be to provide the small arms necessary for close quarter combat to these men. I believe you have H & K MP5's in sufficient number at your disposal you might redirect for this exercise plus a sufficient supply of ammunition." Iran for years has manufactured H & K MP5's under license from H & K in Germany for which the Ministry maintains its own inventory.

"Why only a dozen men? Why not send more?" He asks.

"Sir, as you can appreciate secrecy is paramount in achieving our objective. It will be difficult enough secreting the technical staff that will launch the drones into America let alone a dozen combat personnel any more will surely be detected and alert the authorities.

"Very good I agree. Where would you have me send these weapons?"

"If you could send them under your standard diplomatic currier on the evening 5:00 P.M. flight tomorrow night to Damascus I will arrange for them to be picked up."

"I will see to it" agrees Sayid "one more thing. My sources tell me your second attempt on Jack Hunter was no better than the first plus you lost valuable field assets we will need later. Renew my confidence and tell me I chose the right man for this assignment. This grand plan we are embarking on offers a unique opportunity for us to render a crippling blow to the very soul of America, striking fear into their hearts which allows me to place our great nation at the forefront in the eyes of the world to witness the demise of America's arrogance and influence in world affairs. We must not fail.

Azzir growing weary with this pompous bureaucrat who chooses to stand along the sidelines only to tell others what to do never wanting join the fight himself decides to hold his tongue for now. "All is in order Mr. Kamal. As I reported recently the aircraft are being constructed, I will secure the explosives on my next trip to Damascus and I will arrange for shipping to the western port as soon as they are completed. And with the men I have assembled plus your armament we will succeed. As for Jack Hunter, he knows nothing that can hurt us. Every lead he had died before he could have their CIA extract any useful information."

"I hope for your sake you are right, proceed."

As Azzir leaves the building he calls Jasim and tells him once again in coded fashion to hide the canisters inside the small arms crates at the airport before they are loaded onto tomorrow evenings diplomatic flight to Damascus. He knows in his heart Jack will be coming. He only hopes a dozen armed men will be enough to stop him.

Chapter 15
Damascus, Syria

Azzir arrives on the morning Iran Air flight from Tehran to Damascus. He finds the service is generally poor, not in keeping with western standards but serves its purpose. He laments that all air transportation will be this poor the world over once America and the west are destroyed. But maybe, he reasons, there will be no air transportation at all for the west are the only ones building commercial airlines. Either way he will be content as his mission is in the destruction of the west and not in the aftermath. He proceeds to his car that he left parked before his previous trip. His plan is progressing but feels he must stay engaged with all aspects to insure success. The technicians and scientist are working, he will secure the explosives shortly and the deadly uranium will arrive tonight with Jasim. The unknown element will be to stay ahead of Jack.

Through the years he has built a vast terrorist network of sympathizers, allies, suppliers and fighters he knew he could rely upon to assist his next operation. He is cautious in all his planning and commits to memory the contact numbers for these assets in case his phone should fall into the wrong hands and reveal his contact list. Azzir pulls up to a two story apartment building on the lower east side of the city to meet with a trusted associate, a man who shares his loathing of the west and has been instrumental in planning and supplying personnel for previous attacks Imam Mansur-Al-Hamwi. Azzir climbs the steps and knocks on the door of the first apartment.

"As-salaam 'alaykum my friend come in come in."

"Thank you old friend I have been busy lately and need to rest for a while."

"Come please sit I will get us some tea and you can tell me everything."

The Imam returns with a pot of tea and two cups which he sets before Azzir on the table. "Now, it has been too long, tell me all of what has happened. How is our special surprise for America progressing? And how is that stuffed shirt Sayid? Is he still drunk with power and does he still think he is in control?"

"All is well so far my old friend. Sayid has been useful in supplying the funds for our grand plan to destroy America and yes he still believes he is in charge. He likes to call me in for progress meetings, quizzes me and lets me know that he is in control. If it wasn't so pathetic it would almost be humorous. I am growing tired of the man and putting up with him is harder each day."

He takes a long drink of the warm tea, lies back in the sofa and sighs. "Sayid is a fool. He sees this exercise as his grand plan to make the Americans shake in their boots and finally bow down to the will of Iran so his government may take their rightful place in uniting all Arabs under their leadership. Better men than him have tried to dominate the world. He does not appreciate America's capabilities or have understanding of where their strength lies. He thinks that killing a few thousand people and destroying a few buildings will destroy their will and cause them to retreat from the Middle East leaving a vacuum for Iran to fill and then finally being able to destroy Israel at will. He does not realize that this will only make them angry and that this conflict is not politically or ideologically based. It is only from the sever destruction of the source of their strength that we can then truly begin to wipe this cancer called America from the face of the earth. That is why we have taken over this operation. Let Sayid continue to pay us and believe he is in control while we strike a true crippling blow to the Americans one that they cannot easily recover from. It took them a brief 10 years to nearly complete one of the New York towers but when we detonate the enriched uranium payload an area 10 times as great will be uninhabitable for 1000's of years."

"Allahu Akbar" cries the Imam. "This is good but what of Sayid? How will you stop him if he finds out what we intend to do?"

"He will find out when it is too late. The Americans can only conclude the radioactive material came from Iran's nuclear enrichment plant and the stealth drones are copies from the one they lost over his country. The Americans will only look toward Iran as the perpetrators which will occupy their attention for many years to come and allow us to continue the fight elsewhere. By crippling America Israel will become weaker and more vulnerable. Then we can finally rid ourselves of the abomination called Israel and retake the land for all Arab peoples. We have planned and worked hard for this day to come to pass but nothing is certain."

"What do you mean?"

"There is another man, an American that has proven to be a disturbance in our plans more than once throughout the years."

"Why not just kill him?"

"I've tried but he has been either highly trained or very lucky I am not sure which but I have not been able to kill him. Three of my best men though well-armed including having the element of surprise were not successful on two occasions. I fear I will see this man again and I will have to kill him myself to finally be rid of him."

"Perhaps what we need" suggests the Imam "is to create a distraction to conceal our true objective something to occupy his time while we complete our plans for America."

"What do you have in mind?"

"If we were to plant an explosive at a Sunni mosque in Jerusalem and another at a Jewish commercial site we could turn the world's attention to the escalating violence in the region and have the Jews and the Sunni Arabs at each other's throats. They would blame each other for the death toll and seek revenge. While the American's attention is focused on trying to calm the two sides we will be free to complete our objective."

"You are very cleaver my friend" says Azzir "but for it to be convincing an Arab must be identified as the attacker at the Jewish site How do we accomplish this?"

"Do not fear my friend for there are many who consider martyrdom as an effective way of battling the Zionists hordes. I know of one such young man whom I have been working with for some time and I think he is ready to make the ultimate commitment to his faith for the good of the cause and the destruction if Israel. I would recommend a high value target, something with a large concentration of people."

"You are most imaginative my friend. I will have Jasim take care of the mosque. I will tell him to place the device to cause maximum death and injury. And you will have your man take care of the Jews in a fitting manner. Let us drink a toast to our new apocalypse. One more step towards the destruction of America and the illegitimate invader Israel. Give me some time to acquire the explosives from my supplier. I will be in touch."

Chapter 16
Cairo, Egypt

Jericho arrives at the British Embassy in Cairo dressed in the customary white robe of Saudi dignitaries. Equipped with the necessary papers, provided by the IAAI identifying him as a Saudi attaché temporarily assigned to the local consulate, he enters the building nodding politely to the marine guard stationed at the entryway.

"Excuse me" he says to the guard "would you please direct me to the diplomatic archive section for the embassy."

"I am sorry sir" responds the guard "we do not have a department devoted to that purpose. Perhaps if you would tell me more of what you need I may better direct you."

"Yes of course forgive me. I have recently been sent by the Saudi government to conduct research in an attempt to recover copies of diplomatic documents from our formative years as a nation, for historical purposes you understand."

"I see" says the guard "perhaps one of our Ambassador's assistants could be of aide to you." Extending his arm pointing toward the proper direction the guard politely offers "please take this hallway to the third door on the left."

"Thank you sir" the man says as he nodes and begins walking.

An attractive secretary looks up as the man in white enters the office. "May I help you she asks?"

"Yes, I wish to speak to the assistant Ambassador, here is my identification. As you can see I am on temporary assignment to the local Saudi Consulate" he says as he passes his identification to the woman.

"Please have a seat and I will let the Ambassador's assistant know you are here" she says.

The man does so and as the young woman returns to her desk a well-dressed gentleman emerges from his office and approaches the man. "Mr. Haddad, it is a pleasure to meet you. Please come into my office."

The two men walk into a well-appointed spacious wood paneled office overlooking the open courtyard of the embassy compound. The Ambassador's assistant takes his place behind his oak desk in his padded executive chair and offers the seat facing him to the man. "So, how may we be of assistance to the Saudi government today?"

"Thank you for your time. As I told the guard outside I have been sent on a research assignment in an attempt to reconstruct the events of the early stages of our nation, for historical purposes. I am interested in locating any and all correspondence and documents you have between our two countries between 1910 and 1920.

The assistant thought for moment before responding "regrettably I am sorry but we do not store pertinent documents of national interest here and certainly none of that age. All correspondence, letters of understanding, treaties and agreements of any kind are sent to the Foreign Office in London for archiving and disseminating. Copies are sometimes kept but only for a short time. Again nothing of the age you are looking for exists here."

"Perhaps there is someone you could direct me to in London that can help me in my search" counters the man.

"I am sorry again this is not my area of responsibility. I do not know personally the members in our government that are responsible for this work. However, if you intend to resume your search in London I will call ahead to let them know you will be coming. Perhaps they can get a head start on your search."

"Yes thank you that may be helpful. Thank you for seeing me."

The man leaves and returns to his car parked a half block away and enters the rear door. "Any luck" asks the driver.

"No" answers Jericho "this is going to be harder than I expected. How do you find something everyone believes does not exist? He takes out his cell phone and punches a preprogrammed number. "It's me no luck in Cairo. I'm going to London.

Chapter 17
Israel

Hisham Bashir is the youngest of two brothers and one sister. He was born to a poor Palestinian family living in the Gaza Strip in southwestern Israel. Unemployment is high and his mother made what little money she could as a hair dresser and his father sold bread that he baked from a brick oven in his back yard. By all standards they lived better than most families in their neighborhood yet far below any acceptable level of poverty of most countries. His neighborhood consisted of crumbling buildings pockmarked with bullet and shell holes. Many of the once larger buildings have turned into rubble due to the years of attacks by the Israeli army. If it were not for international aide many would starve. As a small boy Hisham would walk with his friends the few miles to the Israel border and looking across see modern houses, improved roads and fine automobiles. Returning to his home he would ask his parents why they did not live like the people on the other side of the fence. He was only told that the Arabs and Jews have been fighting since the end of the Second World War and after the 1967 war they were told that Palestinians were forced to live here and not in Israel. This now was their land. Periodically Hisham would see newspapers or magazines of the lives of people in other countries. Resentment began to build in his mind for the poverty imposed upon his family and others like him. He would overhear adults discuss this forced internment and oppression by the Jews and wonder why? The Imam at his local mosque spoke of the evil in the world focused upon the Arabs. Little by little resentment and hatred for the Israelis began to consume his mind. When he was 12 he witnessed a group of Palestinian men shoot a number of rockets into Israel toward one of the settlements striking several houses. Within a few minutes he heard the sounds of war planes overhead and saw for the first time the horrors of war as missiles struck his neighborhood killing some of the men who shot the rockets as well as women and children who happened to live in the area. Hisham's own house was heavily damaged in the attack and his older sister and brother were badly hurt.

Soon after, before travel restrictions were put in place, his family was allowed to move from Gaza to the West Bank where many other Palestinian families lived. They settled in Ramallah, 10 miles north of Jerusalem. Life was better but still poor. His father opened a small bakery to provide for the family. Hisham attended the local mosque on a regular basis where the local Imam instructed the young men on the tenants of their faith. It was here that Hisham met another Imam who traveled to neighboring cities to meet and talk to young men such as him. Imam Mansur-Al-Hamwi was a charismatic speaker and quickly drew the attention of the young men in the area. At age 15 Hisham was an impressionable teenager eager to hear of the history of the struggle between the Palestinian people and the Jews. The Imam told of how the world powers carved up the Palestinian homeland following World War Two to create the State of Israel effectively displacing thousands of Palestinians to satisfy their imperialistic demands. Over the years Hisham and the other young men would meet with Mansur whenever he came to town. As he grew older the discussions turned more to seeking the true will of Allah by taking up arms to drive the invaders from their lands. Jihad, he was told, was the true calling of all Muslims. He was told that honor awaits those in paradise who die on the battlefield as a martyr in a holy war. He is assured that there his sins are forgiven, food and wine abound, a crown of glory await, marriage to 70 virgins and the right to intercede on behalf of 70 family relations. The Imam reasoned to Hisham that since we are a poor nation we did not have vast arsenals of guns, planes or tanks to battle the invading Jews therefore a well-planned martyred attack where many would be killed while one of the faithful is lost, but to paradise, is an effective trade. These words did not rest easy on his mind but as time passed Hisham kept in contact with Mansur if only to hear more of the ongoing struggle of his people.

As Hisham reached the age of 20 he has been fortunate to find employment as a baggage handler at the Ben Gurion International

Airport. He maintains a small apartment in the town of Qibya just over the border of the West Bank in an Arab settlement and takes a bus ten miles each day to and from work. His daily routine reminds him of his plight in life that forever he will be a non-citizen never obtaining the dignity he or his people deserve answering daily to the orders of his Jewish task masters. Each day he sees well-dressed American, European and Jewish families freely boarding the planes to faraway places he will never see and the words of Mansur begin to weigh heavy on his mind. He reminds himself of the scars on the face of his sister and the permanent limp that afflicts his brother and after much prayer decides he must do something to right the wrongs that have been perpetrated against his family and people. He prays for courage and strength to carry out his mission. He then calls the Imam for help in carrying out his personal Jihad.

Two days later the Imam arrives at the young man's apartment with a knapsack. The Imam is quick to notice the element of fear in Hisham's voice and by placing a hand on the youth consoles him and tells him that Allah himself must have placed this noble calling upon his heart and it is by the will of Allah you will succeed. He goes on to say that this will bring honor to his family and they will forever be proud of him and that his family will be given $5,000 US dollars for his service as a martyr. The Imam explains what he must do, leaves the knapsack and departs. Hisham spends the rest of the evening alone in prayer asking again for courage and strength and manages only a few hours sleep. In the morning he has a small meal but does not wash. By tradition a martyr should not be washed, to retain his musk on the Day of Judgment. Leaving his apartment for the last time he pulls on the knapsack and heads for the bus.

Hisham reports to work beneath the main concourse and hides his knapsack behind a pile of unclaimed baggage before they are brought to their permanent storage facility. His supervisor a middle aged Israeli directs him to assist loading bags onto flight # 227 at gate #34. Hisham begins loading bags off the conveyor belt onto the baggage cars then accompanies the tractor driver out to the plane to begin the first delivery of luggage to the plane. The plane is an American Airlines

747 Jumbo Jet beginning to fill with passengers. As he works he gazes up at the clear blue Israeli sky and admires it perhaps for the first time knowing he will not see another. He looks also through the large viewing windows at the passengers and notices indifference in their faces as if everything in life is as it should be which further steels his resolve. As the baggage train empties he jumps on to return to the lower concourse for another load. Nearing the baggage handling section he jumps off the tractor and retrieves the knapsack he previously left before. Sprinting to a nearby fuel truck awaiting the arrival of the next plane he jumps into the cab and starts the engine. As he drives off he ignores the shouts of workers to return. Clutching the knapsack in his lap he drives straight toward the front of the plane just aft of the boarding walkway. Bumping his fuel truck into the fuselage of the large plane Hisham raises his face and hands toward heaven and cries *"Allahu Akbar"* then depresses the detonator. Five pounds of semtex quickly vaporizes the truck and its occupant. The resultant shock wave and fire ball from the 10 thousand gallons of jet fuel shred the aluminum skin and airframe of the Jumbo Jet igniting the additional 50 thousand gallons of fuel already on board. The resulting shock wave and fire ball destroy what is left of the airliner and all of the passengers and crew that boarded. The devastation continues to shatter the viewing windows at the gate and destroys five of the neighboring gates and incinerates all of the people inside. All totaled 390 people perish and an additional 200 are injured by shattered glass near the proximity of the blast and on the main concourse.

The evening news reported the death count as 140 American, 165 European, 60 Israeli and 25 Arabs but no one claimed responsibility for the act much to the dismay of the Israeli authorities.

Two days later a studious looking young man wearing glasses and a beard approaches the Al-Aqsa Mosque in Jerusalem as the Friday afternoon Salah or call to prayer sounds. It is the oldest mosque in Jerusalem and the third holiest site in Islam following Mecca and Medina. The mosque was first constructed in 710 A.D. a few decades after the Dome of the Rock. It was destroyed by earthquake twice in its first 60 years and rebuilt five times the last in 1035 by Caliph az-

Zahir. During the crusades the knights Templar used it as a palace and a church and were responsible for designing and constructing the Romanesque arches comprising the front facade. Sultan Saladin, the first sultan of Egypt and Syria, recaptured Jerusalem in 1187 and left the front arches but tore down all other Templar construction except the refectory along the south wall.

The man is dressed in sandals along with a standard white thobe robe and keffiyeh head scarf. He stops at the Absolution Fountain fronting the North entrance to the mosque for the traditional washing of face hands and feet. He then stands for a moment in the warm sun by the arches of the northern entrance and looks back toward the fountain and the Dome of the Rock beyond admiring the ancient culture and architecture and waits for the crowd to begin entering the mosque. The man carries a backpack and enters the mosque with other worshipers and removes his shoes. The hallway is covered by a rich red ornately decorated carpet. The interior of the main prayer hall is arranged in seven aisles comprised of arches supported by 45 columns many of white marble. Stained glass windows in white painted walls surround the hall high above the floor. Richly crafted mosaics adorn the columns and walls. As the faithful take their places kneeling about the carpeted hall the man makes his way to the front of the hall beneath the main dome. The dome having been rebuilt several times through the years and is constructed of concrete and covered in lead sheeting to give it its dark gray color. The interior of the dome is painted white and adorned in mosaics and designs from earlier times. He kneels beside other Muslims beside the wall, removes his knapsack and begins to pray. After a while he slowly pushes the knapsack against the wall and quietly rises to leave being careful not to make eye contact or call attention to himself in any way. He retrieves his sandals and exits the mosque just as the height of the Friday afternoon crowd enters the hall. He makes his way across the stone courtyard to a rental car he parked two blocks away and drives away. Traveling northward a few miles he stops at an abandoned house in a poor and blighted area of the city. Inside he removes his thobe and keffiyeh along with the glasses, wig and beard revealing a short haired olive skin young man in an Izod polo shirt and denim jeans. He replaces the sandals with Nike cross trainers he brought with him and stashes the disguise in the house. Exiting the house he sees a large column of white smoke rising from the area of the mosque he recently left. The knapsack was filled with 10 pounds of semtex and timed to detonate at the height of the mid-day prayer. Returning to his car he heads toward the Ben Gurion International Airport for his return flight. On his way numerous emergency vehicles pass him traveling in the opposite direction eliciting a smile from the face of the deranged terrorist.

The evening news reported the attack on the Al-Aqsa Mosque. The explosion caused the dome and much of the surrounding roof to collapse upon the worshipers inside. In total 83 Muslims died and another 262 were injured due to the large attendance for Friday afternoon prayer time. The mosque was severely damaged and would take years to rebuild. A reporter from a local television station interviewed senior Muslim clergy blaming the attack on Israeli extremists in retaliation for the recent airport bombing. The clergy vowed revenge for the attack on their holy sight escalating an already strained condition.

Senior Israeli officials both denounced the attack and disavowed any involvement in the attack on the Muslim people or their holy sites.

As the initial shock wore away the disclaimer was to no effect. The enraged Muslim community sought to blame the Israeli government plus western powers for the atrocity and vowed to carry the fight to the offending parties. But few could imagine the horrors yet to be unleashed upon the world.

Chapter 18
Washington DC

"What are these people doing?" the President rages. "They think nothing of killing their own. When are they going to learn to outgrow their petty squabbling? I'm trying to curtail Iran's nuclear ambitions and all they want to do is fight like two kids in a sand box. I have enough to do trying to get the Chinese and Russians on board with sanctions and other means of isolation. These attacks are taking attention away from the bigger picture. If I turn my attention now to calming down the rhetoric and easing the hostilities the momentum I've gained on the Iranian front will be lost. I can forget about the UN. They're about as useful as lips on a chicken."

Vice President Ryan Granger rises from his seat and addresses the President "Gordon, I know how you feel but getting excited won't help."

"Thanks Ryan but I'm feeling a little frustrated not only am I sworn to protect this country and its people but it would be nice if I could leave behind some resemblance of a lasting peace after all it was an important part of my campaign. It's like trying to squeeze your hands around a balloon. Once you think you got it it bulges out somewhere else. It's like these people are locked in some eternal struggle and are doomed forever to fight and kill each other for all time to come and nothing can stop it. I just wish there was some way to get their attention and solve the problem once and for all."

Just then the President's Chief of Staff knocks on the door and announces Robert Hammond and Bishop Kincaid. As the two men enter the Oval Office Hammond begins "Mr. President we finally got the report on the explosives used in the attacks from the FBI lab."

The President finds his favorite chair and relaxes briefly. "Go ahead Bob."

"Thank you sir I'll try to be brief. The explosive signature at all three sites the US frigate, the mosque and the airport bombing does conclude semtex was used."

The Vice President interrupts "wait a moment Bob what is semtex and why use it?"

"I think I can address that Mr. Vice President" responds Bishop. "Sir, it is easily obtained on the open market primarily manufactured in the Czech Republic. I've always said that the Czech's greatest export to the world has been semtex and beer. Anyhow, Semtex is a terrorists explosive of choice. Semtex is more powerful than C-4 and easily obtainable. Half a pound of Semtex could destroy a commercial passenger plane while several 1.25 pound blocks of C4 are needed to demolish a truck. It is a pliable odorless product that is virtually invisible to conventional security devices. Semtex was used to bring down Pan Am Flight 103 over Scotland killing 270 people. Over the years the Czechs have sold huge quantities to Iran, Iraq, Libya and Syria plus more has been stolen from Czech factories along with thousands of detonators. Since then illegal sales have been to other extremists and is thus readily obtainable on the black market."

"So how does that help us?" the President asks.

"Mr. President" begins Hammond "now that we know what they are using I can have my people focus on suppliers and supply routes. Once we find who is supplying the explosive we can track them to the perpetrators."

"Bob, why not simply send all our CIA operatives to ground, gather our informants and search for these guys and when you find them send in a hit squad and take them out?" asks Granger.

"Mr. Vice President," Hammond responds, "I believe it will take too long to mount an action of that type to obtain any favorable results plus the fact that those many people snooping around will surely alert our perpetrators and either scare them off or cause them to go further underground."

"How about asking our Israeli friends for help?" suggests Granger again.

"I don't think we want to do that either" responds Hammond "remember they are hip deep in the problem themselves. Anything they are caught doing will only acerbate the problem with the Palestinians and the whole area will blow up."

The President bows his head with his eyes closed and takes a deep breath clearly sensing the frustration of the limited number of options at his disposal to effectively deal with the situation in a quiet covert manner not wishing attention to be diverted from his main concern of controlling Iran's nuclear program.

He runs his fingers through his thinning gray hair and looks up at General Kincaid. "I've now heard suggestions ranging from finding supply routes to flooding operatives into the area to asking the Israelis for help. General what do you think?"

"Sir, although knowledge of the explosive supply chain has value I still think my team has the best shot at finding the terrorists directly and quickly."

"General," the president begins, "a lot is riding on whatever you and your people have planned. For the safety of the country you must stop them and for the safety of the world we need to stop them and the Iranians before it is too late. Make it happen. We're all counting on you."

Chapter 19
England

Arriving in London at Heathrow Airport, Jericho takes a cab to his hotel. After a hot shower and a savory meal delivered by room service he opens up his lap top to begin searching vital records for surviving relatives of Addison. Typing in ancestry.co.uk he enters a site containing the marriage, birth and death records for English families. Once again amazed at the openness of western society and how relatively easy it is to track down people of interest Jericho sips his tea and scrolls through the available data. The first entry to catch his eye is a marriage license issued in Cambridgeshire County to Addison Devencourt and Camille Harper in 1913. Jericho smiles at his early success. Now it is a simple matter to follow the thread he muses to himself. Knowing he is on the right trail he next finds a birth record issued in 1915 from Essex County for a Jonathan Devencourt to parents Addison and Camille Devencourt. Scanning further he finds a 1948 marriage license issued to Jonathan Devencourt and Heather Bowles followed by a birth record for an Elizabeth Devencourt in 1950 to the same couple. Much to his chagrin the English records stop here. No further marriage, birth or death records of heirs. Realizing she may have immigrated to another country he temporarily terminates the search. It will be easy enough to resume the search once he accesses the immigration records of likely countries. Terminating the search for now he decides to get a good night's sleep and renew his search for the document itself tomorrow.

Jericho arrives at the Foreign Office on King Charles Street in London and enters the main visitor's hall. Finding a directory he locates the library on the second floor. Thinking this may be a good place to start he climbs the marble stairs to his left. Jericho is amused once again at how open western countries are. So easily they give up information on themselves and travel restrictions are all but nonexistent. It is easy to see how 911 was accomplished. Entering the library he approaches the attendant at the front desk.

"Excuse me" he asks "can you direct me to copies of all correspondence between your Cairo and London offices between 1910 and 1920?"

"Why yes of course young man" responds the attendant "you may use one of our computers against the far wall. Just enter nationalarchives.gov.uk and then select the Foreign Office Card Index 1910 to 1919 and catalog reference # FO 371."

After an hour of searching not really expecting to find what he was looking for he returns to the attendant. Wanting to confirm at least one piece of information he was given decides to ask "Excuse me mam but can you tell me if a man by the name of Addison Devencourt was assigned to the Cairo Embassy in 1914?"

"Yes, it may take a moment I must access another data base." After navigating through a number of screens the attended remarks "here it is, yes, he was assigned to the Cairo Embassy from 1914 to 1915."

"Does it say where he was assigned after 1915?" the man asks.

"No I am sorry. I have no further record for him" she responds.

"What I was looking for I was not able to obtain through the web site you previously directed me to. I'm looking for documents written by Mr. Devencourt. Can you help me locate those?"

"I'm sorry sir but if you did not find what you were looking for it may be protected under national security and require the authorization of the Prime Minister or the Secretary of State for Foreign Affairs to access the document. That is of course if they exists. For personal letters or documents you would need to prove you are a family member and then obtain permission from the Secretary of State for Foreign Affairs once again. All documents are cleared on the basis of national security before released to the public."

"I see thank you" says the man.

As the man turns away the attendant ads "This must be a popular subject. I wonder why? Another woman contacted us a few weeks ago asking the same questions. She was able to obtain permission from the

Secretary of State for Foreign Affairs to retrieve copies of all documents we stored concerning this man you are researching. She was able to prove she was related to this man thus given access to personal documents."

The man's attention was instantly aroused at this new revelation. "Would you be able to tell me the name of this woman please?" he asks.

"Just a moment let me check my records" she responds. After sifting through a stack of receipts she returns "here it is, the woman's name was Jennifer White an American I believe."

"Thank you. Thank you very much" the man says as he quickly turns and leaves.

Chapter 20
Phoenix, Arizona

Jack and Raul relax back at Jack's office discussing options for seeking the terrorists responsible for the attack on the USS frigate and the two attacks on Jack. Having seen the news reports of the two bombings in Israel they realize things are heating up.

Jack sits behind his desk with his feet up on the polished wood surface, his fingers laced behind his head, and stares out the window. "You know Raul if Azzir IS behind all this it does ring true of something he would do but I also feel something big is in the works. Azzir has always had delusions of grandeur and sees himself as the great Islamic savior of the world."

"I think you are right. I remember the last fire fight we had with him in Afghanistan where he got away. I didn't see him but I can understand the hatred he must have for you interrupting his operation. I wouldn't put it passed him to deviate from his plan a little if it meant taking you out" responds Raul.

Just then Jack's desk phone rings. He picks it up and hits the intercom button so Raul can listen in. "Jason, that you?"

"Yeah Jack it's me, how you two holding up?"

"We're like a dime waiting on a dollar. Raul says hi. What have got for us?"

"Well, after much red tape and a few markers called in by the General I finally got the cell phones belonging to the four dead terrorist. The first one, the one from the traffic accident, didn't have anything useful on it. No calls to the middle-east or any recurring local numbers of any importance. The same can be said for two of the remaining three but on the third one I think we hit pay dirt. This one was probably the leader of the group and did have a recurring Middle East number on his contact list."

Raul interrupts by raising his hand "ah excuse me can I ask a dumb question? How can Jason give us a call list from the guys phone while the guys on the Aegis ship could not?"

"I think I can take this Jack" answers Jason "it's simple I have the actual phone where the call numbers are recorded on the phone's cpu. The guys on the ship simply tapped into the frequency of the call itself something like listening to your favorite radio station once you know the signal frequency. Then it's just a matter of sifting through all the simultaneous calls to focus on the one you want. That's why they need those large sophisticated computers."

"OK Jason," says jack, "can you find out the owner of the number the third terrorist kept calling and download its call list plus the next time it is turned on download that program that activates a constant GPS signal so we can find it?"

"Way ahead of you big guy, I've already ID'd the number. It belongs to an old alias of our friend Azzir and the calls all originated from Tehran. I've also downloaded the sent calls log from it and I've found a recurring number in Damascus belonging to a Mansur-Al-Hamwi a local Imam attached to a small mosque in a poor section of the city and another number used frequently to someone unknown in Tehran. It must be a private blocked land line, no way to determine the owner. Hopefully he uses a cell phone next time."

"Good job Jason. Activate the GPS on Azzir's phone we'll start with him and move out from his if need be. Oh, one other thing is Bishop around?"

Jason contacts Bishop and ties him into the call. "I'm here Jack what's up?"

"General, the two resent attacks at the airport and mosque don't make any sense. If we are supposed to be the targets why do they go after their own? I can see them targeting the Jews at the airport but Muslims where there too. Is this plan of theirs bigger than we thought or is this a smoke screen to take our eye off the ball? Then again if we go after the bombers it may lead us back to the main group. It's another avenue to accomplish the same thing."

"Negative" interrupts Bishop "stay focused on Azzir. The President shares your concerns of the effects these other distraction are having in the area. He's looking at deploying other options to calm the locals."

"I think that would be unwise" reminds Jack "I think that would only make things worse."

"I agree and that's what I told him. I think you and our team are still the best option we have at stopping this before it gets out of hand. Azzir has got to be the link pin in all this. Find him and it all ends. What are you going to do next?"

"I haven't decided, give me back to Jason."

"I'm here Jack, on to item two. Bishop tells me the FBI analyzed the residue from the explosions from the Navy ship, the Tel Aviv Airport and the Mosque all contained semtex. The chemical signature was slightly different for each which suggests the production source was different for each which indicates we are dealing with a black market supplier rather than a dedicated terrorist single manufacturer. I also managed to crack the encryption on the lap top files you sent me from Phoenix. They contained mostly local gibberish but I did find obscure phrases that must relate to something but cannot tell what. I can only conclude it must be a code for something. I'll keep working on it. The words must relate to something but the numbers stump me. They're not an account number, I've contacted banks and brokerage houses they have nothing that matches this format. I'll also keep working on that. Stand by I'll send you the first file to see for yourself."

Jason transmits the file to Jack:

    voice   wife   beautiful

29442029500545
30295149111173
30032139035546
30104329319228

"You're right Jason, it makes no sense to me either. Raul, its time for us to go on offense, feel like a trip to Syria?

Chapter 21
Damascus, Syria

Raul arrives early at Jack's house pulling into the driveway in his Ford F-150 and heads toward the barn out back. Stopping between the house and barn he gives the horn a quick blast to announce his arrival just as Jack exits the rear door. He tosses his duffle bag into the truck bed and hops into the cab.

"Why do you always have me getting up so early in the morning? Mrs. de Martinez's little boy needs his beauty sleep" Raul complains.

"Well good morning to you too sunshine. It's a long flight to Damascus and I told Mitch to meet us early at the airport. If it will make you feel any better I'll spring for a latte at Star Bucks on the way how's that?"

"Add some chorizo and eggs and you got a deal" chides Raul.

"You can put your order in with the flight attendants for whatever you want. Oh that's right there are no flight attendants. Let's get going."

After stopping for coffee the two men continue their drive out to Phoenix's Sky Harbor Airport where Mitch is waiting to fly them to Damascus. As they exit the terminal they see Mitch standing beside the big Gulfstream looking like a kid with a new toy.

"Top of the morning gentlemen" he announces "please stow all carry-ons in the overhead bins or under your seat. Leave all tray tables and seat backs in their upright position for take-off."

"Are you always this happy so early in the morning? asks Raul.

"It is when I'm driving a bus like this" Mitch jokes.

In a few minutes the Gulfstream G650 takes off and powers its way to 35,000 ft. for the first leg of the flight to Ramstein Air Base in Germany for refueling. The time allows the two men to get an extra few hours of sleep which they understand will be much needed before starting their hunt. The second leg into Damascus International

Airport is shorter and allows them to make final preparations to their quest to find and stop Azzir.

"Before we left home Bishop told me he would have a CIA operative meet us and give us a place to stay."

"How thoughtful it is of him to provide us a tour guide. I hope knows all the local hot spots."

"I don't think we'll be doing much touring on this trip. This is a sneak & peek, shoot and loot operation remember" instructs Jack.

Arriving early evening the next day the plane pulls to a stop at the small corporate terminal at the North end of the main concourse where they find a local CIA operative waiting for them standing beside his nondescript Nissan Sentra.

"Gentlemen welcome to the glorious land of camel dung and burning sand. I will be your tour guide during your stay. Oh and General Kincaid sends his regards. My name is Marty Tishman. Come on jump in. I'll take us back to the house where you can get some rest and something to eat. Mr. Grabowski has sent welcoming presents you may find of interest."

"See Jack he is a tour guide and why do people keep calling us gentlemen? Do they know something we don't?" whispers Raul.

"Easy Raul don't offend the natives. Thanks for the hospitality Marty."

The two men retrieve their duffle-bags and follow Marty to his car. As Marty drives off Jack asks "So, how long have you worked in the Middle East?"

"I've been here about five years but not all in Damascus. The company likes to move you around your first few years to give you a broader perspective of the social and political climate of the region. After that you can have your pick if you're lucky. I haven't figured out if I've been lucky or not."

"Hey Marty I want to thank you for all your help we sure appreciate it" Says Jack.

"No problem, always ready to help a fellow warrior and grunt."

"You ex-marine?" asks Raul.

"Sure-nuf, desert storm '02 & '03. After that I knocked around for a few years. Then the company offered me this gig and I couldn't turn it down. They sent me to linguistics school for two years and here I am."

"By the way" asks Jack "just how do you go about collecting local intel? if I may ask."

"Well it's a funny thing. There are those that actually like us and want to help but the majority fall into the more practical line whereby poverty and hunger causes some to adjust their allegiance and don't mind being our eyes and ears for a price. You see a self-sufficient farmer may have little need for money but a poor urban Arab needs it to survive. After that I go to mosques and coffee shops and ease drop on conversations. Once I find a likely source it's not too difficult to plant a bug here and there. But informants are still the tried and true way especially if you can find someone that is discontent with the status quo or a neighboring faction with an axe to grind willing to share information. The spy business hasn't changed very much as far as the mechanics go.

The remainder of the trip is relatively quiet as Marty navigates through the congested local streets and finally arrives and parks in the driveway of the safe house located in a neglected older section of south central Damascus.

"Well this is it, come on inside it's not much but it'll do. Feel free to make yourself comfortable. There are two extra bedrooms and a bathroom for a hot shower. I live a few miles away. We use this place to stash people we intend to smuggle out of the country or to hold private meetings. It really blends into the neighborhood doesn't it? You guys get settled in and cleaned up while I make us something to eat."

Jack and Raul look at each other wondering if they want to enter the rundown establishment. "I've seen better looking places in the poor section of Tijuana" whispers Raul to Jack.

"Maybe it looks better on the inside, come on" answers Jack.

Both men cross the dirt front yard and follow Marty inside. "You were wrong it's worse" declares Raul.

Following a hot shower and a change of clothes the two men return to the kitchen as Marty finishes the lamb stew. "Help yourself to the humus, pita bread and figs on the table while I dish up the stew."

"This smells awfully good. Where did you learn to cook like this?" asks Raul.

"Oh it's more of a skill born out of necessity than anything else. Plus I had a local girl teach me the finer points of local cooking. Say Jack, Chester's care package is over there in the corner. Check it out while I dish up dinner."

Jack opens the duffle bags to examine his latest request of implements of destruction provided by Chester for him and Raul. He mentally checks off two of each item; a Kevlar vest just in case, a Glock 17 with four 30-round magazines concealed in a shoulder holster, a combat vest with pockets, a S&W Model 442 chambered in .38 S&W Special in matte black finish with an ankle holster. The Model 442 is a double action revolver so there is no fumbling with a safety lever and it has a small internal hammer so no protruding parts can catch in your clothing during a quick draw. Also included, as any combat veteran would not want to be caught without, is a Columbia River M16-14ZSF folding tactical knife followed by a small med kit. A light weight nylon jacket serves to conceal their gear as much as possible. Included in a separate small duffle bag is the remainder of the equipment Jack asked for.

As the men sit down for dinner Jack asks "so Marty what can you tell us about the local color? Who are the movers and shakers in the terror community?"

"That's a tough one to answer Jack. The underlings are a fairly transient group. There are always those who are quick to join the fray once pumped up by the local Imam or chief Islamic militant wanna be. The head guys are a different story. The Imams like to talk but they rarely get their hands dirty. The true bad guys keep a low profile and have a select few helpers that run messages for them and also serve as their eyes and ears. These are the guys I'm after."

"As long as we're on the subject" inquires Jack "do your people hear anything about something big coming down or a man by the name of Azzir?"

"I'm sorry Jack but no. This group you're working must be very close-knit. My guess is they have to be small in number as far as the leadership goes. The support group however can be isolated from each other not knowing the other exists. The fewer who know what's going on the quieter they can be. By the way there is a small Renault auto outside around back for your use the keys are under the floor mat."

"Thanks we appreciate it" answers Jack.

"I want you to know that you and Raul have full use of the house and the Renault as long as you need them plus if I can be of any help do not hesitate to ask OK?"

"Thanks Marty we appreciate it."

The three men share an evening meal before Marty leaves to return to his apartment. Jack and Raul soon turn in to get some rest before the next day begins. Rising at mid-morning trying to recover from jet lag the two men grab a few protein bars and check their equipment one last time before heading out for the car.

"Raul, why don't you take the wheel I want to talk to Jason."

As they head off into the heart of Damascus Jack inserts the wireless combo microphone/speaker into his ear and taps it to activate the call to Jason. With his hands free he is now able to talk to and hear Jason as they ride.

"Jason, this set up you gave us works pretty well."

"Thanks Jack. Have Raul tap in so the three of us can talk."

Jack has Raul hook himself into the system. "That you Jason?" asks Raul.

"I'm here loud and clear guys where do we want to start?"

"OK Jason" says Jack "let's start by you turning on Azzir's GPS signal. Can you feed the location to my phone screen so we can track him?"

"Will do Jack. Now, for your info the accuracy of the system will not allow you to walk up and put your hand on his shoulder We're talking a 50 ft. radius at best. Now you're the only guy to know what he looks like so be sure you see him before he sees you. Here it comes."

Jack, staring at the screen directs Raul into the heart of downtown Damascus. "Find a place to park around here as soon as you can the signal locates him a block away."

The men begin walking in the direction indicated by the location signal. While approaching a cafe with a large outside seating area the men slide into an adjoining alley. From their position Jack is able to scan the assembled patrons in search of his quarry.

"According to the GPS signal he is here but I can't make him out" says jack.

"Let's get closer" suggests Raul.

The two men saunter into the dining area as if they have been there many times before while avoiding eye contact with everyone as much as possible. They find an empty table along the perimeter of the dining area allowing them the best vantage point to observe the establishment's clientele. A waiter soon appears and offers the men each a menu as they order a cup of coffee. Jack, concealed behind the menu scans the crowd looking for Azzir.

"We could just have Jason dial his number so we can listen for his ringing phone" offers Raul.

Jack returns his friend a concerned stare "no I think we'll wait."

On the opposite side of the cafe Azzir turns to call attention to one of the waiters. Jack's eye is pulled to the motion of the arm being raised and quickly recognizes the profile of the man known as Azzir.

"Gotcha" Jack whispers to himself. Jack looks over to Raul and tips his head in the direction of the man conversing with the waiter and nods to Raul. Both men observe their quarry from afar sipping his coffee and reading the local newspaper.

Jack taps his ear piece "Jason, we got him. We're in a cafe. Azzir is sitting alone on the opposite side with his back to us eating breakfast. Stand by."

After a few moments the man puts down his paper and retrieves his cell phone from his pocket and dials a number. Jack notices this is not a social call as Azzir appears anything but relaxed.

"I sure wish there was a way to know who he is talking to and what they were saying" Jack says to Jason.

"No problem" Jason offers "Raul, Azzir probably does not recognize you so if you were to walk slowly passed him with your phone I can piggyback onto his signal and we can listen into his conversation."

"Do it" says Jack.

Raul begins walking between the crowded tables toward Azzir. Not wanting to make eye contact and jeopardize the operation he waves to another patron as he passes directly behind the terrorist mindful to allow his phone, hidden in his coat, to pass as close as possible to Azzir. Completing the maneuver he circles around the cafe and returns to the table. "Jason, you got it" he asks.

"Just a moment I'm sending the signal back to you. Here it comes."

Azzir: "The construction is delicate and taking longer than anticipated."

Other Party: "I thought you said all the problems were worked out with the smaller craft you tested.

Azzir: "For the most part yes. The final version is much larger and heavier to carry the required payload and fuel not to mention the larger engine to power the craft therefore the structural design is much different. We've had some problems with cracks in a few of the welds but nothing we cannot correct. Also, our friends in the Russian Federation, though helpful, have not been very timely in supplying the guidance systems that we are generously paying for. You sound overly concerned. Is there a problem I should know about?"

Other Party: "Nothing that concerns you. A lot has been invested in more ways than one I wish only to be assured of the success of the mission. What else do you need?"

Azzir: "My chief engineer informs me that an additional $10 million dollars is required to finalize all work.

Other Party: "You shall have it. But I expect results. I will have it wired to a numbered account as before. Let me know of the final schedule once the work is complete. Check back with me in a few days.

Both men terminate the call. Azzir pockets his phone and sits for a moment longer to finish his coffee angered once again by the impudence of this bureaucrat he is forced to work with. A measure of comfort is realized when he realizes he will be through with this man once the mission is complete. Gathering himself together he stands and leaves enough cash on the table to cover his bill. He strides purposefully toward his rented Peugeot anxious to begin his day.

"Jack, Raul did you get all that?"

"Yeah Jason we did" responds Jack "Raul you run back to get our car I'll watch our friend. I don't want to lose him. I want to see which car he gets in. Pick me up on the way by. Jason, can you access his phone log to see who he called then get me a background check the guy?"

"I'm already working on it. I think we hit the jackpot. The other party used a cell phone this time not a blocked land line. The number traces to a Sayid Kamal. It seems Sayid is the Director of the Ministry of Intelligence and National Security for Iran."

"Jason patch me through to Bishop."

"Kincaid here, what have you got Jack?"

"We found Azzir, you were right he is working on a major event. He is working for Sayid Kamal the chief spook for Iran. You can have Jason give you the details. But evidently Sayid is holding the purse strings and calling the shots. I need to have our people over at CIA take a more thorough look at this guy. I need to know if he is a rogue or party player and where the funds are coming from."

"OK" responds Bishop "I'll get right on it but Jack we need to find the intended targets and stop the attack as soon as possible."

"Trust me I know. Jack out."

Just them Raul pulls up and Jack hops in "which way did he go?" asks Raul."

"Follow that blue Peugeot. Well are you ready? We're about to jump head first into the hornet's nest."

Chapter 22
Damascus, Syria

Azzir snakes his way through the local streets and finally makes his way onto the Damascus Airport Motorway. From here he drives a short 14 miles to the airport. Jack and Raul follow staying far enough back not to be seen knowing they still have the GPS signal from Azzir's phone as back-up in case they lose him.

"Weren't we just on this road with Marty? And where do you suppose this guy's going" wonders Raul.

"I don't know but it can't be good. Watch your speed I don't want to be stopped by local law enforcement. It may be hard to explain the hardware we're carrying."

Azzir parks at the executive terminal, takes a quick look at his surroundings, notices no apparent threats and enters the terminal. Jasim is there waiting in the lounge.

"Where are the crates Jasim?"

"They are safe within the impound room awaiting your arrival. All paperwork is in order and money has changed hands with the proper authorities per your direction."

Jasim takes his leader back to the holding room. "As you can see both crates of MP5's are sealed per your orders. I was able to place the canisters within before the cases were sealed."

"Open one now I wish to see them."

Jasim breaks the diplomatic seal on one of the crates and opens the lid. Inside Azzir finds six Iranian made MP5's nestled in their racks plus two canisters labeled with the universal designation for radioactive substance. A smile creases Azzir's lips. "This is good."

Parking their car near the north end of the main concourse parking lot both Jack and Raul watch through a pair of Steiner 10x50mm Military Binocular Rangefinder glasses as Azzir enters the building. They cannot see what happens inside the terminal but after a few minutes they see Azzir and one other man emerge carrying two cases which they load into their car.

Jack pulls out his cell phone and dials in maximum magnification to take a picture of the men. He keys his ear piece "Jason you still there?"

"I'm still here Jack. What's going on?"

"I'm sending you a picture of Azzir and another man. Azzir is walking in front. Can you give me an I.D. on the second man?"

"Hold on I'll run facial recognition from all data bases. It may take a little while. I'll call you as soon as I get a hit. Jason out."

Let's keep following them Raul. I have a feeling those cases don't contain Christmas dinner."

As the two men follow Azzir back to the city Jason calls Jack. "I've gone through all our databases and did not get a hit. This number two guy is either just as smart as Azzir or new on the job. We have no record of him. But thanks to you we now have one for Azzir."

"That's great but if I have anything to say about it Azzir won't be around long enough for the I.D. to be of any value to you. We're following him back to the city. Hopefully we can find out what is in those cases. I'll call you again when I have something. Jack out."

Back they drive allowing at times for other cars to drift between the two cars to further disguise the tail but still maintaining the GPS fix just in case.

Azzir and Jasim travel northward on the Damascus Airport Motorway toward the city turning west onto the Almotahalik Aljanobi Highway and then south on the Amman Highway. Finally exiting the freeway in one of the old sections of the city he stops in front of a vacant produce market and warehouse in a decayed forgotten section of the city. The warehouse is made of brick with large clear story windows along the front of the building with a loading dock in the rear. Jack and Raul park a block away and watch the terrorist leader stop and enter the building.

"We need to find out what's going on in that warehouse" says Jack. "There is an equally tall building across the street. If we can get on the roof hopefully we can use those tall front windows to our advantage."

The two men quietly approach the rear of the opposing building. Finding no one in the area they break the rusty lock and enter the building making their way up to the roof. From their vantage point concealed behind the north parapet they look across into the windows of the warehouse. Jack opens the duffle bag sent by Chester and pulls out an infrared laser listening device and begins to assemble the three main components; a laser transmitter, a laser receiver and an amplifier unit with audio recorder. The infrared laser is designed to detect the vibrations in the window glass caused by the speech of the occupants. While working Jack notices Raul sniffing the air and gives him a quizzical stare.

"What? I'm doing research for my restaurant. I could swear someone is cooking chorizo. I wonder what they use for spices in this part of the world."

"Will you pay attention? This is serious. We can have lunch later" responds Jack.

Jack finishes setting up the tripod with the listening device and adjusts the direction of the invisible beam to maximize the search tone signifying the best angle for the beam and its return. He next turns on the recorder and inserts an ear bud into his ear giving one also to Raul so both may listen in.

"Raheem, if I have not said so already congratulations on the attack on the American ship with the small scale test drone. It was most effective. I am anxious to see the results of the larger models."

"Yes, thank you. I could not have accomplished such a feat were it not for Sayid and his giving me the American drone as a copy to base the final design. Come let me show you what I and my technicians have accomplished so far."

Jack and Raul cannot see but can hear the background noise of men working and what appears to be the sound of a cover or tarp being removed. "This is the first of four drones" Raheem continues "the skin is applied and the engine installed. It waits only for the servos, guidance and navigation system. Beside it are three more partially completed air frames but as you can see the skins and engines are missing along with the same avionics."

"Have one of your men accompany Jasim out to the car I have a surprise for you." Soon two men return carrying two wooden cases that they place before Azzir and Raheem. Azzir bends to open both cases and reveals the 12 MP5's.

"I hope those are not intended for me. My men and I are not experienced solders."

"No, I will secure the additional security personnel when the time is right but look a little closer. For an added surprise to the Americans I want you to include one canister each of the nuclear material into the fuselage of the drones along with the explosive material. Together they will make a most devastating punch to the Americans. Will they not?"

"Yes, I agree" answers Raheem "it will make a most welcome addition to the Americans. But that reminds me I do not as yet have the explosive material you said was coming."

"I will have the material and detonators shortly. Proceed ahead with your work. We can have no mistakes from this point forward. Much has been planned and spent in achieving this goal. I am counting on you and your men to see it through."

Jack's infrared listening beam is concealed within a ten megapixel digital camera with a 10x lens. The viewing angle from jack's vantage point through the windows of the warehouse offers only a quick glimpse of the two men as they walked by inspecting the progress of the work. It was enough for Jack to obtain a photo of both.

"Tell me more of the avionics and what you need from the Russians."

"It is a much simplified system over what was used in the American drone yet is still complex and expensive. I will not need the high resolution camera nor the ability to release ordinance on commands from a ground base as was used by the American's drone. I will simply insert the target GPS coordinates and the craft will fly directly toward those coordinates along a predetermined altitude. GPS uses a minimum of four satellites to compute exact location in the horizontal and vertical directions. The autopilot is used to control the take-off and landing to the preset target destination coordinates. Detonation will be on impact. If you can persuade the Russians to expedite delivery of the auto pilot, inertial guidance system and GPS navigational receiver we will soon have all that we need. Then it is a somewhat simple matter of incorporating these elements and completing the work. To complete the remaining 3 airframes, skins, engines, hydraulic controls and avionics to the specifications you provided I will need approximately $10 million as I have mentioned before.

"I will have the funds shortly for you to finish. Continue the work. While we are still undetected I will make one cash withdrawal so that if the Americans somehow find out they cannot have their puppet banking institutions freeze the accounts and prevent completion of the work. If you are successful in constructing this undetectable weapon you will be given much more funds by many countries wishing similar capabilities to join our fight and your contribution will be forever remembered by our people as the grand architect of our holy war against the infidels. Allah be praised."

Raheem beams with pride. "What shall I do when I have completed all four drones?"

"When all four drones are complete you are to break them down for transport into two 40ft. shipping container to an address I will provide later. I will be back soon with the explosives."

Azzir and Jasim leave the warehouse and head for their car. Raul looks over at Jack "I've heard enough shall we just shoot them."

"Yeah, but not quite yet we still need to find all the players and Azzir is going to help us. Come on lets go."

As Raul begins to break down the equipment Jack taps his ear piece which connects him to Jason's preset number.

"Jason are you there?"

"I'm here Jack. What have you got?"

"I'm sending to you a photo of Azzir and what appears to be his chief engineer working on the construction of stealth drones. I need you to do a background check on him. Find out as much as you can. Azzir called him Raheem. I'm also sending you a recording of their conversation. Share it with Bishop. Raul and I are going to keep following them. Jack out."

Chapter 23
Damascus, Syria

Jack now confident in his ability to follow Azzir by either his GPS signal or visual contact of his blue Peugeot both he and Raul trail their prey. Weaving through city streets of old Damascus they eventually arrive at a one-story office building in a poor yet populated neighborhood. Commercial buildings consisting of markets, tailors, shoe makers are interspersed with apartment houses of varying sizes. All were designed without thought of modern safety features and few if any had anything resembling a fire escape.

"Let's stop here I don't want to be spotted" directs Jack.

Raul pulls the Renault to the curb as the two men watch Azzir and Jasim enter the building.

"There's a one story building across the street. Let's get on top and listen in as before."

The two men gather up their equipment and enter the back door of the building and make their way to the roof and quickly assemble the listening apparatus.

Peering across the street through the front windows of the old office Raul remarks "I don't see them do we have the right building?"

"Yeah they're in there I'm beginning to pick them up. They must be in a side room" answers Jack "here take one of these buds" as he starts the recorder.

"Azzir my old friend or should I say Utep or Farrokh or whatever name you are using today it is good to see my best customer once again."

"As-salaam 'alaykum my friend with your help our jihad will soon achieve an important victory."

The black marketer has supplied semtex to Azzir and others for some time. He has roots in Eastern Europe but knows allegiance to no borders. He is a business man first and last who will sell his product to anyone able to pay the price. Azzir is but another customer whom he does not trust but is cautious in his dealings. Through the years he has learned to trust no one relying only upon a close group of mercenaries to safeguard his product and enforce the conditions of each sale. His network of suppliers and buyers is preserved through a thorough background check performed on all new members.

"Is that so" the man says as he has one of his men search Azzir and Jasim. "Forgive my men but one cannot be too careful. Wouldn't you say? So, how can I help you today?"

"I require 400 lbs. of product. Can you supply this amount?"

"Azzir you *are* getting ambitious. What do you want to do destroy Israel all by yourself? Ha ha ha." His men also begin laughing at Azzir.

Azzir stands quietly and expressionless. "Are you through yet?" He asks.

The leader approaches Azzir and looks closely into his eyes "yes I can arrange to have that much brought here but are you able to pay for such an amount, it will not be cheap and I do not give discounts?"

"You will have your money, at the same unit rate as before. I will return late this afternoon with the money. You will have the product ready."

"Very well, as you wish. Come alone."

As the two men begin to leave Raul asks "well, shall we shoot them NOW?"

Jack says "yes but we need more fire power. They are heavily armed experienced fighters. We'll be back."

Jack calls Chester and provides a list of equipment he needs as soon as possible.

Chapter 24
Jerusalem

A man dressed in common middle class Israeli fashion wearing blue jeans, tennis shoes, a cotton shirt, sun glasses, a cap and beard strolls along Agrippas St. in old town Jerusalem carrying a knapsack. It is a sunny mid-week afternoon. He makes his way to the Mahane Yehuda Market located between Yafo Rd. and Agrippas St. Many shoppers are scurrying about securing items for the evening meal. The market is a magnet for shoppers, both Israeli and Arab, seeking fruits, vegetables, fish and meat as well as durable goods. It is comprised of individual stalls on both sides of narrow isles crisscrossing a section of the old city. The man slowly makes his way to the center of the market stopping along the way to sample many of the delectable items for sale by the venders. Along the way he takes time to converse with other shoppers on their opinion for the best fruit to serve lamb. Nearing a fish market he engages the proprietor on the best way to cook a certain kind of fish. As they talk he takes off his knapsack and sets it aside so he may reach over the counter to more fully examine the fish on display. The proprietor recommends a certain glaze he carries to coat the fish before broiling. The man accepts both the fish and the condiment and politely pays the owner. Conveniently forgetting his knapsack the man exits the market and walks northwesterly along Yafo Rd when he hears a defining explosion. People scream and cry as debris rains down around him. He smiles at himself, proud of his subterfuge and skill of his trade. He pulls out his cell phone and makes a call.

"It is done."

The evening news reports 28 people died and 40 more injured. Authorities are bewildered that no group has claimed responsibility for the bombing. Even so Israeli authorities condemn the attack and seek to apprehend the Islamic extremists responsible while Palestinian leadership are quick to lay blame at the feet of Israelis seeking retribution for the airport attack a short time ago. Already strained tensions in the region are further heightened. Small outbreaks of rioting have begun in various areas in the West Bank. Armed conflict and further bloodshed seem immanent.

Chapter 25
Oval Office

President Gordon Hatch seated at his desk lowers and shakes his head. "What is with these people? They do not seem willing to be happy unless the entire world is in flames."

Secretary of State Anthony Lomax and Secretary of Defense Robert Hammond are seated opposite the President. "Mr. President" begins Tony "let me send my people in there. Perhaps if we can initiate a dialog soon enough clearer heads may yet prevail."

"By all means go ahead at this point I'll try most anything" responds the President. "If only there was some way I could divert everyone's attention away from petty attacks to focus on the bigger picture of solving land and cultural disputes. Has anyone seen General Kincaid? I have not heard from him recently and I'm curious of the progress he is making on the assignment I gave him."

"On my way here I saw him at the office of your chief of staff. I think he was trying to make an appointment with you" answers Bob Hammond. "Let me go see if I can find him and pull him in here."

Hammond exits the oval office and trots down the hallway where Bishop is waiting. "General, I'm glad I caught you. Do you have time to meet with the President and the rest of us?"

The two men head back to the Oval Office. Bishop greets the President and is offered a seat.

"So, general" the President begins "I have not heard much lately what progress have you made on that assignment I gave you?"

"I'm glad you asked I was outside trying to arrange an audience with you just now. My man on the ground has put eyes on our serial bomber and has recorded damaging conversations between himself and a third party who seems to be financing the entire operation."

"Who is this third man?" the President asks.

"We believe he is Sayid Kamal the Director of the Ministry of Intelligence and National Security for Iran. We traced a cell phone call to a number registered to him. My man has traced Azzir to a warehouse where they are constructing four large drones which they intend to ship by container to an undisclosed location as soon as they are complete. We have the first name of the chief engineer and are attempting to put a dossier together on him. We do not as yet have the intended targets. They are attempting to acquire the avionics and flight control systems from the Russians. But there's a new wrinkle in the plot. Azzir has somehow managed to acquire refined nuclear material. The resultant blast will not trigger a nuclear reaction but will result in the worst kind of dirty bomb which will likely result in poisoning the affected area for a very long time."

I was about to call Jack and tell him what I learned about Sayid."

"By all means call him. I would like to hear myself" says the President.

Bishop reaches for his cell phone, calls Jack and activates the speaker phone.

"Jack here" he answers.

"Jack, this is Bishop. I'm here with the President, the Secretary of State and the Secretary of Defense. How are things going?"

"After we last spoke" begins Jack "We followed Azzir to his explosives contact where he intends to purchase 400 lbs. of what I assume will be semtex based on what you told me before. That would potentially be 100lbs. per drone. General I don't have to tell you what 100 lbs. of semtex can do. We're talking about a significant event."

"I understand. What do you intend to do now?" asks Bishop.

"If all goes well I don't need to determine the intended targets now that we know where and by whom the drones are being made and where the explosive product is coming from. I'm waiting resupply by Chester for the means to eliminate all parties completely and quietly as directed."

"Very good Jack" says Bishop "remember Azzir said he is going to add reinforcements sometime soon and one more thing, my sources over at the CIA say that Sayid does not have the means at his disposal to conduct an operation of this magnitude and if he did the government of Iran, though having a history of supporting terrorist activities, would never directly be involved with an attack on American interests. Therefore, he is a rouge player and is doing this out of the purview of the Islamic Republic, on his own, getting funding from a third party. Jack, Sayid must be stopped. I'm sending you a photo of Sayid so you will be able to recognize him should you see him.

"I hear you General and thanks" responds Jack.

"Gentlemen, this just keeps getting better and better" begins the President "I hope you all can appreciate the magnitude of this situation. Knowing what we do about Iranian involvement in this, even though not sanctioned by its government, brings with it serious international implications. I cannot allow this attack, if successful, to go unanswered as it can only be looked upon as an act of war. Therefore the full might of this nation will come to bare on Iran. I have no choice. I cannot allow the deaths of thousands of American citizens to go unanswered. That region of the globe will burn. May God help us. General, whatever your men have planned I pray they are successful the nation is counting on them because it means life or death to many thousands of people the world over. Now, Tony, get me the Iranian Ambassador. We need to try to cut this off before it's too late."

"Yes sir" responds the Secretary of State as he hurries out the door.

"Ah Mr. President" begins Bishop "one more thing, more of a side note."

"Yes what is it?"

"When this all began Jack told me he came across a reference made to some lost deed conveying ownership of the entire Arabian Peninsula from an Arab king to Great Britain through an attaché assigned to the Cairo office somewhere around the time of the First World War. I don't know if it truly exists or if it can play a part into what's happening now but I told Jack I would mention it to you.

The President stood silent for moment thinking. "Thank you General I'll keep it in mind. This could be just the thing to bring that whole place to a standstill. Keep me informed."

Chapter 26
Damascus, Syria

Jack and Raul anxiously await the overnight delivery of the care package Jack ordered from Chester. Both men are eager to extract vengeance upon those who would do America harm. For years they fought side by side in Afghanistan. In combat each new the others thoughts and lent support or aide when needed without asking.

Sitting together at the kitchen table the two men discuss their next step of the operation "How do you want to do this?" asks Raul.

"These are experienced fighters we need to be prepared for most anything. With what I have coming from Chester we should be able to hold our own. But I think we would have an edge if we knew the layout of the building. Hopefully Jason can help with that."

Jack taps his ear piece to call Jason direct number. "Jason you there?"

"I'm here Jack what do you need?"

"We're about to disrupt a major Middle East black market explosives supplier. You may have heard about it. I was wondering if you could give us an edge by providing the floor plan of the building."

"That will require me to break into the Damascus City building department to look for the original plans on file. My guess is the building is so old plans are not available much less having them in electronic format. You've been watching too many Hollywood movies Jack. Everything is not available on a computer screen."

"Alright what *can* you give me?"

"Well since we will never be granted over flight permission from the Syrian Government for a surveillance plane the next best thing would be to adjust the orbit of our LOGIRS- 12 satellites to coincide with the timing of your assault. LOGIRS stands for Low Orbiting Ground Infra-Red Signal so if I focus in on the building in question the infra-red capabilities of the satellite will give me location of hot spots equating to persons. I can give you locations and numbers of persons graphically directly to the screen on your phone. The bad news is it will not distinguish between you and the bag guys. The other bad news is since the satellite is moving its usefulness to you over the target area will last approximately 10 minutes."

"I'll take my chances. Make it so. If you have been monitoring my GPS location I was directly across the street from the building in question yesterday when I called Chester. I should have my equipment soon. How long would it take to realign the bird?"

"I can have it realigned and over Damascus in eight hours."

"Why so long? Bishop said you were a wiz at this stuff."

"Jack it takes 90 minutes to circle the earth. The path the bird takes changes with each orbit. I need to wait until it is close to Damascus before I can shove it over the required amount to give you the coverage you need. Besides it is very expensive to do and NSA doesn't like people playing with their toys if you know what I mean."

"Ok Ok, let's see eight hours puts us at early evening right after diner time. That building seemed big enough so I'm going to assume the group lives and works there while they are in town and since they just made a large sale I would think they all will be leaving soon to replenish their supply. We need to move now before they are gone. OK thanks Jason make it happen."

A short time later the men hear Marty arrive and look out to see him unloading two large duffle bags from his car.

"Show time Raul let's give our friend a hand."

The two men help Marty in and begin to empty the bags checking the inventory and organizing the contents.

"It's all here Raul. Each of us gets an all-black Nomex BDU, boots, black ski hood, two drop leg pouches, a sound suppressed M4 carbine with an AN/PVS-17 Mini Night Vision Site and M203 grenade launcher, four 30 round magazines for the M4, 10 40mm grenades, we'll swap out the kevlar vest for the Dragon Skin vest and we'll keep the combat vest with ammo pouches and the Glock 17 with four 30 round magazines we had before plus the Columbia River tactical knife and oh yeah our com system from Jason."

"What's with the Dragon Skin?" asks Raul.

"It's the state of the art flexible body armor made by Pinnacle Armor and can stop a steel core 7.62mm round so it should protect us from just about anything they'll throw at us. It's made with silicon carbide ceramic laminates forming overlapping circular disks which distribute the kinetic energy over a broader area than a Kevlar vest. Meaning it hurts less."

"I'm all for that. I would have felt a little safer if I had this during that last fight you took me to in Phoenix."

"Let's get dressed, loaded up and get something to eat. We still have a long drive over to our explosive friends."

****

Jack and Raul head out following the call for the evening Salah as dusk settles over the ancient city of Damascus. Crowds are winding their way home for the evening meal as the two armed men advance upon their prey. They weave through the local streets and make their way once again to the Almotahalik Aljanobi freeway and head east. Nearing the suburb of Irbin they exit the freeway and wind their way through the narrow local streets back to the black market supplier.

Jack taps his ear piece. "Jason are you there?"

"I'm here. In eight minutes you will have satellite support and it will last ten minutes. I will supply the feed showing the personnel hot spots directly to your phone. Good luck."

"I'll innocently drive by once Raul you keep your eye pealed for lookouts."

Jack drives the Renault slowly passed their evenings objective "I see one man with a rifle pacing on the roof" instructs Raul.

"Good, I'll park the car in the alley around back a few doors down and watch."

Jack quietly pulls the car into the alley and cuts the engine. The two men watch as the sentry on the roof continues pacing from front to back of the building.

"It takes him approximately 40 seconds to make a round trip from front to back. The next time he heads toward the front we jump out and hide behind that dumpster on the far side of the alley opposite the building" says Jack. "Ready, go."

The two men in full combat gear run down the alley and crouch behind the dumpster.

"Raul, as soon as I get the feed from Jason and I can verify they're all here we take out the one on the roof and enter the back door. If we're going to do this I want to get them all, not just one or two."

The two men wait for the minutes to tick down. After a brief moment Jack's phone screen comes to life showing an outline of the building they now sit behind with fourteen hot spots showing within the perimeter of the building plus the two in the alley outside. "It's show time."

After a few seconds the guard on the roof makes his obligatory showing along the back edge. Jack rises up from behind the dumpster and squeezes off a three round burst of suppressed 5.56mm rounds making contact with the center of mass of the lone gunman who goes down hard.

"Let's go."

Before entering the rear door Jack takes another look at the screen. "There are three men in the rear of the building on the opposite side of where we are now and the rest are scattered in the front half of the building."

Determining the element of surprise is on their side the two men quietly enter through the back door and notice a narrow unlit room with a water heater beside a small water closet along the perimeter wall. As the men advance a ceiling light is turned on and Jack quickly hides in the alcove beside the water closet and the water heater and Raul crouches beside the far side of the water heater. As the lone black marketer enters the water closet and stands at the toilet. Jack sneaks up from behind and places his right hand on the man's chin and his left hand on the right side of the man's head and quickly turns clockwise about the axis of his spinal column. The neck bones break severing the spinal cord killing the man instantly. Jack lowers him to the ground and closes the door leaving him beside the toilet. Raul looks around the corner and asks "what happened?"

"He'll be out a while. Something he ate no doubt" responds Jack. Let's go times a wasting."

As they reach the entry way of the room Jack turns out the light and peaks around the corner. He sees a large open room. To his left is another doorway to the room containing the three men displayed on his phone screen. To his right he sees a doorway in the center of the far wall spanning the width of the building and knows the remaining men will be beyond this door. He gives hand motions for Raul to take the three men in the next room while Jack advances on the rest.

Raul steps out and raises his M4 and centers the crosshairs of his night scope on the three seated men playing cards. Before they could reach for their guns Raul's rounds plow through chests and heads leaving blood and tissue strewn about the back wall. Hearing the report of the suppressed rounds two more gunmen burst into the room through the center doorway and begin to spray the room with automatic weapon fire upon seeing Jack and Raul. Jack, kneeling at the first doorway fires two controlled bursts of three rounds each from his M4. The angry duo are quickly dispatched leaving their automatic weapons fire to arc the ceiling as their lifeless bodies crumble to the floor in a puddle of their own making.

Jack and Raul advance to take up positions on opposite sides of the center doorway and listen for the remaining gunmen.

Raul looks over at Jack and says "I guess they know we're here now. How do we want to do this?"

Jack looks at his phone screen "We're down to six men. Two appear to be in a room directly to our left and the rest are scattered about the remaining "L" shaped floor space."

Jack peaks around the corner and is met by a hail of automatic weapons fire. "The time for playing nice is over."

Jack chambers a 40mm round into his M203 launcher and nods to Raul. His friend sticks his M4 out from behind the doorway and fires three controlled bursts designed to lower the heads of all those down range. Jack targets the open door of the room next to them and sends the round on its deadly mission. The resulting explosion decimates the room and all those contained inside. Wallboard and framing material rain down upon the entire front half of the building. Jack and Raul were soon covered in the gray and white powder of the wall and ceiling material.

"A little overkill wouldn't you say Jack?" asks Raul.

Hearing no sound from the front of the building Jack decides to advance down the hallway to survey the damage and look for survivors. As he steps out into the hallway the angry remaining gunmen now unleash a torrent of automatic fire directly at him. Three rounds of 7.62mm find their mark directly in the center of his chest thrusting him back through the doorway where Jack lays inertly on his back.

Raul quickly comes to his friend's aide and pulls him aside out of the line of more fire. "Jack, are you alright?"

"Ow. Did you get the number of that truck that just hit me?" He feels his chest and Dragon Skin to check for damage. "I'm I glad I got this thing on."

Both men hear joyous hollering from the front as a small block of semtex attached to an electric timer sails past them. Fortunately their assailants did not know the exact location of the pair, due to the wallboard dust, and the deadly package passes them and continues on into the room containing the three expired card players before exploding. Both men hug the ground as the resulting explosion shatters the roof and back wall of the building. The incendiary power of the blast is enough to start a small fire which quickly grows within the building.

Jack looks over at Raul extracts and slaps in a new magazine and says "let's end this."

Both men swing their weapons around the doorway corner and let loose a barrage of fire power. Both sides trade fire. The black marketers employ both 9mm Uzi and AK-47 rounds on full automatic in an all-out attempt to defend against their unrelenting attackers. As the two men advanced into the larger room Jack stiches two gunmen up their chest and into their face with two 3 round bursts from his M4. Receiving 9mm rounds into their vests both men are still able to advance exchanging fire with the gunmen. Raul follows suit and blows the back of one man's head off with a well-aimed shot to his forehead effectively covering the front window in a mist of pink as the remaining two gunmen flee out the front door.

"Go after them Raul I need to check on the fire."

"Do we need to worry about the fire setting off any of the remaining semtex Jack?"

"No I don't think so. Fire does not usually set it off. You need a blasting cap to do that. Go now I'll handle this."

When Raul exits the front door he sees the passenger door of a black panel truck close as the vehicle begins to accelerate down the street. Quickly loading a 40mm round into his M203 grenade launcher Raul takes aims and lets loose the round at the rear of the fleeing vehicle. The round makes contact with the rear doors of the vehicle and shreds them, the blast wave burrowing itself deeper into the vehicle. As the blast wave progresses it continues to shred the sides, roof, and floor sheet metal until it reaches the gas tank where it ruptures into an exploding fireball flipping the vehicle onto its roof and cooking all inside.

The structure fire now out of control begins to engulf the neighboring two floor apartment building. The semtex explosion has sealed off the rear exit of the building with debris and severely damaged the ground and second floor apartments at the rear of the neighboring building. Jack forces his way into the ground floor of the building through the partially destroyed adjoining wall only to hear the screams and cries of people trapped within. Raul instinctively knowing the location and intent of his friend of many years enters the front of the building and sees Jack standing in the hall of what is left of the rear of the building.

"Raul, clear these apartments we need to get these people out. I'll free the people in the rear."

Shouldering his rifle Jack begins to lift and remove the fallen timbers of the second floor clearing a path to the door of the first apartment nearest the explosion. The rising flames and thickening smoke made seeing and breathing difficult in his efforts to find the occupants of the apartment. Burning his hands on the bedroom door

Jack forces his way in to find a woman barley conscious and two small children already unconscious hiding under the bed. Jack quickly reaches for them and pulls them out. He tucks the two small children under one arm. The woman who is barely able to stand is carried fireman style over his shoulder. Jack, now coughing and his eyes stinging from the smoke stagers out into the hallway where he hears screaming coming from the second floor. Running as best as he can, his lungs on fire, he passes off his recovered victims to Raul at the front of the building.

"Start CPR on the young ones."

"Jack, it's all going up. Did you get them all?"

"No, I heard more screams on the way out there are more. Take these three and get out. I'm going back."

Long ago Jack discovered he could not allow those weaker than himself to be oppressed or be made victims. It began in third grade when his best friend was punched and thrown in a puddle by a group of fifth graders who thought the entire episode was quit humorous. Unable to do much about it he vowed that someday he would stand against injustice wherever he found it. During high school one of the school's perennial bullies would regularly torment a smaller classmate in the lunchroom. By this time Jack's physical size and appearance was beginning to take shape. When the bully began flicking food at the timid classmate Jack simply walked over picked the larger boy off the ground and unceremoniously dumped him headfirst into the trash can much to the cheers of the student body.

Watching the flames begin to engulf the rear of the apartment house brought to mind similar horrors he experienced in Fallujah when seeing the sheer terror on the faces of the children, the hopelessness on the faces of the innocent people caught helplessly in the midst of war was just too much. He was not going to let it happen again even if it took everything he had he was not going to let those people die. Placing one foot on the fallen beam rising himself up and thrusting his foot through the hallway wallboard to make another foot hold up through the ceiling he climbed. With his left arm over his face to filter out the smoke as best he could he advanced on the corner apartment. The hallway wall was severely damaged and the door was aflame. Jack attempted to kick in the door to no avail. On the fourth kick it splintered open. Inside he found the entire apartment in flames. Feeling the flames closing in on his hands and legs Jack drops to the floor to improve his vision through the smoke as much as possible. No longer does he hear the screams of the apartment's occupants. Noticing a piece of fabric sticking out from beneath a closet door he crawls over and opens the door. Inside he finds unconscious two teenage sisters. Quickly he picks each one up over his shoulders and stumbles back out the apartment coughing and choking barely able to see where he is going thankful that the Nomex BDU was protecting his body from the flames. Nearing the hole in the floor he looks down to find his faithful friend reaching up to accept his new charges. Easing the two girls down through the floor Jack quickly follows and the two men carry the young girls out the front door into the fresh air. Initiating CPR the two girls come around and begin crying and thanking the two strangers. A smiling face was all the thanks the two men needed.

Not wanting to be discovered by the local authorities the two men leave feeling determined more than ever to exact out their brand of justice to those responsible for the chaos that surrounded them.

"Let's get out of here. I've got a date with Azzir but first I need to call Chester. I need a special surprise for our friend.

Chapter 27
Oval Office

President Hatch, seated at his desk with his hands behind his head, in the oval office stares out the window into the rose Garden. Vice President Ryan Granger and Secretary of State Anthony Lomax are seated on a sofa facing the President. "You know Tony as President I'm supposed to have all the answers but sometimes I just don't. This whole Middle East thing is more than I can understand." He swivels his chair to face the two men. "Surely these people know that their prosperity will increase and their lives will improve once peace is achieved, but no they seem to draw a sense of self-worth by fighting and killing others. And so it goes on with no end in sight. It seems the only thing they respect is military might."

The Vice President interrupts "Gordon I agree and it is no secret that the Arab world may fear our military might but they do not respect us either. I think because we are viewed as outsiders and an ally of Israel, not to mention all non-Muslims are infidels, that we are unable to broker a meaningful peace arrangement. They will take our money for oil and foreign aid but little else."

"Tony" the President asks "have you had any luck from the diplomatic side? You said your people were working the problem."

"Yes sir we have met privately with both the Israelis and the Palestinians. For the moment some resemblance of a peace is in place. Tensions are high due to the three bombings. I fear one more attack and all hell will break loose. It troubles me that no one has come forward to take responsibility for the attacks. Bragging rights are usually a part of the MO but because no one has come forward it is as if someone is purposely trying to incite the region. Who and for what purpose I do not know."

The President's phone rings and he taps the speaker button allowing the two other men in the room to listen in. "Yes?"

The Whitehouse Chief of Staff comes on "Mr. President the Iranian Ambassador is here at your request."

"Thank you Leonard. Have one of the Secret Service agents escort him down here will you please."

"Yes sir."

"Normally I would have Leonard do the honors of escorting Ambassadors back to the Oval Office but after hearing what's been going on I no longer respect the SOB.

The agent knocks briefly and ushers the Iranian Ambassador into the president's office.

The President steps around from his desk to greet the Ambassador purposely not using his given name "Mr. Ambassador thank you for coming. You know Secretary Lomax and Vice President Granger."

"Yes indeed I do. Good afternoon gentlemen."

"Please everyone take a seat make yourselves comfortable" directs the President as he sits in his favorite chair once again facing the men.

The President begins "Mr. Ambassador I hope you realize why I asked you to come today. Recent developments in the Middle East have given us a moment of pause to consider the implications of further bloodshed. As you are aware tensions on both sides have heightened and I hope you can agree that de-escalation in tensions is warranted at this point."

"I agree that peace is always the preferred route but why have you asked to speak to my government?"

The President not wanting to tip his hand regarding knowledge of Iranian involvement in the previous attacks for the time being attempts to appeal to the Ambassadors ego "Mr. Ambassador your government is not without certain influence in the region. What can you do to help the cause of peace and avoid further bloodshed?"

"But Mr. President surely you know this has been an ongoing struggle between the Palestinian people and Israel for some time. We neither take sides nor do we participate in the conflict. We are a peaceful people."

The President secretly fumes inside at the sound of the Ambassador's words but restrains himself not wishing to show his emotion and violate the first rule of diplomacy: never get angry. "Come come the whole world knows you supply Hamas, Syria and Hezbollah with weapons of all kinds. Why? And now an American airline has been attacked. Are you looking to escalate this hostility?"

"We admit to nothing but you must realize much of this is a result of America's foreign policy and America's arrogance in the world. All nations should be free to determine their own identity and place in the world and not be dictated to be America. The whole Middle East can and should be an Islamic Arabic region. We only wish to see come to pass that which is a natural evolution of the region and an attempt to create a unified kingdom for all Arabs.

"And of course" interrupts the President "you would create this unified kingdom under the guidance of Iran."

"Again we seek only the natural evolution of the region. We are merely the facilitators. The Arab peoples themselves will decide the means of government within their individual countries."

"But you want to dictate terms in the region" the President presses.

"This is no different than what you sought to do in Vietnam. You attempted to interfere in the natural direction of an evolving society into communism and replace it with a democratic form of government. You lent your military might to force the political and cultural trends toward a direction of your choosing. In the end you did not succeed and eventually neither will you do so here. All hostility would decline if America would leave the region entirely."

The President asks "Does this mean eliminating aide to Israel?"

"Yes."

"You would replace Israel with an Arab state?"

"Yes, just as you would have replaced North Vietnam with a democratic government. The difference is the will of the Arab people surrounding Israel is in agreement with this. We are only assisting them in their quest just as you inserted yourself into an Indo China civil war and sought to invoke your will. We only seek the natural order of things for the Middle East. Again please remember the Arab people greatly outnumber the Israelis and have lived here for many hundreds of years and have never left. The Jews chose to migrate to Russia, Europe and elsewhere through the centuries. Yes a few Jews never left but only a small number. In the 19th and 20th century they started to migrate back and thought to renew their nation. It is only that after the Second World War a few misguided bureaucrats in Europe decided by themselves to give land they had no right to give to a people that once left and now wish to return. How is this fair? No, the Middle East belongs to the Arabs and we have sought for a unified Arab region since World War I. It is you that must make room for us. The Arab world will unite again under Iranian leadership. We only seek the natural order of things and support the will of the majority. Does not your democracy espouse to the will of the majority of the people? We seek the same. I promise you this though, if you leave all hostility will cease against your nation."

The President growing irritated by this pompous bureaucrat decides to determine his end play. "So to achieve this unification of Arab lands you speak of and to preserve the will of the Arab peoples you seek to develop a nuclear option to destroy the invading Israelites once and for all?"

"Mr. President my government has always maintained that all countries have the right to develop safe nuclear power. Again we will not succumb to the dictates of America nor your sanctions. Our nuclear program will be for power generation and medical research. This we have said many times. As for the Israelis time will tell. The world view is slowly changing. Israel no longer enjoys the full support of the entire world. Many countries in the west are beginning to soften their position on a home for the Palestinians. Perhaps with continued pressure things will change."

"So is this where you see the future going? Continued bloodshed until Israel is wiped out? You do realize America is committed to Israel and will protect her with our full capabilities?"

The Ambassador shrugs and says "Perhaps, we shall see."

The president now totally beside himself over the audacity of this senior official stares directly at him wondering who will blink first "Very well Mr. Ambassador. Thank you for coming. Tony will you escort our guest out please? I believe an agent is waiting to escort the Ambassador to his car."

The President waits for Tony to return then retreats back to his desk lays his head back and takes a deep breath. "Good grief these people are crazy. They would lay siege to an entire nation to satisfy some archaic dream of uniting all Arabs within a selected region.

"Well Gordon I think it's like the man said this has been an ongoing struggle between the Palestinian people and Israel for some time" Remarks Ryan Granger.

"That's fine Ryan but it does not help us solve the problem of escalating unbridled hostilities between Israel and surrounding Arabs and Iran with a runaway nuclear program in the hands of psychotic nationalists with depraved intentions on one of our allies. Pray we find an answer before it's too late."

Chapter 28
Damascus, Syria

"Do we know who was responsible?"

"No Azzir. My man only told me their entire operation was wiped out. All of them were killed and their location was burned down. They are no more. You will need to find another source for your explosives."

"This is of no matter Raheem. We now have all that we need for this operation. There is plenty more out there and new sources will be easy to find. But tell me more. What do the authorities say?"

"All is quiet. It was not the police or the military otherwise news of the fight, who was responsible and what happened would be broadcasted on the radio and television. So far no one knows nor is anyone claiming responsibility and no arrests have been made. My man says the authorities came to put out the fire and collect the bodies including those in a burned out vehicle. They are asking questions of those in the area but no one knows."

"Umph, it sounds like our friends could have bit off more than they could chew. Perhaps it was a deal gone sour, an unhappy customer, a supplier was cheated or perhaps it was a competitor looking to expand his market. It does not concern us and since they are all dead, we have the last shipment and there is no one left to talk. All is well my friend."

"I hope you are right."

"Come, show me more of the progress on your flying machines."

"I am afraid I have little more to show you. However once I receive the additional funds we spoke of I will be able to finish."

"Ah yes the funding. I have secured the final funding you requested. It will be arriving soon."

"I would feel better if you could secure additional fighters for security purposes."

"I already have. They will join me when I go to retrieve the funds. I have acquired the entire amount in cash as I mentioned before so that the funds cannot be traced or frozen if we are discovered. But once you have the funds you requested you must finish quickly."

"I will. Our Russian friends say they are holding the avionic systems until they receive payment. I have also already lined up the remaining servos, actuators, cables and aluminum stock. I have also fitted the explosives and uranium canisters appropriately."

"Very good Raheem it will not be long now."

After a good night's sleep following the previous evenings sortie to eliminate the source of the explosives component Jack and Raul are up early the next day and once again perched outside the warehouse listening to the conversations below.

"Jack, are you getting all this? It sounds like our performance last night is receiving great reviews. I think it deserves an encore. What do you think?"

"I think you're right let's not disappoint them."

Chapter 29
Damascus, Syria

As evening descends upon the suburbs of Damascus the hustle and bustle of the day's activities begin to wind down. Some enjoy a late evening meal others allow their children one last chance to play outside before coming for bed. As in any desert community the temperature noticeably drops as the sun sets behind the western skyline and as the evening lights come on the remnants of a typical Middle East sunset fills the horizon with radiant colors of red and gold.

Anxious to hear how the previous day's mission played out Marty quietly pulls up to the safe house. Down the street he can hear a woman calling to her children to come inside it's getting late. As Marty approaches the house Jack opens the front door holding a large bag of trash in his hand.

"Marty, when was the last time you cleaned this place. You weren't kidding when you said you wanted to blend in to a depressed neighborhood."

"Jack, you don't have to do that."

Jack returns an icy glare as he passes Marty on his way to the communal trash bin. Marty steps inside to see Raul actively sweeping the floor. "What's up with Jack?"

"Oh don't mind him. He thinks better when his hands are busy doing something. He's probably cooking up something special for our friend Azzir. What can we do for ya?"

"I came by to ask about your little op late yesterday. It seems there was a disturbance and fire across town. Did you guys have anything to do with that?"

"Yeah that was us" admits Raul.

"The locals say two strangers saved them from a burning building including some kids. I thought you were supposed to be quiet about this. Take care of business, in and out with no one knowing about it?"

"Look Marty, let me tell you something about Jack. He's the kind of guy that will give you the shirt off his back. Look what he did for me. I'd not seen him for 2 or 3 years, show up at his door step, he invites me in and treats me like one of the family. He hates injustice and looks after those weaker than himself. That's why he went into the fire to save those people. He's as faithful and loving as a blue tick hound. He can be your best friend in the world but don't mess with the less fortunate or those that belong to him. He'll shove a stick up your ass and break it off."

"Ah, thanks for the heads up Raul."

Jack re-enters the house and looks around for his next chore.

"Hi Jack, what's happening?" asks Marty.

"Keeping my hands busy helps me think. What have you heard?"

"Not much. The authorities have ID'd the men you smoked as black marketers with known terrorist involvement. No great loss but they are looking for two men seen in the area. You know I want to help you guys but I was told to lay low, hands off, this is a solo operation.

"Yeah we know that's why we got someone else" admits Jack.

Just then they hear a thump on the front door. Raul strides over to see who's there. As he opens the door Mitch steps in carrying a large duffle bag. "Hi guys what's happening?"

Jack and Raul greet their new friend at the front door of the safe house shaking hands. "Bishop had me fly in your latest care package from Chester right away special delivery.

"Thanks for coming Mitch you're right on time we sure could use an extra hand on this one. Come on in." Gesturing a hand toward Marty he continues "This is Marty the proprietor of this humble abode if you have any problems with it take it up with him."

"Thanks Jack glad to meet you Marty I hear you guys have been making progress."

"Yes we have made some inroads, come on in to the kitchen, Raul poor a cup of coffee for our new friend. Put your feet up relax."

"Uh oh, this doesn't sound good already" responds Mitch.

The four men seat themselves around the kitchen table. Raul pours them all a cup. "OK lay it on me what are we going to do? Remember I'm just a plane jockey."

Jack and Raul look at each other for a moment then at Mitch "well to tell you the truth we're going to steal Azzir's money."

"Although not exactly in our normal playbook this does sound quite imaginative. But I thought the game plan was just to eliminate the offending parties why concern ourselves with the money?" asks Mitch.

"Bishop said the President told him he wanted the problem to go away. That means taking out all the players. We cannot afford to have this technology falling into the wrong hands. And because if we do it right it will lead us to the rest" answers Jack.

"OK I'm in what do we do?"

****

A black SUV and a black van pull up beside the warehouse. Azzir and Jasim exit the two vehicles and enter the drone factory. A short while later twelve hard looking men of local decent begin to arrive.

"Ah my brothers it is good of you to come, glory awaits those that serve Allah in our holy jihad" announces Azzir. "Come, take up your arms" as he directs the men to the two wooden cases. "Today you are the right hand of Allah as you protect the plan he has devised to render a crippling blow to America."

Azzir pulls Raheem aside "you see my friend every precaution has been made. You not only will safely have the money you need to finish the work in a few weeks now but have the additional security necessary to insure your success."

Azzir turns to the new arrivals "it is time, come my friends your first assignment awaits."

The men exit the warehouse and climb into the waiting vehicles. Azzir and Jasim enter the front seat of the SUV with four gunmen behind them. The remaining eight gunmen all enter into the trailing van.

"Jack, did you get all that?" Asks Mitch as the three men listen from across the street. "What do you want to do?"

"We'll work the plan. Mitch, you follow the two vehicles in our Renault. Don't let them see you. If you lose them ask Jason to help reestablish location through Azzir's GPS signal. Keep in touch. Get going" directs Jack grateful that he got an additional phone and headset for Mitch.

"Raul, you're with me, grab your equipment come on we have work to do" says jack.

The two men climb down from the roof of the building with their listening equipment and head toward a pickup truck Marty acquired the day before.

I saw them drive off to the North so I will assume they will return the same way. There are three roads that lead back to this warehouse from the main street. We are going to block off the other two to channel them down the street of our choosing.

"Where did you get all those street barricades in the back of the truck" asks Raul.

"I requisitioned a supply from a neighborhood construction site late last night while you were getting your beauty sleep" answers Jack.

The two men drive out to the main road to review their choices of access routes the gunmen will have on their return. The first contains a number of local businesses with numerous pedestrians and children running about. "Too many innocents around when the lead starts flying" decides Jack. "Let's move on."

They drive to the second intersection. It too has many pedestrians but offers the most direct access to the warehouse. "Although they will prefer this route we can't take the chance of hurting innocent civilians. Let's look at the last one" decides Jack.

The third access road coming off the main street abuts up to the rear of commercial establishments. Fronting the street are garage doors, dumpsters and loading docks. "Of the three roads I chose this one. It may not offer the most direct access to the warehouse but it's the safest for civilians. Let's get to work and set the barricades on the other two intersections" directs Jack.

The two men work quickly luckily to have the orange vests and hardhats normal construction crews wear so as not to draw attention to their efforts, items Jack also requisitioned the night before. Finishing the work on the barricades the men head down the third road.

"This is good, we'll stop here. I'll park the truck in that alley behind us. Help me set the claymore" says Jack.

"Ah, Jack this road is paved we're going to need a jack hammer to dig"

"Nah, look at the pavement. See all the cracks. The asphalt binder has mostly washed away leaving the exposed aggregate. It will be easy digging. Get the shovel. Besides our pothole will look like all the others. No one will know the difference."

As the two men begin working Raul asks "Why are we using a claymore rather than a couple pound block of C-4?"

"Standard explosives have a spherical destructive pattern which radiates in all directions. I want to minimize peripheral damage to property and civilians. The claymore has a 60^0 blast angle which I will direct upward toward the underside of the vehicle away from the neighbors. Besides it does contain 1.5 pounds of C-4 plenty to do the job. You finish hiding the claymore and run the wire back to the alley. Cover it with some dirt I'll start setting up the traffic cones that will guide them directly over the mine."

A few minutes more and the trap is set. The two men retreat back to the alley and wait behind the truck. "I better call Mitch to find out what's happening" says Jack. "Jack taps his ear piece "Mitch you there?"

"I'm here. We've stopped at a bank down town. They're coming out now. Two men are carrying one large suitcase each and are placing them in the rear of the van. Eight men in the van and six are in the SUV same as before. They're heading back your way."

"Head back this way too Mitch and keep your head down. Let me know when they near the third street into this neighborhood. CK Raul, show time. Let's lock and load and get our vests on."

As the men get ready and hide themselves beside their vehicle in the alley Raul asks Jack, "why did we plant the claymore 15 yds. downstream of the alley? Wouldn't it be better to have them right in front of us so we can hit them quickly?"

"If we did that we'd be caught between the two vehicles when the lead started flying. Not good. This way we also don't get caught by any flying debris and the lead vehicle is far enough away that they won't be an immediate threat once the shooting starts. Hand me the clacker it won't be long now."

"Jack, it's Mitch. The lead vehicle just passed the first street."

"I hear ya Mitch stay sharp."

The two vehicles enter the third street approximately 20 yds. apart and begin accelerating down the street. The two men now positioned beside the truck and located behind a dumpster placed at the head of the alley as they watch the first then second vehicle pass their position. Both men cover their ears as the second vehicle begins to pass over the claymore concealed in a pothole as Jack triggers the clacker. The resulting explosion and shockwave sends 700 steel balls at close to 4,000 feet per second vertically into the air effectively shredding the van in two directly behind the driver's seat killing the two occupants up front and seriously injuring the two in the first row of seats. Jack and Raul keep their heads down as debris lands all around. The remaining four men though dazed spill out the far side cargo doors like disturbed bees out of a nest and begin firing their automatic weapons on anything that moves. The first vehicle having heard the explosion quickly stops. Its occupants disembark with guns drawn searching for targets. One man stepping around the back of the van is quickly dispatched by Raul with a well-placed three round burst of 5.56mm steel jacketed lead to his neck and face. Jack crouches behind the dumpster and begins to exchange fire with members of the lead vehicle as Raul races to take up position behind the van where the first man fell. The three remaining gunman who exited the van quickly advance further down the street to take up defensive positions in front of a car 20 ft. ahead of the van. The group from the first vehicle conceal themselves in front of their SUV and behind a dumpster positioned to the left of their vehicle as they pour 9mm rounds down the street at Jack and Raul. The two groups exchange gunfire each unable to achieve an advantage due to the tight quarters. As Jack and Azzir pause to replace magazines in their weapons they each peer around their cover to make eye contact for the first time. Upon recognizing Jack, Azzir's first expression of amazement quickly turns to rage. Jack returns the icy glare with a large grin and a nod of his head. "Good to see you too Azzir" Jack says to himself."

As each group has the other pinned down Jack realized that he must move to improve the angle of fire upon his adversaries. Jack taps his ear piece to hale Raul. "Cover me."

Raul inserts a new magazine and releases a torrent of 5.56mm rounds down range in an attempt to keep the heads of the gunmen down as Jack races forward to reach concealment beside a car parked with its nose pointed into the building on the left side of the alley effectively shielding Jack from fire from the SUV and from the three gunmen hold up directly across the street. The three men now realizing that if they stay in front of the car they are exposed to Jack from across the street and if they move to the side of the car they are exposed to Raul decide to lay a barrage of fire in the direction of the two men and fall back closer to their comrades hoping to find safety in numbers.

Their plan was doomed from the start. As each man stands to release a hail of 9mm lead Jack rises to stitched one man center of mass with a single burst from his M4 just as one round from the lead vehicle impacts the center of his vest knocking him to the ground. Raul quickly diving to the pavement from behind the van effectively terminates the remaining two gunmen as they race down the street. One man receiving a through and through behind his right ear which causes the left side of his head to disappear in a cloud of blood and brain tissue the other receiving a round slightly left of center of his spinal column and halfway between his collar bone and center of his chest severing his carotid artery his arms and legs flailing as he falls headfirst into an awaiting trash can.

Azzir seeing Jack fall begins to feel elated at the final demise of Jack Hunter. But his joy starts to sour as he sees Jack slowly get back up.

Raul keyed his headset "Jack, you alright?"

"Yeah time to end this." Now crouching behind the car Jack raised the barrel of his carbine to insert a 40mm grenade into his M203 launcher. Azzir and his men, witnessing their impending demise release a steady stream of automatic fire in the direction of the two men. One lucky round impacts the launch tube beneath the barrel of Jack's weapon making it operable and nearly wrenching it from Jack's hand. The overwhelming firepower of Azzir, Jasim and their four gunmen allows them to reenter the SUV and escape. As they flee Jack and Raul pepper the SUV with rounds from their M4's to no avail.

The two men stand in the center of the roadway watching the SUV drive off. "I guess we know where they're going" observes Raul.

"Yeah we know where they're going but do they know we know" answers Jack. "You go get the suitcases out the back of the van and find someplace safe for them I'll go see if our friends left anything else of use behind. We gotta get out of here fast before government troops arrive."

"OK Jack. We did pretty well so far haven't we? By the way I never did tell you what my last name means in Spanish did I? It means son of the god of war."

"I knew I brought you along for a reason. Come on buddy. Let's get outta here." Jack taps his ear piece "Mitch you there?"

"I'm still here Jack. Good shooting you guys."

"Head back to the house. Raul and I will meet you there. We're not done yet."

Chapter 30
Damascus, Syria

The team weaves their way through town as quickly as traffic will allow. Jack concludes that a city planning director or a traffic engineer was just not on the payroll or up to the task as the city grew. Narrow streets and inadequate traffic control devices hamper the free flow of movement. Jack wonders why there are not more accidents. Mitch arrives at the safe house in the Renault about the same time as Jack and Raul do in the pickup. The men carry their equipment inside to clean and reload their weapons before heading back to the warehouse for the final confrontation with Azzir and his crew. Placing their gear on the kitchen table Jack removes his vest and shirt to inspect the bruise on his chest from the 9mm round and the one from the previous day's assault on the arms dealer. Wincing a little from the soreness he decides all is well. The one sustained in the assault on the black marketers was sore but beginning to heal.

Watching from across the table Raul remarks "sure beats the alternative doesn't it Jack?"

Jack nods, sits down gently and taps his ear piece now reset for Jason. "Jason, you there?"

"I'm here Jack. How's it going?"

Jack fills Jason in on the latest events. "I need you to monitor Azzir's phone ASAP. I have a feeling he's going to be calling Sayid soon to tell him what we did and ask for more money. Oh and you might as well bring Bishop up to speed also." Jack terminates the call. "Ok let's load up and get back out there. Mitch I have a special assignment for you this time."

****

Azzir, Jasim and the four remaining gunmen storm back into the warehouse. Raheem notices the look of distress upon the man's face.

"What is wrong my friend did the bank not have the money that was promised to you?"

"Oh they had the money but on our return that meddling devil Jack Hunter ambushed us killed eight of our men and took the money. I need for you and your technicians to pack up the entire project and move to a new location. Hurry I fear he will be here soon. Start filling your truck and I will have another here in ten minutes."

"But where are we going?"

"Just get moving now. I will tell you on the way."

"It is a good thing I do not have all the remaining material and equipment. If we did I could never move it fast enough. I will get my men started."

Azzir turns to Jasim. "Help them load and then go with them. You know where to go. I will join you there later."

As the men begin work breaking down the partially completed drones Azzir steps off to a quiet corner and calls Sayid and tells him what has transpired.

"What! How did they know? I knew that letting this Jack Hunter live would come back to haunt us. This is your doing Azzir. You have failed twice before to kill him. Now we are on the brink of losing control of the whole operation. We cannot afford to fail or stop now. How are you planning to salvage this undertaking we have invested so much in?"

Azzir thinks for a moment "they must be listening to us somehow and probably right now. We must destroy all of our cell phones. We cannot use landlines or email either. This is how they must have learned where we will be and what we are doing. But they do not know everything."

"So how will we communicate?" asks Sayid.

"From now on we must use once again the system we used for our operation in Afghanistan. It is not as efficient but is much safer. I will tell the others."

Sayid thought for a moment remembering the failed attempts and the observance of Azzir exiting the Intelligence Records Section and fraternizing with the clerk and now begins to wonder if he can fully trust this man to complete the final stage of the assault. He wants nothing to interfere with his planned attack on America. Sayid realizing this attack must go off exactly as planned because if not and word came back to his government that he conducted an unsanctioned attack on American soil his career and most probably his life would be over. "You will have a lot on your mind to complete this assignment so I will assist you by sending to you ten new men to provide security services for the operation."

"That is not necessary Sayid besides it does not matter what Jack knows I can stay one jump ahead of him."

"Oh but I insist. You must not fail. Contact me when it is done and do not return until it is done. Do you understand?"

Azzir now feeling pressure from both Jack and Sayid becomes fully incensed by the disrespect shown to him by this overbearing bureaucrat after all he has done conducting the war against the West decides to kill the man himself after all this is over which helps to calm his rage. "Yes I understand."

"Good, and I will send additional funding as before to a numbered account of your choosing. Keep me informed."

Azzir closes the call and motions for Raheem to join him. "We have a security leak. You and your men must destroy all of your cell phones and you must not use any land lines for communication. All communication must be either face to face or by the method I will provide to you soon. Now hurry clean out this warehouse."

A few miles away at the safe house Jack taps his ear piece "yeah?"

"Jack it's me Jason. Azzir just got off the phone with Sayid. They figured out that we've been listening in and decided to go to a backup system they used before in Afghanistan. Whatever that means also you were right Sayid is sending more money."

"Thanks Jason see if you can figure out anything they may use to replace the phones. Give Bishop the update, we have an appointment with some misguided friends. Jack out."

Chapter 31
Damascus, Syria

Jack, Raul and Mitch arrive at the warehouse by midafternoon expecting trouble. Jack parks the Renault in the alley behind the building they last used for a lookout. They exit and remove their equipment.

"Let's sink up our headsets so we can stay in touch with each other. Mitch, I want you up top this building providing cover. Give us a heads up on our headsets if you see anyone coming that looks suspicious. You'll be fine. Raul, you're with me let's go."

The two men fully decked out in their BDUs, Dragon Skin, combat vests, M4s, spare magazines and side arms watch from afar and seeing no movement advance on the warehouse.

"Let's go around back. I never was much for grand entrances" says Jack.

The two men loop around the block not wanting to be seen from the front of the warehouse and enter the alley. "It looks a little too quiet to me. No sentries no nothing" remarks Raul.

Finding the rear door unlocked they both quietly enter. To their amazement they find little left in the warehouse where before there was welding equipment, hand tools, machine tools, drill presses, and aluminum stock plus varied and sundried implements for constructing the deadly drones. Also missing was the four partially completed stealth drones themselves. The only items remaining were heaps of canvas tarpaulin that lay against the floor and walls on both sides of the warehouse. "I think we're too late" laments Jack. "How could they have moved it so quickly?"

"Perhaps they had a falling out with the landlord and found cheaper accommodations" quips Raul.

Lowering their weapons and walking around the empty expanse looking for clues of the whereabouts of the now relocated drone factory and finding none the men decide to leave. "Hold up Raul let me call Bishop."

In an instant four gunmen jump from beneath the piled tarpaulin on each side of the empty room and advance on the two men with muzzles pointed at their heads. Jack and Raul freeze knowing they were outnumbered and at a clear disadvantage. "Drop your weapons" one of the gunmen demands.

The two men lay down their carbines. As they stand with hands slightly raised Azzir calmly walks forward and stands before Jack and smiles looking deeply into his eyes. "Jack, Jack you've been a busy boy haven't you? I had a feeling you would return here" he says.

"Azzir, is that you? Long time no see. I like what you did to the place" responds Jack.

"Jack, Jack you have been interfering with my plans for quite some time. I'm beginning to take it personal."

"Oh don't do that. I'd put a bullet into the head of any two bit terrorist who would harm innocent women and children."

Remembering seeing Jack shot earlier in his chest and realizing his vest stopped the bullet but still leaving a tender bruise Azzir steps forward and punches Jack directly in the affected area. Jack winces and sags slightly to the ground. "I owed you that and much more. How did you find me Jack? Can you listen in to private phone conversations and emails now with your fancy technology?"

Jack, recovering from the punch, just shrugs "then again maybe your organization is not as secure as you think." he says as he looks at one of the men trying to instill a measure of discourse into the ranks of the terrorists.

Azzir slowly stiffens in anger, steps forward and backhands Jack across the face before stepping back to the ring of gunmen. "I like you Jack but not that much. You have interfered for the last time. Search them, remove all weapons."

Four gunmen approach and take their weapons. "Tie them up" he orders.

Two wooden chairs are brought and placed behind the men. They are next shoved, side by side, into the chairs with their hands bound tightly behind them.

"So, Azzir you might as well tell me what are the targets you have identified for your psychotic attack?"

"Now where would the fun be in that? Don't you like surprises? This isn't personal Jack. Your way of life is a cancer upon the earth that must be wiped out so it cannot spread any further than it already has. Even now your decadent society has invaded the minds of young Muslims turning them from the true faith. This is only the beginning" he says as he sweeps his hands across the room.

"Surly you cannot hope to destroy us with only four drones."

"No, but we can seriously impact the essence of your might plus now that we know how to build them more drones can and will be constructed."

"Azzir, we both know you have no great spiritual aspiration which drives you so why do you do this?"

"For me I think nothing more about it than I do stepping on ants. You are an infestation that needs to be eradicated nothing more nothing less."

"You are sick and will not get away with this."

Azzir chuckles "I don't think you are in any position to be making predictions of this kind. Jack I'd love to stay and chat longer but you caught me at a bad time. Unfortunately I can't stay to catch up on old times I have some important business to attend to, schedules to keep, you understand. But you will have fun getting to know some of my new associates." Azzir turns to go "I have work to do." As he slowly walks away he turns to look over his shoulder at his men and says "kill them both, goodbye Mr. Hunter."

Chapter 32
Damascus, Syria

Jack hears Mitch call into his ear piece "Jack I heard everything. I can't see you though. What do you want me to do?"

Jack wanting to inform Mitch of what's happening hollers after Azzir "aren't four against two a little unfair?"

As Azzir leaves the four gunmen surround the two men, smile and hoist their guns toward Jack and Raul.

"Hey fella's does it really take all four of you to kill two guys tied up in chairs? Besides shouldn't some of you stand guard outside or something? You wouldn't want a police car driving by just as you fired. It might be hard for you to explain to them two fresh bodies in here."

The leader of the group sneers down at Jack then turns to one of his associates "go outside and have a look around."

Hoping Mitch understands Jack ads "only one man going outside. Are you sure that's enough?"

The man exits the side door of the warehouse and slowly walks to the front looking for anyone that may interrupt plans for the demise of the two men. Mitch, watching from the second floor across the street concealed behind the roof parapet tosses a stone which lands in the alley on the far side of warehouse. The gunman hearing the sound of the stone landing looks around then slowly proceeds to the far side of the warehouse. Entering the alley and finding no one he stands still long enough for Mitch to paint crosshairs from his Advanced Combat Optical Gunsight or ACOG on the center of mass of the lone gunman's back and sends a suppressed 5.56mm steel jacketed round through his body dropping him lifelessly to the ground.

"One down Jack" he announces into Jack's earpiece.

Jack calls out to the leader "Hey Marwan or whatever your name is your man's been outside an awful long time maybe he needs help."

The man growls to himself and nods to another man "go see what is taking so long and don't take any chances."

The second man exits the same side door and walks to the front of the warehouse. He calls out for his associate to no avail and becomes concerned. Mitch tosses another stone toward the far alley as before. Upon hearing the stone the man begins walking in the direction of the sound calling the others name thinking the man was relieving himself in the alley. Upon entering the alley and finding the man lying face down with a small red hole in his back he turns to run. The man is able to take one step before another deadly round from Mitch's suppressed M4 enters just to the left of center of his chest and explodes his heart killing him instantly before he collapses to the ground like a rag doll.

"Two down Jack" is announced over his ear piece.

Although his hands tied behind his back Jack is able to grip one of the back rungs of the chair. Jack looks over at Raul and gives a quick nod of his head. He then calls over to the leader trying to incite him to approach closer "Where are the two guys you sent out? Oh that's right they're probably playing with each other that's what you guys do isn't it? You guys sure are inept no wonder you live a cesspool third world dump of a country."

"Yeah, I'll say they're inept four of your buddies went down faster than toilet water on steroids" ads Raul.

The two remaining gunmen covering Jack and Raul turn and advance quickly attempting to backhand the two seated men into submission. As they near Jack he jumps up, his hands firmly griping the back of the chair, and does a forward summersault crashing the chair into the head of the advancing guard. As the man falls Jack jumps again and pulls his feet between his hands thus placing his hands in front of him. As soon as Jack made his move Raul also jumps up and giving his best defensive lineman interpretation lowers his shoulder and thrusts himself into the solar plexus of the second guard driving him backwards until he impacts against the wall effectively pinning him there before Raul drops to the ground. The second man has the wind knocked out of him but quickly recovers to see Jack having attacked the leader and raises his rifle to finish Jack off. Jack lunges for the dizzy leader and spins him around just in time for the man to receive a burst of 7.62mm rounds mid chest as Jack grasps the man's rifle and returns two quick rounds into the head of the second man depositing blood and brain matter on the wall of the warehouse.

"That was close Jack nice move."

"You did pretty well yourself. Faster than toilet water on steroids? What's that all about?"

"You caught me at a bad time. That's all I could think of" says Raul as he shrugs his shoulders.

"Alright buddy no harm done." After the two men untie their hands Jack taps his ear piece "Mitch, thanks for the backup good shooting. Jack keys Jason on his headset. "Jason, patch me through to Bishop."

"Bishop here Jack what's going on?"

"It looks like they figured out that we're on to them and went to ground. They're using another means to communicate. How I do not know. We missed taking out Azzir. I'll give you a full report later but as of right now we have no idea where they are or when and where they will strike. I need you to do something for me."

"What is it?"

"I need you to have the CIA put eyes on Sayid. He will, I'm sure, lead us to the money man to replenish the funds we stole. Then we can wrap this whole thing up. I'm convinced now more than ever that Azzir and Jasim are a couple knights short of a crusade and are capable of anything. Jason, are you still there?"

"I'm here Jack. Go."

"I need for you to figure out what new communication format they will use now that they discovered we can listen to them. Perhaps the key is in that code we found at that Phoenix apartment. Do the best you can and keep in touch. Since we lost Azzir the three of us are heading back home to regroup and maybe work this thing from another angle. Jack out.

Chapter 33
Houston, Texas

"Hey Duncan hurry up sergeant Hickman's about to start roll call."

"I'm coming."

After a late night chaperoning his daughter's high school dance and his young son coming down with something this morning, requiring a quick trip to the pharmacy, this day was not starting off well. Arriving late at the station house Duncan McDonald races through the locker room securing his personnel gear before joining his fellow deputies in the squad room obtaining the last open seat which happened to be in the front row directly in front of the sergeant.

The sergeant, standing behind the podium, tips his head down toward Duncan allowing his bifocals to slide down his nose and pears over them directly at Duncan. "McDonald it's nice of you to join us today. Can I get you anything perhaps a bagel or some coffee?" A slight chuckle runs through the team of men.

"No sir I'm fine."

The arrays of men comprising Harris County Texas finest are a lean mix of seasoned veterans and rookies. Though varied in experience they are a close knit group of deputies ever mindful of ensuring the safety of their fellow officer. They may joke with each other but the sense of unity runs strong.

"Alright men listen up" begins the Sergeant "I have a few general announcements. 1) The new personnel rules are now in effect. All annual fitness reports will now include a side arm proficiency exam and a general physical fitness exam."

An officer in the rear exclaims "does that mean Benson can only eat five donuts a day?" Another excited chuckle runs through the room.

"Alright, alright you guys simmer down. Moving on, number 2) all leave requests must be submitted a minimum of two weeks in advance for scheduling purposes, 3) we have received report of an increased number of petty robberies in and around the Pasadena and Deer Park Cities area so stay focused, 4) as many of you know there was an armed robbery at Alberto's Market on Center Street in Deer Park last night. The clerk was shot but will pull through. The description of the perp and his car has been uploaded to your vehicle scanners. Any questions? Stay safe gentlemen, dismissed."

Duncan sits for a moment longer deep in thought as his fellow deputies file out. The events of last week go over and over in his mind of how he somehow feels responsible for a young women's death. If only he had checked she might still be alive. The Sergeant sees the man mentally chastising himself aware of what happened and decides to intervene.

"Duncan, don't do this to yourself. It's an honest mistake. You've been with us for six years and you're a good deputy. Let it go or it will eat you up inside and then you'll be no good to anyone. Life is about making choices and learning from the ones we get wrong."

"I know but I feel responsible in some way and I can't let go of it. Something inside me that night said to check out that parked van But my head said I'm making something out of nothing. The van is fine. No sign of trouble move on. That young girl did not have to die that night in that van. If only I'd listen to myself."

"I know, I know. Son listen you have good instincts use them, learn from them, listen to them. Let it go. You are not responsible for her death. That SOB killed her not you and we're going to nail him you'll see."

"Thanks sarge I'll try. I'd better get going on patrol."

Still feeling down but determined to make a difference because in the end that is why he joined the Sheriff's department in the first place, to help people, to protect them and make a difference. At least that is what he tells himself. Duncan heads out to the motor pool to collect his Crown Victoria patrol car. He does a quick inspection; shotgun, flares *"yup it's all here"* he says to himself. Texas county deputies are given county wide jurisdiction and may exercise their authority in incorporated and unincorporated areas of the county but their primary responsibility is to serve the unincorporated areas yielding to municipal police to service the incorporated areas as needed. Deputies are also empowered to make state-wide warrantless arrests for any criminal offense committed in their presence. His patrol area today is South Deer park and the unincorporated area to the East and South.

Duncan pulls out of the yard and heads toward Deer Park a suburb east of Houston comprised of middle income housing, light industrial, commercial establishments with a heavy industrial section north of the Pasadena Freeway. He has no set patrol route equally dividing his time throughout the area. Duncan relishes this time alone where he can ponder the things life throws at you on and off the job. How should he react when his teenage daughter starts bringing boys home soon? How is he going to pay for college for two children on a deputies salary? How to respond to a life or death situation on the job? These and other questions he uses as tools to enable him to have a well formulated response for many situations ahead of time realizing early in life knee jerk reactions to events were not always the best response but a well thought out logical response is always the best policy.

While cruising through a modest neighborhood he notices, ahead of his patrol car, a teenage girl about his daughters age roll through a stop sign while talking on her cell phone. Duncan gives a quick flash of his lights and siren to which the young driver sees and quickly pulls to the curb. He approaches the vehicle as she lowers her driver's side window and in his mind sees his daughter in a year or two. "Good grief" he thinks to himself.

"Excuse me miss but did you know you failed to make a complete stop back there?"

"I'm sorry I thought I did. I looked both ways."

Duncan, seeing the future embodiment of his daughter in a few short years in this young woman before him is moved with the compassion of a loving father. "Yes I know miss that's why I'm giving you only a warning this time. Studies have shown that talking on a cell phone is a distraction while driving and I would not want to see you get hurt or anyone else. I'm going to ask you not to use your phone while driving anymore. Ok?"

"Yes officer I'll be more careful. Thank you."

As he turns to walk back to his patrol car he hears an all points call over his portable radio announcing a Pasadena City Wells Fargo Bank has just been robbed. Witnesses report the suspect fleeing the scene East on East Edgebrook Dr. in a mid-1980's dark blue Isuzu Trooper with Texas plates.

Not responding in hast since he was some distance from the event concluding others would reach the suspect before he would Duncan returns to his car and continues to cruise slowly northward until he reaches Fairmont Pkwy, the name changing to East Edgebrook Dr. as you cross from the City of Pasadena to the City of Deer Park. While listening attentively to his radio hearing local police units were in pursuit but some distance back the vehicle in question passes his position at a high rate of speed. Duncan immediately flicks on his flashing lights and siren and hits the gas leaving a rooster tail of dirt and gravel as he makes a sharp right turn accelerating after the suspect.

"Harris County Dispatch this is car 212 I am in pursuit of a dark blue mid-1980's Isuzu Trooper wanted in connection of a robbery to a Pasadena City Wells Fargo Bank. I am traveling east on Fairmont Pkwy. Over."

"Car 212 give us your position. Over."

"Harris Dispatch I am just crossing Red Bluff Rd. and am still accelerating. This guy is going way too fast for this road. Request assistance. Over."

"Car 212 this is Lieutenant Dover, can you overtake the suspect and affect the stop? Over."

"Harris Dispatch that's a negative. The suspect is traveling too fast. Over."

"Car 212 there are no other cars in the area that can reach you in time. Can you affect a PIT maneuver to terminate the pursuit? Over."

"Harris Dispatch stand by. Over."

Thankful that he was in a relatively rural section of the county with no traffic signals to impede his pursuit Duncan accelerates further and closes the gap with the escaping felon. The suspect in the Isuzu Trooper notices the approach of the patrol car with flashing lights and begins to swerve back and forth from lane to lane in an attempt to block the sheriff's cruiser to keep the advancing deputy behind him.

"Harris Dispatch this is car 212. PIT is a negative. Say again PIT is a negative we are approaching 70 now. In my opinion a PIT at this speed is ill advised on this road and very dangerous both for the suspect's car and mine. Over."

"Car 212 you must stop that car before it crosses State Route 146. There are schools and neighborhoods east of Route 146 that will have significant numbers of children in the area. We cannot have him reach that area. Over"

Recalling the words of his Sergeant earlier in the day *"you have good instincts use them"* he calls the Lieutenant once again.

"Harris Dispatch this is car 212. Lieutenant, perhaps if I backed off and he saw I was no longer chasing him he would slow also before reaching the school. Over."

"Car 212 we cannot take that chance. I am ordering you to affect that PIT maneuver now and terminate this pursuit. Do you understand? Over."

"Harris Dispatch this is car 212. I understand. Stand by. Over."

Duncan says a quick prayer. Quickly pictures his wife and kids in his mind and says I love you to them and begins to accelerate toward the menacing vehicle. The mid-1980's Isuzu Trooper contained a design flaw. It was top heavy making it subject to rolling over when sharp turning movements were introduced into the vehicle. As the vehicle weaved from lane to lane attempting to keep the deputy at bay Duncan timed his approach perfectly. As the Trooper swerved right Duncan tucked his right bumper behind the left quarter panel of the fleeing vehicle. As the vehicle swerved back to the left contact was made. With his front wheels turned slightly left to complete the move to the left lane and the rear of his car unable to move left due to the position of the deputy's car the Trooper begins to slide sideways. As its wheels make contact with the center median grass and dirt strip it begins to roll violently. The 70+ MPH initial speed before the accident was enough to carry the rolling vehicle through the median strip carrying it airborne as it exited the depressed median.

Duncan's vehicle also begins to slide after the impact but does not roll and comes to rest on the right shoulder of the roadway.

A mother traveling westbound on Fairmont Pkwy in a Dodge Caravan with her three year old son strapped in his car seat in the rear of the vehicle did not see the careening Trooper until it was too late. The tumbling Trooper impacts the minivan squarely in the windshield killing the mother instantly. The child receives minor lacerations from broken glass but survives.

The newspapers reported a mother of two was killed in a head on collision following a high speed pursuit by a Harris County deputy. The escaping suspect's car was pushed off the road during pursuit by the deputy into the path of the mother and one of her young sons. The child will survive his wounds. An investigation into the cause of the accident is ongoing.

Weeks later a lengthy investigation by the department concludes that Duncan was not at fault. No intent of malice and neither gross dereliction of duties nor incompetence was found. The cause of the accident was a result of a horrible series of regrettable circumstances. However things did not go as smoothly during a private conversation with Lieutenant Dover.

"McDonald do you know how much heat I had to endure as a result of your screw up. I had to call in a number of markers and do some quick dancing to stay out of the fire on this one."

"I don't know what you mean sir."

"I mean if you had given that PIT maneuver to that SOB when I told you to that mother and her minivan would not have been in the picture. Get what I mean?"

"Yes sir but I knew it was a dangerous move at any time during the pursuit."

"You don't get it McDonald. You almost made me look bad. I won't forget it. The board of inquire cleared you but I won't. Until I deem otherwise you are going to get every lame assignment I can think of starting with patrolling the marshes out by the river. Now get out."

Chapter 34
Macau, China

The CIA agent calls into his ear piece to his team leader back at their office "I got him. He's getting on a flight now from Tehran on China Southern Airlines to Beijing and after a short layover Air China to Macau China"

"Are you sure it's Sayid Kamal?" answers the lead agent.

"I'm as right as rain falling on a parched desert. Minus the fancy suit and entourage my guess he's trying not to call attention to himself."

"Alright come on in we'll have another agent pick him up in Macau. Good work."

After 17 hours and 1 stops the Air China Airbus A321 lands at Macau International and taxis up to the gate. A local CIA agent dressed in typical tourist fashion in a flowered shirt and Khaki pants stands in the concourse against a support column pretending to read a newspaper while scanning the passengers exiting the flight.

"I got him. I'll follow him down to baggage claim."

"The agent stands off to the side pretending to be waiting for a family members who are retrieving their bags. He watches Sayid gather his bags and head for the line of taxis just outside the doors. The agent follows and taps his ear piece to connect him to his partner who is waiting in the departure Queue with all the other taxis and shuttles.

"Come on up he's getting into cab # 265."

"Wouldn't it have been easier to just put a bug on him? This way we could lose him."

"Maybe so but if he ever discovered it we'd lose our edge and then he may never make the contact. No in this case the old way is the best way."

The two cars exit the airport and turn directly onto the Ponte da Amizade bridge which spans the harbor connecting the island airport to the mainland. Upon reaching the mainline the two cars turn left onto Avenida da Amizade which passes the ferry terminal serving passengers between Macau and Hong Kong. Once passed the ferry terminal the taxi turns left once more onto Avenida Dr. Sun Yat-Sen before stopping at the Sands Macao Hotel and Casino.

"Ok you're up." The driver says to a third agent waiting in the back seat. "Remember get his room number if you can then you can attach the motion detector to the door so you will know when he leaves the room. Another agent will be here in a few hours to relieve you. Good luck."

Sayid spends the rest of the evening in his room coming out only once to have diner in the main floor dining room of the hotel before returning to his room. The agents begin to worry that they have been sent on a wild goose chase expending assets for a worthless cause that they believe can be better spent elsewhere. Mid-morning the next day Sayid leaves his room much to the delight of the agent assigned to the morning shift.

"I got him we're moving. He's crossing the street headed for the Arabian style theme park."

"Don't lose him but don't let him see you either. Another agent will be right there to take over."

In covert surveillance it is beneficial to substitute the trailing member on a regular basis making it more difficult for the subject to spot a reoccurring face.

"I've got him now. He's stopped at an outdoor cafe and is sitting at a center table."

The replacement agent watches from behind a stand of trees. After approximately ten minutes another man approaches and sits opposite Sayid. They each order a coffee.

"Ok he's here I'm going in."

The agent finds a nearby table where he can view the two men in profile from behind a menu and places a very sensitive miniaturized directional microphone and digital camera behind the table's centerpiece pointed at the pair.

"I can't get a good look at him. He's wearing a hat, dark glasses and his jacket collar is rolled up. Wait let me turn on the mic."

"Omar thank you for agreeing to meet with me on such a short notice. I trust the agent I sent to see you to request this meeting did not overly alarm you."

"I have told you never to call me that name in public. So what is so important that you had to travel all the way to Macau and why could you not contact me through our normal channels?"

"I believe the Americans have found a way to listen into all of our conversations either phone or email. They are close to defeating our plans."

"So use another way to communicate, one they cannot break."

"We have instituted a backup method that has worked effectively in the past. It is not as efficient but will serve our purposes. Depending upon how much they know we might yet prove victorious. But that is not the main reason for my coming here today. Your last deposit of funding for the construction of the drones was stolen by the Americans."

"They have what? How could you let that happen?"

"We had 12 armed men and many died but they still were able to take the money."

"Is this Jack Hunter you spoke of involved with this?"

"Yes."

"I want his head on a stick. Assign more men if you have to. There is too much riding on this to be defeated now. You were chosen for this task because of your access to the original American made stealth drone. Do not let me down again or it is you I will replace. Our organization has far reaching plans for the destruction of the west. We cannot tolerate setbacks due to incompetence. Do I make myself clear? I will make one more deposit same as before. I want those drones completed and sent off as soon as possible. No delays. Do not fail me again."

"I will see to it. Do not fear."

Sayid gets up and leaves the cafe. The other man sits for a moment longer, collects himself, and takes a sip of water then leaves. The agent walks over to their table and using a pair of latex gloves collects the mystery man's water glass and seals it into a plastic bag for later DNA testing.

"Did we get all that?"

"Yeah, let's complete our report and send it along with a copy of the audio and video back to Langley. Maybe they can get an ID on this guy."

Sayid returns to his hotel, pulls out his laptop and conveys a message to Azzir that funding has been reestablished and he is to complete the work and ship the weapons to America as soon as possible.

Chapter 35
Washington

Mitch lands the Gulfstream at Andrews Air force Base outside DC. Tired after the last few days Jack asks if there is a place they can get some rest and a shower.

"Sure thing General Kincaid has arranged temporary officer accommodations for you two here at the base. I'll drive you over. You can get a quick shower and put on some clean clothes then the General wants to see you."

After an hour or two of R & R the two men were ready and piled back into Mitch's borrowed government car. Exiting the air base they travel north on Pennsylvania Ave. Before reaching the Anacostia waterway they turn left onto Minnesota Ave SE and travel an additional block and a half and park behind a non-descript two story building.

"Here we are gentlemen your home away from home. Come on in" invites Mitch.

The three men enter the rear door of the building to find a richly appointed foyer complete with an armed security guard at the front desk.

"Hey Mitch welcome back are these the two guys I've been hearing so much about?"

"A fan club already? I hope you heard only the good things" jokes Raul.

The guard gives Raul a bemused look and nods his head in the direction of the hallway. "The General is in his office waiting for you."

Mitch gives a quick knock on Bishop's door as they enter. "Mitch, Jack, Raul welcome back" Bishop gets up from his desk and walks around to greet the men. "I've read your report. Good work so far. Too bad we lost Azzir so soon. I guess they caught on to us sooner than I would have liked."

"Before we go much further" interrupts Jack "I need you to know that we would not be standing here today if it was not for Mitch. He saved our tails back there and I just wanted you to know that. Mitch, if I hadn't said it enough thanks for your help."

Mitch beams with pride as Bishop concurs "here here, good work all of you. So, now what do we do?"

"Let's go see Jason" suggests Jack "and see what we can come up with regarding potential targets and the new communication system Azzir mentioned using."

"Come let me show you around" suggests Bishop. "This is your first trip to our nerve center. The GOA had a number of vacant buildings in and around Washington. I managed to find this one for a good price. You'll have to excuse the seemingly disarray, the President did not give me much time to get this program up and running."

As they leave Bishop's office and head down the hallway they see a large room with a long table surrounded by padded executive chairs behind a glass paneled wall facing the hallway the General continues "this is our conference room. You'll notice the same view screen and work station as in the Gulfstream. We can video chat with most anyone anywhere." The men walk on where the hallway opens up into a large room filled with overhead monitors lining the walls on one side with a large computer console fronting the wall. Behind the console and work desk are a series of computer servers and data storage racks in support of the mammoth computing power contained in the room. A constant humming filled the room as massive air handlers provided the cooling necessary to preserve the electronic hardware.

"And this is Jason's lair" begins Bishop as he spreads his arms in an attempt to display the room "you already know what he can do. Jason are you in here?"

Jason pops his head out from behind one of the servers. "Hey guys welcome back. It's good to finally meet you in person."

Jack and Raul step forward to shake Jason's hand. "You don't know the half of it. We're glad to be back. Thanks for all you do" says Jack.

Jack sees a short stocky man built like a tank walk up. "Chester" exclaims Jack as he extends his hand the two men testing each other's grip "good to finally meet you and thank you also for all your help."

"My pleasure Jackie. And this must be Raul" he says as he pumps the younger man's hand.

"Let's head back to the conference room" directs Bishop "we can all decide where we go from here."

Filling in the seats around the table Jack begins "there are two things I want to discuss with you all. The first is the envelope we found in Phoenix suggests the intended targets are in New York. Possible targets are either Giants stadium during the Super bowl or New Year's Eve in Times Square or the New York Stock Exchange. But for this to happen where would they launch the drones from? They certainly do not have an aircraft carrier and how can you hide four drones at a public or even a private airport? Someone is bound to see something. Any ideas?"

The team members all grumble and shake their heads no. No clue.

"Jason, based upon what we know so far and the few pictures we sent what would you estimate the range to be on one of these drones?" asks Jack.

"Based upon the dimensions and engine configuration you gave me I'd say about 700 to 800 miles."

"Good Grief" says Bishop "Jason can you be looking for large private estates within that radius of New York City that have the privacy and area to hold and launch a drone of the size we are talking about?"

"Sure, I'll get right on it."

"Moving on to number two" begins Jack "since knowing what these guys are going to do before they do it has been helpful to us so far I think we need to concentrate on figuring out what new communication technique they will employ to complete the attack."

"Jack the field is wide open. It could be anything" admits Jason.

"Let's see if we can narrow this down" begins Jack. "These guys don't have a lot of high tech hardware to play with. It has to be something somewhat simple using things they readily have access to. What do you think?"

Bishop begins "well what do we know now? Email is out and so is cell phones and land lines. Could they use some modified or deviation of any of these three?"

Jason steps in "they could use a code of some kind encompassing a series of letters and numbers."

"I don't know" answers Jack "that sounds kinda sophisticated for these guys plus remember Azzir said they employed the technique before in Afghanistan. Bishop, do we have any intell of a sophisticated code being used by terrorist groups in Afghanistan?"

"I can check with CIA and NSA but I highly doubt it. We would have heard about something like this by now. It must be something else. Again some low tech variance on the big three mentioned."

"They could use curriers to carry messages like the old Roman army" offers Raul.

"That's right. The CIA report I saw said Sayid sent a currier to Macau to set up the meeting with the head money man" suggests Bishop.

"It does sound simple and foolproof admits Jack but not very efficient. Remember they want to make this happen soon. Shuttling people back and forth across the Atlantic is not efficient.

"I have a suggestion" interrupts Jason "it sounds a little silly but it does work. It's been used for years by covert operatives by utilizing an email account known only to the operatives."

"I thought we just said no email" exclaims Raul.

"That's right" answers Jason "but these emails are written but never sent. They are placed into the draft box and held. Since they are not sent out, but reside on a server at the ISP's central data hub, they cannot be read on the world wide web but only by other members who have access to the account with a user name and password. It's simple but effective."

"That's ingenious" says Jack "but how does that help us? How do we find the correct user name and password in the millions used with each provider? Plus they may have more than one account so even if we are lucky to find one account they may have others. We don't have time to explore them all. We're going to be hit soon."

"I'll work on it" says Jason.

"So right now we don't know where they are going to launch from and we don't know how they are going to communicate" says Jack as he looks over at Bishop "we'll think of something."

Chapter 36
Phoenix, Arizona

It is early evening, the house lights glow through the front windows of the homes on the tranquil residential street. Jericho sits quietly in his rented car parked a few doors down from the home of Jennifer White. His flight from London was long and so decided to spend the night in New York to rest. While there he accessed ancestry.com typing in the name Elizabeth Devencourt, he obtained from the attendant at the National Archives in London, plus an approximate date she may have immigrated to America. Immigration records revealed she arrived in the US in 1974. Further review disclosed a marriage license issued to a Louis White and Elizabeth Devencourt in 1975. Birth records indicate they were parents to a child born in 1980 given the name Jennifer White and born in New York. From this he confirms Jennifer is the great granddaughter of Addison Devencourt given in the diary shown to him by Omar. The 2000 census data showed Elizabeth and Louis White residing in Phoenix Arizona. A quick look through the on line phone book showed a Jennifer White also residing in Phoenix. The following day he boards a plane to Phoenix.

Jericho, remembering his orders to not do anything untoward so as not to arouse suspicion decides to observe the young woman for signs that she too was actively seeking the deed. After watching her home well into the evening and finding no visitors calling or seeing her traveling out he leaves only to return early the next day as she leaves for work. Satisfied the woman will be away for some time he quietly walks around to the back of the house and picks the rear lock and enters the house. So as not to give away his presence he is very careful not to disturb anything he touches. In attempting to find the documents he was told she obtained from the London office he opens her cabinets, desk draws and filing cabinet all to no avail. Noticing the boxes in the dining room he begins to examine the family correspondence. Recognizing the boxes were arranged by the age of the documents he quickly focuses his attention on the box containing her great grandfather's letters. After some time he too finds the letter bearing witness to the existence of the deed. Satisfied he is on the right trail and that the woman now also is aware of the deed he quietly leaves. Returning to his car he punches a preprogrammed number into his cell phone.

"Yes?"

"It's me. I found the great granddaughter of the Englishman in the diary. I searched her house she does not have the deed but she has an old letter written by him to his wife alluding to the existence of the deed you seek."

"This news is most extraordinary. I did not believe you would be successful so quickly. So where is the deed?"

"All record of the Englishman once he leaves Cairo is either lost or held in secret by the English government. I still feel certain they do not have it. It would have been found by now through the efforts of cataloging and making electronic copies of all government documents. I feel certain it is either lost or hidden."

Omar thinks for a moment "the woman must know something more."

"She does not appear to be mounting a search of her own but I too cannot help but feel she knows more than she may be willing to say. Perhaps she needs some persuasion to tell all that she knows."

"Yes, an excellent idea. Watch her for a few days. If she does not make an effort to mount a search of her own then you are free to question her in any matter you like but if she leaves follow her. Let her lead you to the document."

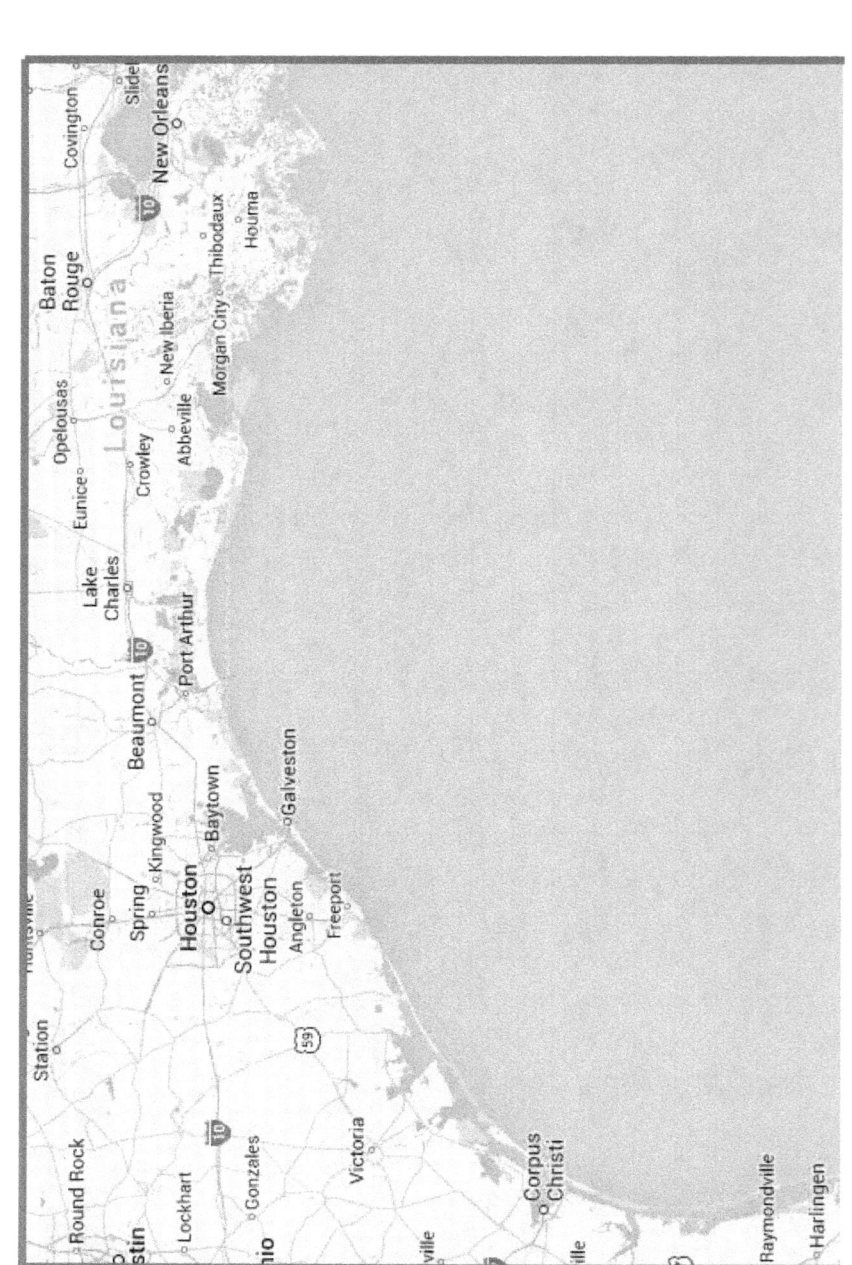

Gulf of
Mexico

Raymondville

Harlingen

Matamoros

Valle
ermoso

aguna Madre
y Delta del
Río Bravo

ramar

Tampico

Chapter 37
Tampico, Mexico

The 70,000 ton Panamax class container ship the *Guiding Star* arrives at port in Tampico Mexico. Azzir has entitled the contents of the two containers on the manifest as experimental model aircraft parts. Not wanting to have the contents inspected he bribes the Mexican customs officials to clear the containers for offloading onto two flatbed trucks he has rented for the purpose. He is amazed at how easy it is to conduct illegal activity in third world countries. All that is required is to pay the right people. Duty and honor are compensable commodities like anything else. Raheem and his technicians having arrived the day before on tourist visas supervise the loading of the containers then board the two trucks themselves.

"The abandoned airfield I found will perfectly fit your needs Raheem" instructs Azzir. "The old hanger has doors that can be closed for you to reassemble the drones in privacy and there is a chain winch affixed to the roof truss you can use to hoist the engines before setting them into the air frame. The landing strip was once used by crop dusters so it is rather short but you told me you do not need much for your smaller drones."

Azzir and Jasim each drive a truck north and west of town to the deserted air field. The field is located on the outskirts of town. Barren desert and cultivated fields both mark the landscape. Privacy was not going to be a problem. Upon reaching the old air field the trucks were driven into the hanger to unload the containers.

"I have located an old tractor you can use to remove the containers from the trucks after you unload them. They can double as living quarters for the few days we are here" announces Azzir.

As Raheem's men begin organizing and setting up the hanger to reassemble the drones ten of Sayid's new security detail arrive. The leader approaches Azzir "I was told to follow you on the next available transport and you would be expecting us. Sayid ordered us to provide oversight to insure the success of this operation."

At the word oversight Azzir shutters thinking in his mind the sound of that worthless Sayid's voice and his pompous prattling which brings further anger. Realizing he must play the part until he can figure out a way to deal with his unwelcome guests he maintains a professional tone.

"Yes welcome. As you can see we are very busy. Do as you seem fit but do not hamper the work of the technicians."

The leader gathered his men against the far wall of the hanger. "We will set up our quarters here. For the time being I want two roving sentries outside at all-time replaced every two hours. Go."

The leader stood for a moment to survey his surroundings. He vaguely remembers Sayid saying something about an attack on a city well within the heartland of America. If so why are they in Mexico? The thought troubled him.

"Jasim" Azzir waves his friend over "I am concerned about our uninvited guests. I fear their allegiance is with Sayid and their duty is less in protecting us and more in following Sayid's orders."

"I think you are right. What shall we do?"

"Let us watch and listen and determine the threat level they pose."

Azzir and Jasim begin work with Raheem and his team to empty the containers and organize the drone parts for assembly.

Chapter 38
Washington

"This is hopeless. For all we know they're using a string and two tin cans" says Raul as he and Jack brainstorm Azzir's new communication strategy in the conference room of their Washington Headquarters.

"I wouldn't give up hope yet we'll think of something" answers Jack.

Just then Jason bursts in. "Jack I think I got it. The laptop you found at the original terrorist's apartment in Phoenix must of had the internet account and password in code. If they lost communications this is all they had for backup to recreate a new system. All we need to do is break the code.

"Whoa slow down Jason. Explain" says Jack.

"Don't you remember there were three words plus a series of numbers in one of the encrypted files? The words were wife, beautiful and voice. To open an email account you need an ISP or internet service provider's name like Internet Explorer or Google Chrome plus a user name and a password, three words. We just have to figure out how these three words relate to the task at hand.

"It sounds pretty sketchy. How do you relate these words to the real names on the desired account?" asks Raul.

"If it was easy you wouldn't need me" responds Jason. "Now about the numbers, I still don't know what the numbers represent they could be part of a different code. I asked around at some banking institutions and they do not translate to any account format and they do not equate to a frequency or a shipping code or anything I'm aware of. I'll keep trying.

"Well you do the best you can Raul and I are going to go see Bishop and find out what the CIA found out about Sayid and his financial friends."

****

The Oval Office has been a hotbed of activity lately. In recent years CNN and Fox News have been just as efficient as the state Department itself for generating up to date information on developing stories around the world. The President, the Vice President, the Secretary of Defense and the Secretary of State are all seated facing the big flat panel TV watching events unfold in the Middle East. The Palestinians have resumed rocket attacks on Israel. Israel has responded with aerial attacks. Egypt and Syria are building troop strength at the border with Israel . Iran's ruling party has called for the elimination of the Zionist regime in Israel. Their inflaming rhetoric seems to be having its desired effect.

"Gentlemen" begins the President "it's all going south and a little too fast. Tony, have your efforts at diplomacy gained us anything?"

"No Mr. President, we've gained little. It seems they tell us one thing in meetings but do something else once we adjourn. We've had meetings with our counterparts in Israel, the Palestinian leadership, the Syrians, the Egyptians and the Iranians. Although they outwardly want peace inwardly I think they are in agreement that most all of their problems would fade if Israel no longer existed. Iran seems to be the driving force behind this movement garnering support from the other countries. The recent bombings we've talked about have seemed to be a catalyst to further embolden Arab groups against Israel. I fear things will get worse before they get better.

"Mr. President" offers Bob Hammond "What if we send the fleet into the Med. kind of like a show of force to keep things from spiraling out of control?"

"Bob I appreciate the thought but I think that would be an empty threat. What are we going to do shell Damascus and Jerusalem? I certainly cannot afford to get us involved in another shooting war The American people don't want another foreign war and we sure don't want to be burdened with the debt of another."

"We could threaten to withhold foreign aid" says the VP.

"Thanks Ryan I appreciate the thought also but much of the money has been formally promised under separate agreements. Reneging on them would make them trust us even less in the future" responds the President. "No, we need something to get their attention completely and quickly. If there was only some way to convince Iran that it was in their best interest to back off this aggressive posture with Israel."

Chapter 39
Washington

"Jack, Jack I think I got it." Jason clutching an arm load of printouts races into the conference room as Bishop is explaining the results of the CIA's surveillance of Sayid to Jack and Raul as Mitch listens in. "Remember how I said the three words must have equated to the name of the internet browser, the user name and the password. Well, starting with the browser I exhausted the worlds known supply of ISP addresses and there are none that have the name of the three words given. So next I started translating the three words into other languages. I tried French, German, Spanish, Arabic and Russian. Again I found no match. Then on a wild hunch I tried Farsi and guess what? The word voice translates to Neda in Farsi and there is a browser named Neda. So I assumed the other two words were also English translations of Farsi words. There were no user names or passwords using the words wife and beautiful for the browser Neda. I next wrote a program designed to use all the synonyms for wife and beautiful in Farsi as either the user name or password associated with the browser and again no hits. I next tried the same thing using the Farsi antonyms for the two words and again nothing. I finally tried a simple word association which gave me handsome and husband instead of wife and beautiful and bingo we hit pay dirt. The Farsi words for handsome and husband are shohar and ghashang. I now have their account, shohar@Neda.net with password ghashang."

"I accessed the account and found communiques between Sayid and Azzir. I also played around some more with those numbers and I think they refer to latitude and longitude coordinates. Since I don't know the given designation North or South, East or West I plotted all combinations. Jack, the targets are not in New York but rather four of the largest oil refineries in the US which happen to be on the gulf coast and only approximately 250 miles apart, two are Exxon Mobil one in Baytown Texas and one in Baton Rouge Louisiana, Marathon

Petroleum in Garyville Louisiana and PDV America in Lake Charles Louisiana."

"A drone attack on these facilities with 100 lbs. of semtex and refined uranium will not only decimate the plant by fire but will cause the area to be inhabitable for hundreds if not thousands of years" ads Bishop. "If they are successful this will surely start a war the likes of which we've never seen and all evidence points to Iran as the originator of the plan and the supplier of the uranium. I've got to alert the President."

Everyone around the table is stunned and speechless by the ruthlessness and magnitude of the plan. Jack hardens his glare and sets his jaw. "Well I guess it's up to us to stop him."

"But how?" asks Jason.

Jack plants his feet firmly on the floor and leans into the table. "We concluded earlier that they cannot hide something like this on US soil. Someone is bound to see something therefore the base must be in Mexico where direct line of flight is over water so as not to be visible by ground personnel. They don't have a C-130 to fly these things in so they must have been transported by a container ship. Jason, where is the nearest shipping port to the US on the Mexican gulf coast?"

"Wait a moment let me pull that up on my screen." Jason quickly accesses the computer work station. His fingers dancing across the keyboard like Mozart playing a concerto searching for Mexican ports rated to service container ships. "Got it, it's in Tampico Mexico. It's approximately 250 miles South of Texas and 700 miles from the farthest refinery located in Garyville Louisiana well within the range of the drones."

"That must be it. Raul, mount up we've got a war to stop. Jason get me real-time satellite imagery. Look for a warehouse large enough to hold drones plus a nearby cleared field for takeoffs. Chester, we need to resupply armament plus some new items I'll give you shortly. Bishop, we need the Air Force on stand-by and get an AWACS in the air over the Houston Gulf coast area now. Mitch, feel like taking a flight to sunny Mexico?"

"What will an AWACS do for us" asks Bishop "the drones don't show up on radar anyhow, remember?"

"They may not have to. Trust me" responds Jack.

Chapter 40
Tampico, Mexico

In slightly more time than it took to disassemble the drones, Raheem and his men have meticulously reconstructed them. The auto pilot and inertial navigation systems have been installed and tested awaiting only Azzir's input of the target coordinates. The explosive payload and uranium canister have been secured within the nose of each aircraft but not yet armed. The four drones are arrayed in two rows of two in front of the large hanger doors. Parked within the hanger near the large sliding doors is a Cessna 150 Azzir has reserved for himself and Jasim for a quick exit should the need arise. The leader of Sayid's security detail has been watching carefully the reconstruction operation with a puzzled look recalling Sayid's comment about striking America's heartland and finally approaches Azzir.

"Excuse me but I have a question. These drones of yours look small how far can they fly given we are already 250 miles from the border?"

Azzir stops what he is doing and turns to face his troublesome guest and responds flatly "it will fly as far as it needs to go."

"But where is that? Sayid has told me a mighty blow will be struck into America's heartland that will strike fear into their hearts" the leader returns.

Angered by the interference and the intrusion by Sayid's proxy Azzir's anger builds. "I do not question your duties do not question mine."

The guard slowly walks back to his men eyeing Azzir over his shoulder and assigns four men to watch over the drones full time and report back to him anything suspicious.

Azzir sensing there may be a problem approaches Jasim who is readying the fuel delivery to the drones. "Jasim, it is time. Our new friends are sensing all is not as they were informed to be. Do you have any semtex remaining from our initial supply?"

"Yes my friend I have one pound remaining plus a wireless detonator."

"Excellent. Place it beside the gas tank of one of the trucks then when you are done raise the hood on the second truck and pretend you are working on the motor."

As Jasim leaves, Azzir returns to Raheem and his men to continue final preparations. When he hears Jasim open the hood of the second truck Azzir approaches the leader. "It would be helpful if you and a few of your men would go to town to pick up some food. In our hast to get started I have forgotten to acquire such provisions. Have five of your men take the truck outside."

The leader gives a questioning looks toward Azzir then relents. "Very well we will go."

He selects three men from the hanger and walks outside and orders the two sentries to drive to town before returning to the hanger. As the truck and five men drive off Azzir exits a side door and stands beside Jasim at the second truck slowly placing his hand on a Tech-9 machine pistol resting on the passenger's seat. "Is all in order Jasim?"

"It is."

As the truck travels approximately a quarter mile Jasim presses the detonator. The report is heard throughout the hanger briefly shaking the walls as the truck and its contents are engulfed in a fiery inferno. The security leader and the remaining four guards race outside and around the corner of the hanger to investigate only to be met by Azzir's merciless onslaught of 9mm rounds chopping the guards like a sickle cutting wheat.

****

"How far out are we" asks Jack through the intercom of the Gulfstream.

"We're about 20 minutes out" responds Mitch.

Jack and Raul have discussed and planned their assault on the hanger compound since leaving Washington. Realizing no plan is perfect and the unexpected most always makes its presents known at some point the men check and recheck their armament, BDUs and Dragon Skin protective vests.

"Jack" Mitch calls back "I just got a message from Jason. He says 90 minutes ago he saw two large trucks parked beside the hanger and a number of armed men patrolling the perimeter. Now he says he sees one truck no sentries and a smoldering wreck a quarter mile away."

Jack and Raul look at each other. "Perhaps a falling out among friends?" suggests Raul.

"Either way it sounds like our job just got a little easier. I'll take it" says jack.

"10 minutes" announces Mitch

"Mitch, take us down to 10,000 feet. Ok son of the god of war let's get our chutes on and open that rear hatch."

"I've never done this before from a plane like this" says Raul.

"Neither have I but there's a first time for everything" answers Jack "remember this is a HALO jump so that our chutes won't be visible for long. Wait for the last second to pull your chute. Ok?"

Each man helps the other secure the harness of his parachute, then Raul opens the rear bulkhead door and activates the motor to lower the ramp.

"How does it go back up after we vacate the premises" asks Raul.

"I would assume Mitch turns on the auto pilot comes back here and hits the up button" answers Jack.

"Oh yeah I knew that."

As the ramp lowers Mitch can feel the added drag on the plane. The ramp acts like a second set of flaps slowing the sleek fuselage of the Gulfstream. The noise from the slipstream entering the cabin makes conversation near impossible. Forgoing the ineffectual intercom Mitch reverts back to Jack's ear piece. "The reduced speed should make your egress easier. Three minutes. Happy hunting."

Mitch counts down the last few seconds "three, two, one go."

Jack and Raul exit the plane on cue.

****

"Azzir, what have you done?" exclaims Raheed. "They were here to protect us and insure our success."

"I have just insured the success of our plan. It appears Sayid did not share in our vision for a glorious attack on America. He had a less than ingenious plan for America one not worthy of our efforts and sacrifice. But it is of no matter it is too late to stop us now anyhow and with the extra weapons I brought your men will be able to defend our plan."

"I hope you are right."

Azzir walks over to the Cessna and starts the engine giving it time to warm up before returning to the task of sending the deadly drones on their way. "Come my friend it is time, help me roll the implements of our might out onto the runway where I can set the coordinates for their final destination. Raheem, you initiate takeoff from your control panel in here as soon as I arm the explosives and start the engines. Once airborne they cannot be stopped."

Jack and Raul hit the ground and roll absorbing the energy of their descent. They quickly gather their chutes and conceal them behind native creosote bushes scattered in abundance throughout the desert.

"Mitch got us pretty close I can see the hanger just over there" remarks Jack.

"And I don't see any sentries" ads Raul "come on."

The two men race forward dodging from one bush to the next mindful to conceal their presence until they reach the last row of bushes along the perimeter of the old airport to the rear of the hanger where they stop to rest. Raul turns and begins to sniff the air. Jack turns and notices how easily his friend is enticed by the smell of food and just lowers and shakes his head. "What?" says Raul. "Don't you smell that fresh menudo cooking?"

"It looks quiet but I hear the sound of a light aircraft engine idling" observes Jack. "On the count of three we'll race to the rear corner of the hanger. One, two, three go."

The two men sprint to the hanger and stop. "There's the truck parked off to the side of the hanger. We'll swing around the far side for cover and hopefully we can see into the hanger" directs Jack. "Ready, go."

As they reach the truck they can see all four drones lined up on the runway their engines running and Azzir reaching into the cowling of the nose of one of the drones. As he turns to step away he sees Jack standing beside the rear of the truck raising his M4. Azzir pulls his Tech-9 releases a barrage of 9mm rounds at Jack as he runs into the hanger for cover. Jack and Raul return fire tearing shards out of the hanger door's wooden frame just missing Azzir. At the sound of gunfire Jasim joins the fray unloading a full clip of 7.62mm jacketed lead from his AK-47 effectively pinning the duo behind the truck. As the gun battle rages the four drones take off under Raheem's direction.

"Jack we're too late they're taking off" screams Raul against the noise of the gunfire.

"First things first let's take care of these guys. Then we'll worry about the drones. The next time Jasim stops to change magazines you open up on Azzir while I rush to the corner of the hanger."

As expected Jasim stops to reload and Jack dashes for the corner of the hanger nearest the big open doors as Raul unloads his M4 magazine into the hanger. Azzir and Jasim see Jack approach and retreat further into the hanger. As Jack pears around the hanger door he is met by a cacophony of assorted gunfire from within. Raul races up and peaks around the corner. "I see four men huddled in a shipping container firing Tech-9's" he says. As pieces of the wood door and frame concealing Jack and Raul are splintered away from impacting rounds Raul calmly loads a 40mm grenade into his M203 launcher, quickly pivots around the corner and fires into the open container. The blast from firing into the open door of the container momentarily lifts it off the floor before crashing back to earth destroying one wall of the container and leaving tissue, blood and body parts behind which only the finest forensic examiner would later recognize as human.

Jack and Raul rush in and dive for cover wherever they can find it and trade gunfire with the two terrorists. Magazines are replaced as the firing continues neither side gaining an advantage.

"Raul that far wall is filled with fuel drums, be careful where you fire or we all may go up" exhorts Jack.

The four men hide, duck and race around the hanger trying to gain a tactical advantage over their opponents to no avail. Jasim hides behind a barrel of used oil as he trades fire with Raul. Raul fires a three round burst hitting the barrel which causes the oil to leak out. He then leaps across a gap between two rows of pallets. Anticipating the move Jasim raises and fires striking Raul in the center of his chest with a 7.62mm round. Raul crumbles behind the row of pallets in pain and cries out. Jasim smelling victory advances upon his prey stepping through the spilled oil to finish him off. Hearing him approach Raul rolls to his side into the isle and fires blindly. Jasim attempting to avoid the stream of hot lead turns quickly his feet slipping in the oil and falls headfirst into an empty drum. Raul jumps up racing forward pulls the pin and drops a grenade into the drum and slams the lid down tight before diving for cover. The detonation completely disintegrates the drum. Pieces of Jasim become a colorful collage against the blank bare sheetrock wall of the hanger.

Jack and Azzir trade fire each seeking cover where they can find it in and around the idling Cessna. Jack finds cover behind a large trash bin. Azzir decides the only way to flush Jack out would be to fire from above down into jack's position. Quietly climbing a ladder hidden behind storage shelves he advances to a catwalk which traverses the hanger above the large open doors. Additional debris and trash on the floor of the catwalk further masks his advance on Jack's position. Nearing a point over the open door he sees Jack behind the bin and slowly raises his Tech-9.

His combat senses on full alert Jack sees Azzir out the corner of his eye at the last moment and spins and fires striking Azzir in the shoulder spinning him around where he stumbles and falls over the railing. As he falls his legs get tangled in the chains of the winch preventing him from hitting the floor. Having lost his Tech-9 during the fall Azzir is left dangling upside down and attempts to free himself using his one good arm from the chain now wrapped tightly around his legs. Jack, mesmerized by the sight approaches the hanging man and stares up at him in amazement. As Azzir struggles to free himself his action causes the winch to slowly lower him closer and closer to the awaiting idling prop of his Cessna. Azzir now looks down and sees the approaching spinning blades and cries out for help.

Raul hobbles over to Jack rubbing his chest thankful the Dragon Skin did its job once again. The two men stand watching in disbelief as Azzir slowly descends inverted toward his demise.

"Do you think we should help him?" asks Raul.

"We are. We're helping him die" responds Jack.

Lower and lower the screaming deranged terrorist drops until the whirling sharp blades of the Cessna's prop sever the man in half leaving two legs each attached to half a body dangling from the chains, a river of blood traces a line across the hanger floor from the spinning blades.

"It couldn't have happened to a nicer guy" says Raul.

"I hate to say it but it was entertaining" answers Jack.

"By the way did we get them all?" asks Raul.

"I think so, come look over here I found some kind of control panel."

As Raul stands besides Jack at a work bench examining the control panel Raheem used to launch the drones. They hear a shuffling sound behind them. Jack begins to turn and Raul removes the safety strap on his Glock 17 thigh mounted quick draw holster. Standing before them with his machine pistol pointed into Jack's face is Raheem. Blood drips from his face and arms as his hand holding the Tech-9 begins to shake as he grows ever weaker. With his jaw set in grim determination and with eyes that burn with hate he stares at Jack.

"This is all your doing. We have labored for over a year and sacrificed much to seek the will of Allah. For it is the will of Allah that all who are not of the true faith be put to death. You may have defeated us here but a surprise still awaits you American infidels. One you cannot stop. The mighty hand of Allah will strike your harlot of a nation this day. I may not see it come to pass but neither will you. You will die here and now."

As Raheem points his weapon a foot from Jack's face and begins to squeeze the trigger Raul's flashing right hand draws his Glock and fires at the menacing drone builder. The 9mm lead round enters Raheem's right eye, travels through 6 inches of brain tissue and exits through the top of his head in a volcanic eruption of gray matter and red bodily fluid removing the top half of his skull. The deranged terrorist dies before hitting the ground in a puddle of his own making.

"Good shooting Raul what took you so long?"

"It was a nice speech I wanted to hear it all. Will this control panel help us stop the drones or not?"

"I think not" says Jack "it looks like a simple remote control only designed to give the command to take off. Once airborne the auto pilot takes over."

Jack taps his ear piece "Jason give me Bishop."

"Bishop here Jack."

"Azzir and his team are dead, the drones have taken off. Call Mitch have him follow the birds and maintain visual contact as long as possible."

"Will do Jack but how do we stop them? There is no radar signature to lock missiles or guns on. Where are they?"

"We'll think of something."

Chapter 41
Houston, Texas

Jack and Raul quickly look around hanger. "Just as I feared there is no control function here. The drones must have an auto pilot which guides it by way of a GPS signal to the coordinates Jason found. The drone used on the Nathanael Greene was a test drone not incorporating the sophisticated flight controls that's why they needed the fishing trawler to guide it to the ship."

"How are we going to stop them Jack?"

Jack taps his ear piece. "I got an idea. Jason get me Bishop."

"Bishop here Jack."

"Does Mitch have a visual on the drones yet."

"Yeah he's flying slow and steady about a mile behind them. Why?"

"Have the AWACS locate and move closer to Mitch tell them the drones are a mile ahead of him and have them focus a jamming signal on the GPS satellite signal over that area. They need to hurry because the drones will start diverging soon to seek their own targets. My guess is the autopilot is slaved to the GPS signal and without it they won't know where they are or where they are going and hopefully fall into the sea."

"I'll get on it stand by."

Not being able to do anything else Jack and Raul nervously await Bishops call. "What happens if it doesn't work?" asks Raul.

"Then we pray they are poor craftsmen and the thing doesn't work or we prepare for world war three."

Minutes seem like hours as the men await Bishops call. Finally the call comes through. "Jack it's working. Mitch reports three of the four drones have veered off course and are continuing in a large circle we're hoping they will fall into the Gulf when they run out of fuel but one is staying straight and true and it's headed for Houston."

"Listen carefully" answers Jack "it must have a second controller guiding it in just like the fishing trawler did when they attacked the Nathanael Greene. It must also operate on a different frequency than the satellite GPS signal that's why the jamming has no effect. Instruct the AWACS to find the source of the second signal. It's the same as identifying the source of enemy radar locking onto airborne targets so as to target return fire. When you've located the source of the control signal contact the FBI to vector in and destroy the transmitter."

****

Patrolling the outlying unincorporated areas did have its benefits. Events requiring his attention rarely happened which afforded him down time to think about the things that mattered most in life like his wife and two children. Duncan McDonald was a confident man secure in who he was and what he knew. Many times he replayed the events of that day over and over in his mind when his supervisor told him to take out that escaping felon's car. Each time he arrived at the same conclusion. It was just too dangerous. He knew his instincts were correct and if given the chance to relive that fateful day he knew he would make the same decision and request not to affect the high speed stop. However, knowing he was right did not ease the despair of being relegated to the lonely post of patrolling the county outlying areas, his penitence for defying his supervisor. This was not why he joined the department. He joined because the desire to serve the people of Harris County and to make a difference was a part of who he was. Even from an early age he knew this was his calling. He needed to find a way to return to the good graces of the department for his career to flourish and to reach his full potential. But what could he do while relegated to this obscure landscape?

Duncan's current assigned patrol area was a large region along the western shore of the San Jacinto River from the City of La Porte to Independence Parkway and north of the Pasadena Freeway. It was mostly an industrial area of freight rail lines and storage areas for the loading and unloading of container shipping. The northern most point of his patrol area was the San Jacinto State Park where Duncan would go to eat his lunch each day and to watch the ships ply the river. It was the only area that afforded an unobstructed view of the harbor in a peaceful park like setting.

His activity most days revolved around issuing citations for the rare speeder and the not so rare stop sign rollers and the occasional red light runner. Certainly not the exciting activity he had hoped for to help pass the time. The mundane routine begins to ware on his mind and decides to take a trip up to the park to clear his head. At this time of the day and week there are few people in the park save for the lonely tourist and stay at home mom seeking a safe place her children may release their pent-up energy. Traveling northward on Independence Parkway approaching San Jacinto State Park Duncan notices the San Jacinto Monument which immortalized the decisive battle in the Texas Revolution of 1836. Far off to his right on a grassy knoll he notices a seemingly unoccupied lone white van parked near the bank of the river. Duncan's mind quickly flashes back to that fateful day those many months ago when he failed to investigate a seemingly innocuous parked vehicle in a lonely stretch of road where a young woman died never knowing if he could have saved her life if he had only listened to his instincts to stop and look. Erring on the side of caution not wishing to repeat his previous lack of judgment he drives slowly over to the van, activates his flashing lights and gives a quick blast of his siren as he approaches the vehicle.

"What was that sound? Go see what it is" directs Abdul.

His assistant puts down the binoculars he was using to scan the horizon and climbs to the rear window to pear out. "It is a police officer. He's getting out of his car."

"We are too close to be stopped now." As the Imam passes over the transmitter to his assistant he gives further direction. "Here, you maintain the guidance signal on the drone and continue to scan the sky to make visual contact I will take care of the intruder. We need only a few minutes longer to complete our mission well before any help for our friend arrives."

Abdul retrieves his venerable AK-47 and opens the side door of the van and steps out just as Duncan rises besides his patrol car looking over the roof toward the exiting Imam. Noticing the raising AK-47 Duncan pulls his Smith & Wesson Model SD 40 VE chambered in .40 caliber. The Imam fires first, the 7.62mm rounds obliterating the windows on both sides of the patrol car. Duncan dives beside the front of his vehicle utilizing the engine block to protect him from the penetrating powerful rounds and rises to his knees behind the hood of the car returns fire tearing holes through the van body's sheet metal. Abdul continues firing on full automatic peppering the patrolman's car deflating both near side tires and rendering the car body to look like an obscene piece of modern art. Duncan able to rise up to return fire only when Abdul stops to replace a magazine and likewise attempts to subdue his opponent by firing through the van body protecting the man. Both men exchange fire replacing magazines as needed to continue the onslaught each changing position in an attempt to exploit a weakness in the other. Duncan dives behind the rear axle attempting a better angle on his foe. As he begins to rise to return fire over the rear deck of the cruiser a high velocity 7.62mm round passes through the trunk of the car striking and passing through Duncan's left arm causing him to cry out and collapse to the ground. Filled with his warped zeal of superiority Abdul strides to the rear of the car eager to finish off the impudent infidel. Duncan realizing the end one way or another was near launches himself from behind the car and firing from the prone position on his right side delivers a 40 caliber S&W round to the middle of the forehead of the advancing man who then drops like a stone.

Duncan kicks the downed gunman's rifle away and advancing on the van holding his injured left arm against his chest. As he pears into the van from the side door he sees a younger man seated at some electronic device of unknown purpose and with one hand points his gun at the man.

"Come out with your hands up."

Duncan is ignored and although tired and in pain he repeats the command. The young man turns quickly brandishing a pistol which is all Duncan needed and methodically empties his clip into the van killing the man and inadvertently destroying the transmitter. As a result and unknown to Duncan the drone now without a controlling signal soon begins to spiral into the ocean and is observed by Mitch high overhead.

Dropping to the ground in exhaustion and pain Duncan sits for a moment trying to collect himself. If this is what the lieutenant had in mind for penitence duty he wanted no more of it. Lifting himself up and staggering back to his patrol car Duncan attempts to radio for assistance only to find the radio in worse shape than he. Deciding to sit and wait hoping to survive until help arrives he begins to hear the sound of an approaching helicopter and advancing cars.

Skidding to a stop near his destroyed cruiser four men in suits jump out and run to his position. As two men view the shot up vehicles and two dead men a third approaches him.

"What's your name deputy?"

"Who are you guys?" he answers.

"Houston FBI. You just did your country a great service son."

Not knowing who the gunmen were or why they opened up on him a confused Duncan asks "What do you mean?"

The fourth man after surveying the interior of the van reports to the agent in charge. "Mike, it's them. The transmitter is in the van but shot up. The antennas on the roof seal's the deal it's them it's over."

The lead agent turns to Duncan and eyes his nametag. "Deputy McDonald these men were wanted terrorists that were in the process of carrying out a heinous act targeting the Bay Side refinery. Your quick action saved the facility and countless lives. Congratulations. By the way how did you know to stop them?"

Not knowing what to say Duncan shrugs and says "just doing my job. And by the way can one of you give me a lift to the local hospital I don't seem to be able to drive myself" as he looks toward his destroyed cruiser.

"No problem, we'll load you into the chopper and have there in a few minutes. Good job."

The lead agent turns to his associates "you two help this man to the chopper and take him in for medical treatment and get a complete statement from him. Frank, you get photos of the two dead perps and send them to General Bishop. And get the coroner down here."

Chapter 42
Tampico, Mexico

Jack and Raul sit in the old hanger and agonizingly wait for Bishop's call reporting on the status of the drones wondering if his last ditch idea was enough or should they be planning for a bigger war.

"What do you think Jack?"

"I think it's out of our hands. It's in the hands of the Air Force, the guys on the ground or a higher power. It depends on the next call from Bishop for what we do next."

The two men do not have to wait long as Jack's com link rings in his ear announcing Bishop's call. "Jack, we got them all. Your plan worked. Mitch reports seeing the last drone spiral into the sea. The FBI reported a local Harris County deputy was ambushed but managed to shoot and kill two men involved in suspicious activity. They are attempting to analyze the electronic equipment in their possession at the time of the gunfight. Initial reports seem to indicate they got the guys controlling the drone. They forwarded photos of the two dead gunmen to me and I'm sending them to you know."

Jack studies the photos of the two men on the screen of his cell phone and shares it with Raul.

"Look familiar to you Raul?"

"I'll say. Those are our old buddies from Phoenix, Imam Abdul - Al - Malik and his weird assistant Faruq Nassar. Nice shooting by someone, it could not have happened to a nicer pair."

"My thoughts exactly, Bishop you still there? We've seen these two before at the Phoenix mosque. The older one is the Imam I told you about who gave us the phony info about an attack on New York and the younger one is his assistant the guy with the funny antennas on his van I thought was for his stereo radio. It appears that this was their plan all along, to have a backup control system for the drones. Those three other men we killed in Phoenix must have been assigned to cover the other three drones. Azzir was not able to replace them in time and so took the chance they would not be needed. Lucky for us we got them when we did or we could not have intercepted the controllers of the other three drones."

"But do you think we got them all Jack?" asks Bishop.

"Yeah I do. That apartment Raul and I went through showed five men living there, the three we killed in Phoenix plus Faruq Nassar plus Mohammed Sharif the young man killed in the accident. That accounts for all five. We also found the bodies, here in Mexico, of five other men plus a wreckage of a truck with additional bodies and body parts. It looks like some type of falling out between the group and Azzir. We also have accounted for Raheem and his technicians here at the hanger."

"Great work men" reports Bishop "I'll make a complete report to the President.

"You know Bishop" continues Jack "all and all they had a good plan. The American economy is built on energy. Seriously interrupting our production capabilities would render a devastating blow to nation's economy for some time. We have other refineries but not all of those are assessable by tanker ships as these were. Plus others cannot produce the output that these four can which means our demand for energy would greatly outpace our supply capabilities resulting in inflation hitting every sector in our economy and triggering a new recession at a time our President is trying to pull us out of the last one.

"Good point Jack I'll mention that to the President too. I've also given the Navy the rough coordinates of the locations of the four downed drones that Mitch sent me. They will start salvage operations on the uranium canisters as soon as possible."

"Ah, I have a question" interrupts Raul "While we're on the subject why didn't the drones explode on impact with the sea?"

Jack thinks for a moment. "The best I can figure they were designed to impact the refinery. The severe impact would be enough to trigger the detonator. When the drones spiraled into the gulf I guess the impact was not substantial enough to actuate the detonator. Lucky for us unlucky for them."

"Well once again good job men. It's all over come on home. We can celebrate."

"I disagree" says Jack "there's still one more. Jason you there?"

"I'm here Jack."

"Sayid does not know we broke his little code does he?"

"I can't see how Jack. What do you have in mind?"

"I need you to send a message to Sayid as if you were Azzir. You will need to mimic the sentence structure, greeting and salutations from previous correspondence. Can you do that?"

"Sure Jack what do you want me to say?"

"Tell him, as Azzir, to meet me at Tishreen Park in Damascus at 1:00 P.M. tomorrow afternoon. Tell him to enter the park from the south parking lot and walk north up the main side walk 110m and sit on the bench on the left side. Tell him I will meet him to share great news. Got it?"

"Will do Jack."

"Oh, and Bishop, have Chester fill one last requisition for me and have it dropped off at the British Embassy in Damascus tomorrow morning, tell them we're coming and have Mitch pick Raul and me up ASAP.

Chapter 43
Damascus, Syria

Jack and Raul are able to rest and decompress from their harrowing last few hours as Mitch glides them across the Atlantic in the sleek Gulfstream. Void now of much of their combat equipment they can focus on the one remaining perpetrator of the vicious attack on America.

"Do you think he will come?" inquires Raul.

"Yeah I think his ego won't let him forgo an opportunity to gloat in the success of his plan to punish America. Most madmen in history seem to have a superiority complex enabling them to think they are acting by the will of a higher authority or in seeking the greater good for all. Well, not today, not on our watch. It ends here. I'm sure there will be others, in time, to take their place. We can leave that to the General Bishops of the world although it was satisfying bringing to justice those that would harm America this time."

"I hear ya Jack" responds Raul.

"Get some sleep buddy we've earned it."

After a brief fuel stop in Germany and a hearty meal the two men arrive once again in Damascus. Mitch taxis the big jet up to the executive terminal.

"Mitch, keep the motor running we won't be long" instructs Jack over his shoulder as he and Raul exit the plane.

Devoid of their combat gear they quickly pass through customs and proceed to the awaiting line of cabs fronting the airport service roads. Entering the nearest cab Jack directs the driver "British Embassy Mohammad Kourd Aly Street please."

The 20 mile ride from the International Airport on the far southeast side of the city to the British Embassy located on the northwest part of city went smoothly and quickly, freeways and major streets encompassing much of the route. Paying the cabbie the two men enter the Embassy and are met by a Royal Marine soldier.

"I'm Jack Hunter and this is Raul de Martinez I believe we are expected."

"Follow me gentlemen" as they are led into the office of the duty station they are met by the stations most senior military officer.

"Gentlemen, welcome. Always good to see you yanks from across the pond. Come in. I was told to expect you and to offer any assistance you request."

"Thank you sergeant" begins Jack "it's nearing 12 noon and we'd like to get to work. Do you have a couple packages for us?"

"Yes we do right over here."

"We thank you for your hospitality and if you will kindly direct us to the elevator we will be on our way" says Jack.

Both men ride quietly to the top floor, exit the elevator and find the maintenance stairwell to the roof at the end of the hall. Exiting the stairs they are offered a panoramic view of the downtown area of Damascus.

"Great view" observes Raul.

Standing near the edge of the roof on the south side of the building Jack looks out over the city. "Let's set up here" he decides. "Open up that duffle bag and help me erect the blind."

Raul pulls from the bag a camo fabric and inserts the supplied wire rods into tabs stitched into the material to add stiffness which forms a flat bottom tubular shape big enough for two men to lay prone inside. Raul takes out the spotter's scope from the bag and lies down beside Jack.

"I can see why you wanted to come here" remarks Raul "the street below us, Abdel Mounawm Riad, runs radially from the embassy and ends at Tishreen Park. We have an unobstructed view all the way down the street to the park."

Jack opens up the reinforced plastic case and removes a CheyTac M-200 Intervention sniper rifle in .408 "I think this will do the trick" he says.

"Why did you pick that?" inquires Raul.

It has a sub minute angle of accuracy at 2500 yards and the 419 grain bullet carries enough kinetic energy to take out almost any target.

"Let's get set up. Give me a range to the bench Sayid was told to sit and wait on. "

Raul adjusts his spotter's scope to focus in on the bench. He activates the laser range finder. "I get 930 yards to target, zero wind."

Jack enters the data into the handheld computer provided by the weapon's manufacturer along with temperature and bullet weight to determine the correction to be dialed into the weapons scope based on bullet drop.

"Got it" he says "now we wait."

At 12:56 P.M. Raul spots a man dressed in a dark suit walking up the center sidewalk of the park and after looking around sits at the prescribed bench.

"I got him" reports Raul as he views through his scope "he matches the picture that Bishop showed us from the CIA. He's looking around probably for Azzir."

Jack rechecks his corrections steadies the crosshairs on his target, lets out a breath and gently squeezes the trigger waiting and feeling for that imperceptible break. The weapons report was loud but was masked by the constant roar of the city's traffic far below. The bullet struck Sayid's head just above his left eye 1.2 seconds after leaving the muzzle of the sniper rifle with enough kinetic energy to cause his head to explode like a watermelon leaving a headless body alone on the bench. No one heard the shot or where it came from. Little if any forensic evidence remained to guide investigators back to the British Embassy.

"Mission accomplished lets go" invites Jack.

"Is that it? Did we get them all" asks Raul.

"All those who played a direct role in the bombing of the *USS Nathanael Green* and the attempt on America are all dead and I believe the secrets of stealth drone construction died with them. Let's go home."

The two men return the equipment to their British friends with their thanks and bid fare well taking a cab back to the airport. Before long Mitch has the two men heading out over the Mediterranean back to the US. The men get some well-deserved rest on the flight home.

Upon arrival in Phoenix Mitch steps from the cockpit to offer his thanks to Jack and Raul. "It's been a wild ride. Sorry to see this team break up."

"Well, all good things must come to an end" says Jack. "Take care Mitch."

As the two men head toward the car rental agency Jack turns to Raul "Will you contact Bishop and report what has happened I have one more thing left to do. I'll meet you back at the office in a couple days. Ok?"

Chapter 44
Phoenix, Arizona

After renting separate cars Jack and Raul head back home to Wickenburg. After a long shower, a change of clothes and a bite to eat Jack heads back toward down town Phoenix to Jennifer's House. It is early evening as Jack pulls up outside her home. Jack notices the light is on inside her front window and calls her from his cell phone.

The evening sun has set. Jericho decides to waits in his car down the street from Jennifer's house until late evening before entering the woman's home. Extracting information from women has always been something he has relished and discovered he had quite a talent for. While waiting looking forward to the evening's foray he noticing a blue sedan pull up in front of the woman's house and decides to wait hoping the disturbing visit will be a short one.

"Hi it's me. Care to give an old sailor a warm seat by your fire?"

"I guess any port in a storm will do. Where are you?"

"I'm outside by the curb."

"Well get in here before the neighbors report you for a peeping tom silly."

Jack was forever grateful for Jennifer's sense of humor even in times of uncertainty which is one of the reasons why they've grown closer over the preceding months. Meeting him at the front door she gives him a big hug. Jack feels the warmth of her embrace as she takes a deep breath and lets out a sigh as if to say *all is now well*.

"Well, don't just stand there come on in. Can I get you something to eat?"

"No that's Ok I had something a short while ago."

Taking him by the hand and leading him to the living room sofa Jennifer asks "So tell me where have you been? I've been trying to call you?"

"I've kinda had my hands full lately" he says. "I can tell you more about it later but I came to see you and to ask if you made any progress in finding out more about your great grandfather?"

"Well yes I have though a funny thing happened recently. A few days ago I came home to find the boxes of my family's papers moved. It is not my imagination. I also found one of my grandmother's letters on the floor. Jack I think someone has been going through my things but why? Do you think someone else is interested in my great grandfather's letter? I still have the letter it was not taken but they could have seen it. At first I thought they took the Red Cross report because I could not find it but I later found it behind my desk. I was reading it over and over and it must have fallen and lodged behind my desk when I got up to answer the phone quickly. I had to leave for a business appointment so I did not return to my desk right away. This must be when they came in. Jack, what is happening?"

"Whoa whoa slow down, what Red Cross report? Let's take it one step at a time. First tell me what you've found about your great grandfather."

"Well I did manage to contact the British Foreign Office and after a lengthy discourse of whom I was and why I wanted the information. And after sending them documentation of my identity I finally got them to give me copies of all the information they had. They gave me a Red Cross field report stating when and where my great grandfather died along with a cursory exam by a medical team which indicated death by gunshot. They must have been the ones called in to collect the bodies. Oh Jack it must have been horrible for him and for my great grandmother finding out this way."

"Jennifer, wait slow down. What bodies?"

"The Red Cross report indicated that a train, on its way to Paris from Naples, was attacked by German's in the beginning of the war high up in the Alps. My great grandfather was on that train."

"Did they say why he was on the train?"

"The Foreign Office had no record of that. By their information he was assigned to the Cairo Embassy and should have been there. No one knows why he was on the train."

"Hum" Jack says to himself out loud "unless he did not want anyone to know he was traveling back to England."

"Why would he want to do that?" she asks.

"Perhaps he did not want anyone to know he had the documents. Did the foreign Office have any records of correspondence with him concerning the documents or copies of them?"

"No, they had no record of them or their existence. I don't think they knew they existed much less that great granddad had them."

Jack looks deep into Jennifer's eyes "how would you like to go on a treasure hunt?"

Chapter 45
Italy

For Jennifer's safety Jack decides to spend the night. The next day Jack returns his rental car and the two begin packing and making reservations for a late morning Delta Airlines flight leaving Phoenix the following morning all under the watchful eye of Jericho. Jack and Jennifer take a cab to the airport the next day. Jericho follows in his car, parks on the second floor departure area and races into the main terminal intent on not losing sight of the pair. Having donned a disguise of a wig and dark glasses he follows the pair into the Phoenix airport. Knowing his rented car will soon be towed from the curb is of no interest to him as the credit card and identification given to the rental agency will never be traced back to him. He maneuvers himself near the couple so as to discover their destination and flight number. He next purchases a similar ticket to continue his surveillance through to their final destination and follows the pair through security to their gate assignment. As they wait for the boarding announcement Jericho reaches into his pocket to retrieve his cell phone and punches the same preprogrammed number.

"It's me. The woman and a man are just boarding Delta flight 623 to Rome with one stop in Atlanta. I have secured a seat on the same flight and will follow them."

"Good, we will have our people join you when you get to Rome. Do not lose them. Be sure to send pictures of the man and woman. I will forward them on to our people in Rome."

After a brief stopover in Atlanta the two are soon on their way to Rome. "It's been a long while since I've been on a real vacation. Thanks for asking me Jack" beams Jennifer.

"You don't have to thank me. It's my pleasure besides this is a working vacation remember? Hopefully we get lucky and find your great grandfather's documents. It'll be fun I promise. Now tell me more of where we're going."

"Not much more to tell really the report says great granddad was found outside the sanctuary at Casa Alpina Padre Semeria a monastery in Courmayeur Aosta Italy. It shouldn't be hard to find. How many old monasteries can there be in one town?"

"I hope you're right. And if not we'll think of something."

The two settled in for the long flight and began to catch up on their relationship. "So tell me Jack did those plants you bought at the nursery where you met me ever take hold?

"Barely, I give them a 50-50 chance of survival. I guess I don't have much of a green thumb. My father taught me a lot of things around the ranch but gardening was not one of them."

"Tell me more about life on the ranch as a young man. I grew up in more of a city setting. I bet you have some interesting stories."

"Well, in addition to tending to the herd and working the fields my father took me hunting frequently and taught me how to track. Rather than sit in a blind all day like most guys do he taught me how to follow the signs left by animals that would lead us right to them."

"That's fascinating how do you do it."

"It doesn't come easy and takes a lot of practice to get good at it. In time you notice things most people do not even see. Many things come into play when tracking an animal like recognizing the imprint of the type of animal, the weather, temperature, the gate, the shape of the imprint will tell you if the animal was running or walking, hurt or healthy, the contour of the impression will tell how old the track is, droppings will tell you how long it was in the area and whether it was foraging or passing through, size and depth of the imprint will tell how large the animal is and much more. The condition of the grass or ground cover will tell how long ago the animal was in the area plus many other signs. It is quit an involved talent that takes a long time to master."

"So, can you use it to track men and did it come in handy during the war?

Jack stops and stares at Jennifer not knowing what to say. To this point he has not told her much of his war years not wanting her to see the other Jack that lurks just beneath the surface.

"Don't be upset Raul told me some things but not all. I can see why you two are so close. You must have shared many life or death moments together. I'm glad you two were able to watch over each other otherwise I may never have met you. Jack, don't hide from who you are and what you've done. I have come to believe you to be a caring and honorable man. If I didn't I wouldn't be here. So, tell me more about tracking."

"Well OK, when I was a senior in high school the family in the neighboring ranch had a 10 year old boy. As young boys sometimes do he got it in his head one day to run away from home. His parents became seriously concerned when he did not return for 24 hours. When I heard about it I went to see the parents. They were visibly shaken and distraught over their missing boy and had just called the sheriff's office. The father told me what he was wearing and his general direction when he left. I headed out on foot on my own before the sheriff's search and rescue could get organized. Fortunately it had not rained nor was the wind blowing to disturb the tracks but after a few hours I found his trail. Following the signs and backtracking a few times when I lost the trail I finally found him 8 hours later, cold and hungry hiding under a tree."

"That was amazing Jack. I can tell there is more to you than meets the eye.

Jack just smiled and gave his boyish grin. "Now tell me something about you I do not already know."

The two laid back and enjoyed small talk. Jack told Jennifer of his early years on the ranch along with experiences he had and other things his mother and father taught him. Jennifer told him of her years growing up in New York before coming out to Arizona to attend Arizona State University and then starting her interior design business.

Time went by quickly. They laughed about funny things that happened in their lives. Each enjoyed the comfort found in spending time with the other and was amazed at the number of things they had in common. Jack was drawn to Jennifer's sense of humor, kindness and trusting nature. Jennifer was drawn to Jack's confidence and charm not to mention his good looks. The two began to sense the attraction they had for each other grow and become something real and lasting.

Following the inflight meal and a brief cat nap the plane arrives at Leonardo da Vinci - Fiumicino Airport mid-afternoon of the following day. Walking through the airport in route to the baggage claim area Jennifer was moved by the colorful murals and paintings that garnered the walls of the main concourse.

"I keep forgetting the art history that abounds in this city. I wish we could stay for a month to see everything" she adds.

"I think I would like that too" he says.

Jack eyes the many signs written in Italian, German, French, English and Spanish around the airport directing patrons to areas of interest. He finds the one that says baggage claim in English and holding Jennifer's arm says "I found it let's go".

Unbeknownst to the pair a set of prying eyes watches their every move.

Collecting their bags Jennifer now assumes the lead "we need to find a cab outside. I booked a lovely hotel a short distance from the train station. Our train for the trip north does not leave until tomorrow morning."

Standing at the terminal curb Jack hails a cab. As they enter the cab Jennifer anticipating the language barrier produces a note with the address and name of the hotel which she gives the driver. The hotel is a pre-World War II structure that has been fully renovated to modern standards yet still maintains its old world charm.

Unaware they are being watched a man slips a cell phone from his pocket and activates a pre-programmed number. "It is me. I have followed them to a hotel not far from the airport. What do you want me to do?"

"Keep watching them. Tomorrow I will take over the surveillance."

After a shower and a change of clothes the two enjoy an elegant evening meal in the hotel's restaurant followed by a lengthy walk hand in hand admiring the culture and architecture of the city after which the two return to their room for a good night's sleep. Rising early they head to the station where Jennifer collects their tickets from the will-call window having ordered them before they left home.

Looking at the tickets Jack remarks "these say Ugine. I thought we were going to Courmayeur?"

"We are but they rebuilt the railroad after the First World War in a different location. We will need to ride to Ugine France and rent a car for a 45 to 50 mile trip eastward and through a tunnel under Mount Blanc to the monastery in Courmayeur Italy."

Boarding the train the two travelers settle into their berth. The quarters are spartan yet comfortable. The space consists of a small bathroom and a high back sofa which converts into sleeping accommodations.

"How long will we be on this train?" asks Jack eyeing the sofa and wondering if his 6 ft. 2 inch frame would survive the night.

"Oh it should not take very long at all. We should be in Ugine in about 6 hours. The last 50 miles by car should put us in Courmayeur by late afternoon just in time for dinner" she responds.

They both spend the rest of the trip relaxing and enjoying the view of the lush green scenery slipping by the large picture window. The time they spent together passes quickly as it usually does as the two come to realize how much they enjoyed each other's company.

The train arrives on time in Ugine. They had to ask more than once the directions to the rental car company but finally found someone who spoke passible English. The drive through the Alps was even more enjoyable than the train ride. Tall trees and flowery meadows and snow kissed mountain tops fill the landscape further heightening the enjoyment of the trip and their time together.

Finally arriving in Courmayeur they find a quaint hotel, check in and walk around town taking in the ambiance of the old Alpine village. "Isn't the scenery amazing Jack? it's just like the pictures you see in the travel brochures" exclaims Jennifer "I wish we could stay for weeks."

The couples find a quaint cafe not far from their hotel and decide to have dinner before starting their quest in the morning.

"What do you want to do after we find the monastery Jack?"

"I'm not sure. Ask a lot of questions I think look for clues research the past as best we can and hope for the best. I've come to believe your great grandfather did have something with him that night and somehow it became lost."

"What makes you believe the account in the letter was true?"

"Think about it, why else would a man abandon a government post he worked many years to obtain? He must have come across something so significant it warranted his hasty departure back to London. He did not tell anyone because he felt the discovery was so profound that it may be taken by others if they knew of its existence. Your great grandfather was an educated man so he would appreciate the importance and value of whatever he had. Besides the war just started and I'm sure he wanted to do his part. My thoughts now are can the documents be retrieved or were they destroyed those many years ago?"

"I guess we'll find out tomorrow Jack. Let's eat dinner and get some rest."

The two rise early the next morning and enjoying a leisurely breakfast in the hotel dining room. Jack inquires at the hotel's front desk for directions to the Casa Alpina Padre Semeria before heading out.

"Signore it's two blocks down and one block to the right. You can't miss it. It is white with red accents. The name is on a small sign in the wall by the front door. Enjoy your stay in Courmayeur" he adds.

"Thank you very much" Jennifer responds as she turns and raps her arm around Jack's.

Following the directions given by the hotel manager the two head out enjoying the picturesque setting of an authentic Alpine village and soon arrive at the monastery. Its pristine facade and small parking lot out front give Jack pause wondering if they may have been misled.

"Well, as long as we're here let's go inside and look around" suggests Jack.

The two enter and find a well-appointed lobby complete with a warm fireplace, a sofa with four lounge chairs, a chandelier and a refreshment table with coffee and tea. Jack and Jennifer look inquisitively at each other not believing what they are seeing. Behind the counter was what appeared to be a friar dressed in standard long brown tunic and hood with a rope belt.

"Excuse me" asks Jack "but is this the Casa Alpina Padre Semeria monastery?"

"Yes it is may I help you" replies the portly and friendly gentleman.

"Forgive me but this is not what I had expected for a monastery" Jack remarks as he jesters his hand toward the spacious room.

"Oh it is indeed" says the man "currently our order has 16 members in residence. Economic realities being what they are we also maintain a bed & breakfast on the grounds for travelers such as yourselves to make ends meet you understand."

"I see" responds Jack "but your Inn looks so new I thought your order was quite old."

"It is" the man replies "this monastery is run by the Barnabiti Friars of Genoa. The buildings here were built in early 1950's and since then converted to also serve as a bed & breakfast."

Remembering the Red Cross field report that Jennifer's great grandfather died outside a sanctuary Jack asks "do you still have the original sanctuary?"

"I am sorry signore we never had a sanctuary here."

Jack and Jennifer feeling their quest quickly becoming a lost cause and a dead end remember that Jennifer's great grandfather was here in 1914 ask "but what happened before this facility was built?"

"I do not know" the man replies "perhaps brother Aldo may know. He is the oldest member of our order. You can usually find him on the grounds somewhere or in the meditation chapel."

"Thank you very much for your help" says Jennifer as she and Jack turn to leave.

"Well, let's look for brother Aldo" says Jennifer.

Jack and Jennifer search the hallways and chapels encompassing the new monastery and inquire other monks as to the location of brother Aldo but to no avail. Deciding to rest for a while they retreat to the courtyard where they find an elderly man praying beside an olive tree. Slowly approaching the man not wishing to disturb him the old man looks up.

"Please excuse us" begins Jennifer "but are you brother Aldo?"

"Why yes my child I am. May I help you?"

"Yes, if you will be so kind she says. We're inquiring into the history of the monastery you see my great grandfather was here in 1914."

The old man thought for a moment then replied "I'm sorry miss but I do not think that was possible. The original structures you see here were built around 1930 and rebuilt in the early 1950's.

"I am aware of the current structures" says Jack "but what did you use before the 1930's?"

The old man thought for a while again then said "I remember being told that when our order was originally formed back in the early 1800's we were once a part of the Greater St. Bernard Abby. The monks of St Bernard loaned us use of some of their out buildings on their grounds for our residence, meditation and sanctuary."

"Were these what were used in 1914?" asks Jack.

"Why yes they would be."

"Do they still exist?" asks Jack getting tired of playing 20 questions

"I do not know" replies the old Friar "the monastery of St Bernard is about 10 kilometers further up the mountain."

"Can we get there from here?" asks Jack.

"Yes just follow the road and look for signs."

Jack and Jennifer look at each other with renewed interest and race back to the hotel, hop into their car and drive up the mountain hanging on to a glimmer of hope that they may, for the first time, be on the right trail. The higher up they drive the sharper the switch backs become. Not wanting to miss the sign Jack drives slowly.

"Look" Jennifer exclaims "a sign. It says St. Bernard Abby."

Jack slows further and makes a right turn onto a graded gravel road that winds its way through the lush dense mountain pines. No longer traveling up the mountain the road meanders at a somewhat constant elevation until reaching a large clearing where they see stone buildings nestled around a circular driveway. Parking the car off to the side of the driveway the two get out and admire the beauty of the buildings and grounds of the Abby.

"I don't see anyone around" remarks Jennifer.

"Perhaps they're out to lunch" jokes Jack. "Let's look around."

Taking Jennifer's hand they begin exploring the grounds. Marveling at the workmanship and age of the stone buildings they make their way around to the back of what looked to be the main sanctuary. Exiting one of the side buildings a lone monk appears and noticing Jack and Jennifer approach the pair.

"Escusa signore, may I be of assistance to you?"

"Yes padre we......."

"Please, you may call me Brother Timothy."

Jack nods his head respectively and begins again "Thank you Brother Timothy. We were told that the friars from the Casa Alpina Padre Semeria in town had, at one time, facilities here at the Abby. Is this correct?"

"Yes, I believe they did but I'm afraid that was very long ago."

"We were told that you allowed them use of some of your buildings to start up their order here in Courmayeur and were wondering if those buildings still existed."

"We do have some rather old facilities that are no longer in use but I do not know for certain if these were the ones used by the order in town."

"With your permission may we see these facilities?"

"But of course. Come I will show you."

The three set out on a winding trail through the forest lead by Brother Timothy. "Our order was begun in the 16th century. This particular Abby was begun in the early 1800's. When our permanent facilities were constructed we allowed the order, the ones you seek, to utilize our old facilities."

The trio continued on their path Jennifer enjoying the sunlight filtering through the leaves of the trees, the cool mountain breeze and the smell of pine. The trail finally opens to a clearing now covered in wild flowers containing the remains of two very old structures. Both Jack and Jennifer stand for a moment moved by the age and history of the buildings. Though a shadow of their former glory the buildings, now ravaged by time, left to decay sit as a reminder of a lost era.

Feeling their hopes of success dwindle for a second time Jack and Jennifer decide to explore the grounds. Standing off to the side of both buildings and pointing to the smaller of the two on their left Jack remarks "that one must have contained the living quarters, kitchen, dining hall and meditating rooms. The report said your great grandfather died beside a sanctuary." Pointing to the building on the right he adds "this one looks to be the sanctuary. Early churches were built in the outline of a cross pointing east toward Jerusalem with the main alter on the far east end, doors were placed at the west end and sometimes two more at the termini of the north/south extensions of the cross."

Walking around the south side of the sanctuary they notice that much of the east half of the building is perched beside a rocky cliff giving the south side windows a breathtaking view of the valley below.

Standing back they see the structure for what it has become, faded clapboard mar the sides with some boards missing allowing the elements to further ravage the inside of the building. A section of the roof was missing, caved in years ago by the weight of fallen snow further contributing to the decay of the inside and outside of the structure. The windows were all but gone adding to the dismal appearance. "Ya know" begins Jack "it may look like its seen its last days but it was a handsome structure in its time. As long as we're here let's have a look inside."

Entering the nave through the west door and weaving their way between the fallen roof trusses they notice missing and upended pews ravaged by years of wind, rain and snow. Leaves and twigs cover the floor throughout. The rotting floor groaned beneath their feet with each step caused by years of rain through the holes in the roof and walls. Gone are the red carpet, tapestries and fine wood finished pews. While navigating a path around the fallen trusses and debris Jack's foot breaks through a group of weakened floor boards near one of the Southside windows eliciting from him a cry of surprise.

"Watch that first step" teases Jennifer "it's a long way down."

Now standing at the center of the sanctuary saddened by the decay of a once great church Jack stands silently and looks around to face Jennifer and gently remarks "The report by the Red Cross said this is where your great grandfather must have come that night."

Jennifer realizes she is in the presence of a distant piece of her history develops a tear in her eye and comes to stand next to Jack and takes his arm in her hands. "Yeah I know."

The east end of the church is called the chancel. It is built on a raised three step platform to separate the rector, or clergy, from the parishioners of the nave. It is here that the alter, now devoid of its finery, resides amongst the same debris. The east end of the church fared slightly better than the rest, the rain and snow not yet reaching this far as the holes in the roof and walls were relegated mostly to the rear portions of the building.

"With this church in its current state of decay finding evidence of my great grandfather's visit and the whereabouts of the documents appears lost once again."

"Perhaps" says Jack "but let's just give the old place a moment. It may yet speak to us."

Feeling saddened by the loss of hope of finding any further sign of her great grandfather and no other clues to guide them the two sit on the edge of the chancel and quietly imagine the history and activity that took place here those many years ago. They listened to the breeze as it gently blows through the old church. While taking in the moment Brother Timothy enters and says "Is this what you were looking for? Sorry it does not look better but it hasn't been used for many years."

Wishing to at least learn something for his trip Jack asks Brother Timothy the purpose of the two tables at the front of the chancel.

"The one on the left" responds the monk "when facing the congregation is the communion table for the offering of the sacraments. The one on the right is the baptismal containing the basin of water to signify new birth."

Jack stands up and walks over to the first table noting the once beauty and simplicity of its design amazed at the craftsmanship of bygone generations. He then walks over to the second and admires its workmanship. "Tell me Brother Timothy why does the baptismal have eight sides?"

"The eight sides are because Christ arose on Sunday the 8ᵗʰ day or the first day of the week which equates to a new day or a new beginning for believers following the symbolic rebirth from the water."

"I see. Thank you."

Jack continues to inspect the baptismal more closely noticing each of the eight sides is composed of eight vertical panels comprising the cabinet holding the water basin with a strip of molding above the panels and directly below the basin and another strip of molding at the bottom by the floor. Along the upper molding of each panel contains lettering barely legible from the years of weathered abuse. Looking closely he notices that the words are in Latin. "Excuse me Brother Timothy but can you translate this writing for me please?"

"Yes certainly I will try."

The priest steps closer and puts on his glasses. "Let's see, *Dei gratia* means by the grace of God, *Deus vobiscum* means may God be with you, *Agnus Dei* means the lamb of God, *Laus Deo* means praise to God, *Deo volente* means God willing, *Deo gratias* means thanks be to God, *Dante Deo* means by the gift of God and *Deus misereatur* means may God have mercy."

Jack quickly steps forward and places his hand on Brother Timothy's shoulder. "Please read that last one again."

The man does so and Jack says "Oh can it be?" Jack quickly turns toward Jennifer and asks "Jennifer let me see that letter from your great grandfather again please."

Jennifer quickly pulls the old letter from her purse. They both view the closing of the letter. "My great grandfather signed the letter with the same words, *May God have mercy.*"

They both look at each other with renewed exhilaration. "Stand back we need to be sure" he says.

Jack brushes away the leaves and dirt piled against the lower edges of the cabinet and pulls at the lower molding strip beneath the panel containing the matching words found in the letter surprised at how easily it separated. Reaching his hand deep inside the cabinet he removes an aged leather pouch. Jennifer kneels beside him eager to see the contents of the pouch both wondering if this could be her great grandfather's lost documents. Gently opening the pouch and removing two pieces of paper they both read with delight finding a deed conveying ownership and a letter of authenticity.

"Jack we found it" Jennifer screams in delight.

Jack just sits staring at the documents and begins to grin.

Brother Timothy noting the elation approaches and asks "signore what are those?"

"These are either an implement of peace unto the world or the beginning of untold bloodshed" responds Jack seriously.

"Perhaps then it is best that they stay hidden, no?" the good priest responds.

Jack and Jennifer sit on the edge of the chancel holding the documents. "Perhaps Brother Timothy is right Jack" she says "maybe we should leave them if they can cause as much harm as you say."

"But should it be up to us to decide or should mankind be allowed to choose for themselves once and for all when faced with either destruction or peace?"

"Is your faith in mankind great enough to know that they will make the right choice?" she asks.

"Yeah it has to be. I believe we were allowed to find these for a reason and wiser minds than mine are going to have to make the call."

Jack stands and turns to the priest, smiles and says "Brother Timothy we thank you for your contribution in helping us recover these documents. Hopefully the world will be a better place soon."

"Go in peace my son. Let it be as you say" proclaims Brother Timothy as he turns to leave.

Standing outside the church two determined men listen through the hole in the wall "I've heard enough" says Jericho "let us relieve our friends of the prize."

As Brother Timothy leaves Jack and Jennifer stand together by the chancel steps enjoying the moment of the miraculous find. A few moments later the two sinister men enter the church and slowly approach the pair.

"Ms. White I presume. Thank you for recovering those documents for us. You and your friend are quite resourceful."

"And just who would you be?" asks Jack.

As the man slowly pulls a short barrel semi-automatic pistol from his pocket and points it at Jack says "let's just say I represent a group interested in maintaining the status quo so to speak."

"What you are really saying is you want the constant tension and fighting to continue" responds Jack.

"Oh it may not continue much longer if certain people I know are successful in their efforts. But that document you hold certainly complicates things. That is why I must relieve you of it. You understand."

"No I do not" Jennifer cries angrily "you would kill and destroy people rather than accept a lasting peace? You people are mad."

"Tsk tsk Ms. White sticks and stones. Now if you would hand over the document please."

"Wait just a moment" Jack responds as he holds his hand out toward the man with the gun "how did you know the deed even existed? Jennifer had the only letter from her great grandfather alluding to its existence."

"Yes I know I saw it" answers the man "but one other remnant of that fateful night survived the test of time. A diary was found written by Muhammad Hamid al-Din himself the unwitting pawn of your Addison Devencourt who undoubtedly would be beheaded if he lived today. The diary spoke of this vile deed that no one either knew about or could find until you came along. As a descendant of Addison you were difficult to track down but certainly worth the effort. I thank you for your resourcefulness. Now if you would be so kind" he says as he stretches out his hand.

Jack looks over at Jennifer with his head turned so only she can see and gives her a wink. Turning back to the man with the gun Jack lowers his head in resignation attempting to put the man at ease. "Very well" he says solemnly.

With blinding speed and accuracy Jack flings the pouch at the man's face blinding him long enough for Jack to close the distance between the two in a flash and grabs the man's gun hand with both his hands. Attempting to counter Jericho lends his other hand where both men grapple for control of the weapon. As each man attempts to twist and gain leverage over the other Jennifer begins hurling sticks and broken wood at the second man in an attempted to keep him busy and not come to the aide of his friend against Jack. Jack and Jericho continue to twist around the floor surprising Jack of the hand to hand combat skills of the man. On more than one occasion Jack attempts to trip the man by placing his leg behind the man and pushing him over it to no avail. His skill appearing equal to Jack's in evading attempts of dominance and control. The two men continue to turn and twist knocking into pews and walls in an epic struggle of survival. Jack attempts to lessen the man's grip by driving his knee into the man's mid-section as they wrestle for control of the gun but the man counters by raising his leg effectively blocking the kick. As they twist and turn and careen around the nave they begin to approach the open window. Jack, remembering the hole he fell through earlier twists and pushes his opponent ever closer. Not seeing the hole Jericho's leg falls through and reflexively lets go of the gun with one hand in an attempt to gain purchase on a stable surface. As the man stumbles backward he falls half out the open window which is all the opening Jack needs. Holding the gun in one hand Jack reaches down and lifts the man's leg and flips him out the window. Falling 20 feet he lands breaking his spine over a sharp rock severing his spinal cord. Still clutching the gun the man, paralyzed from the neck down, stares at Jack through the window and slowly dies.

Turning quickly toward the second man he sees the man advancing on Jennifer with a large curved double edged khanjar knife. Now out of objects to throw she backs slowly toward the wall.

"Hey" Jack calls out "your friend wants a word with you."

Noticing his friend missing he turns his attention from the helpless woman to Jack eager to cut him till he dies so he may have his way with the woman at his leisure. Advancing on Jack he lashes out a sweeping arc of blade intending to cut Jack's midsection. Jack jumps back just missing the sharp blade. Round and around they circle each other Jack jumping just out of the reach of each menacing swing of the deadly knife. Knowing he must time his move perfectly Jack waits for the next large swing of the blade. As the man swings the knife once more at his chest Jack steps forward within the man's reach as the blade passes. Before the man can recover and advance another stroke Jack takes hold of the man's wrist holding the knife. Both men claw for control of the knife. Face to face they struggle a look of anger and hate fills the man's eyes contrasted by a look of sheer determination and confidence in Jack's eyes. Each man attempts to point the blade toward the other but neither is able to gain the advantage. With their hands locked together around the knife Jack pushes the man backwards with all his strength but as the man comes forward back to him Jack rolls over on his side effectively flipping the man over his hip. As the two men hit the floor Jack rolls on top of the man. With the added weight of Jack's body to assist him he is able to drive the blade down through the man's sternum severing a major artery. As Jack slowly stands with blood over his shirt and arms Jennifer runs over to him.

"Jack, Jack" she cries "are you all right?"

"Yeah I'm Ok it's not my blood. Thanks for the help back there. Jack wipes himself off the best he can and retrieves the pouch. We better get going I've found that these guys are never alone. There are bound to be more."

Taking hold of Jennifer's hand they race back up the path that brother Timothy first showed them. Rounding the stone buildings of St. Bernard they jump into their car not noticing the dark sedan with two men sitting parked across the courtyard. Jack fires up his rented Mercedes and heads down the mountain.

"Jack, don't you think you're going a little too fast" Jennifer exclaims.

"Don't look now" he says "but I think we're being followed."

Driving with one eye on the road and one on the rear view mirror Jack clearly sees the second car beginning to close on them. Reaching the next hair pin turn Jack downshifts the big car and drifts through the turn. At the next straight away the second car catches up and rams

Jack's rear bumper attempting to push him off the road and down the mountainside. Mashing the accelerator Jack pulls ahead once more. Braking hard then powering through the next turn Jack gains a slight lead on his attackers. Again at the next straight away the trailing car hits Jack's car even harder causing his rear tires to break traction and fishtail across both lanes of traffic thankful that there were no cars traveling in the opposite direction.

"Jack, we can't keep this up. Sooner or later we're going to wreck" exclaims Jennifer.

Desiring to end the chase before reaching town the passenger of the second vehicle points his Sig Sauer P220 out his side windows and begins firing at the fleeing Mercedes.

"Jennifer, get down" shouts Jack as 45 ACP rounds ripe through the rear window and trunk lid of their car.

Now covered in broken glass and piloting a vehicle at speeds greatly exceeding the safety limit of the narrow two lane mountain road Jack earnestly looks for a solution to their problem. Hurtling downhill the two vehicles weave from side to side with Jack attempting to keep the second vehicle behind him at all costs.

"Jack, what are we going to do?"

"Hold on I've got an idea. Stay down."

Careening down hill approaching a left hair pin turn Jack allows the second vehicle to inch up along his right side. The driver of the second car seeing an opportunity to shoot and kill the pair quickly takes the bait. Nearing the turn Jack stands on the brakes and slides toward the curve, the second vehicle now pulls even with the intent to shoot into the front seat of the fleeing duo's car killing both occupants. As the gunman points his weapon out the window Jack quickly cranks the wheel hard left and mashes the accelerator. The abrupt change in momentum causes the rear of Jack's car to break loose sliding out and into the second vehicle as he rounds the corner with enough force to prevent the second car from completing the turn. The second vehicle no longer able to maintain traction is propelled through the stone fence protecting the apex of the curve and sails out into space tumbling over and over on its decent to the valley floor below.

Jack immediately skids to a stop, gets out and walks back to the curve with Jennifer. Looking at the smoldering wreckage far below relieved that the deadly duel is over and he and Jennifer are safe once again stands quietly for a moment then turns to her and says "I hope their insurance was paid up."

Pulling close to him she looks up at him and playfully slaps his arm "you're incorrigible. Who were those guys anyhow?"

"I don't know but you heard the man. He went through your house looking for these documents. Whoever he worked for is very powerful and has no qualms about killing innocent people. These documents mean a great deal to them. Whoever controls them controls the Middle-East. We've got to get these out of our hands and into someone else's."

"To whom are you going to give those documents Jack?"

"I know just the man." Come on, let's go home."

Chapter 46
Washington

J ack and Jennifer check out of their hotel and drive back to Ugine France. The Frenchman running the rental car agency is outraged over the damage done to his vehicle begins to berate Jack amid wild arm gestures and calling into questioning his paternal lineage and upbringing. Jack, thankful he does not understand French tells the angry French rental agent his insurance agent will be in touch to make good on the damage to his car.

As the two comely walk back toward the train station Jennifer asks "Jack, did you understand what that man was saying?"

"No. Why? Should I?"

"No I guess not. Maybe it's just as well you don't. I took one year of French in high school and was only able to pick up bits and pieces of it. I'd hate to see what you would have done to the poor man if you understood what he said."

"What? You mean gentle easy going me?" They both begin to laugh as they continue their walk.

Jack is quiet most of the way back on the train contemplating his decision to share the documents with those in authority. He wrestles in his mind whether Bishop and the President can be trusted to do the right thing or was this really too hot to handle. He could not tell which but knew he would feel better once the documents left his possession and became someone else's problem.

"Jack I do wish we could stay longer. It has been my dream for a long time to visit Rome and visit the places I have only read about for years."

"I wish we could too but we need to get these back to Washington as quickly as possible. I promise to make it up to you. We'll go on another trip real soon."

The promise makes her feel a little better and she soon begins to relax and enjoy the ride again through the Alpine countryside. The rest of the trip back to Rome went quickly and soon the pair was flying back to Washington.

The final leg of their journey was underway and Jack was anxious for it to be over. Settling back in his seat once the plane reached cruising altitude over the Atlantic Jack allowed thoughts of Jennifer to begin filling his mind. The long flight gave him the opportunity he was waiting for to tell Jennifer of his exploits and what he was really doing the past few months. He knew his feelings for her have grown since they first met and knew that a lasting relationship must be built on honesty and truth decides to tell her everything. He reasoned that if she bolted it was best to know now or to at least find out what she felt about him and his past exploits.

"Ah Jennifer I'd like to tell you things about me that you probably are not aware of. I wish to tell you this to be honest and open with you and I believe relationships are best built on honesty and trust."

Jennifer turns her head and looks into his eyes "go ahead Jack."

Jack begins by telling her of his tours of duty in Iraq and Afghanistan for the Marines, of the fire fights he has engaged in, the covert operations he conducted, the fellow marines and families he has rescued and of the horrors of war he has seen firsthand along with the hate and cruelty he has seen in life on the front lines of a seemingly unending war. He also tells her of his most recent assignment for General Bishop Kincaid, why he was chosen, the plot to attack America and how he stopped it along with the help of Raul and some other very talented people. He adds "although I am proud to have played a successful part and feel that I am good at what I can do, most of all I am saddened by the loss of good people and further saddened that actions like this are necessary at all." Jack looks deep into her eyes wondering what she may think of him now and finally asks "so do you still want to hang around with a simple engineer that gets reluctantly pulled into operations to save the world doing things best left unsaid?"

Jennifer still looking at him smiles with the look of pure admiration in her eyes answers "Jack, the people I meet through my business are self-centered egotistical and shallow who care more about their image and what others think of them than of being who they truly are. Their goals in life are to chase money, fame, possessions, power, and influence trying to fill a void within them which when they fail find their lives then turn to envy, depression, despair gilt and hate. They are empty and they fail because they are looking in the wrong place. Jack you saved my life not once but twice. You are the most honorable man I have ever met. You unselfishly put yourself on the line to protect those you do not even know and those that cannot protect themselves. You do what others cannot and ask for nothing in return. You are like the knight at the city gate offering a last line of defense for a sleeping city whose members do not even know you are there. The people who know you love you and deeply respect you. I wish more people did. I think our country needs someone to look up to these days. Heaven knows we've lost respect for our leaders in Washington over the years.

"Be careful don't lift me up too high it makes for a harder fall."

"You fall? Never. Your sense of duty and honor and belief in ideals greater than yourself is what gives you the strength and sets you apart.

"What I learned many years ago by some very wise men has served me well."

It shows and yes Jack I do want to be with you and I am very proud of you."

She moves closer and kisses him deeply and tucks her arm under his and gives it a hug then lays her head on his shoulder "but I have one request."

"What's that?" he asks.

"Please no more shoot outs while we are having lunch or driving in the car."

They both laugh and he gives her a big hug and kiss "it's a deal."

As they sit enjoying the flight with Jennifer's head on Jack's shoulder he adds "it's not true you know. I did ask for something. Bishop promised to pay my standard consultants fee for the time I was away from the office."

Their eyes meet and they begin to laugh again before finally settling down for the long flight. As she dozes against his shoulder Jack pulls out his phone and taps Bishop's number.

"Bishop here."

"Hi it's me. I found the documents I told you about. It turns out we were not the only ones looking for them. There is a very powerful group out there who will stop at nothing to destroy these documents to maintain their position in the region. A region they say they have big plans for. I'll send you a full report of what has happened so far. We're midway over the Atlantic and should be landing in DC in a couple hours. Can you meet me at the White House?"

"That's amazing Jack. Sure I can meet you there. I'll have a pass waiting for you at the gate."

"If you have not done so already" Jack adds "you may want to share a copy of all the correspondence and audio recordings Jason has collected with the President to bring him up to speed regarding Iran's involvement in all this. And one more thing, it may be a good idea to have someone authenticate the signatures of Sharif Hussein bin Ali and Abdulla ibn Hussein and the documents themselves from 1914 Cairo plus have the British Ambassador on hand as this concerns them."

"Will do Jack. We'll be waiting."

As the plane begins its final approach into Reagan International Jack asks "Jennifer will you be alright going on to Phoenix without me I need to give these documents to Bishop and the President? I'll be back in a day or so."

"Sure Jack go ahead. I'll be fine. Good luck."

As they exit the plane Jennifer heads toward another gate for her connecting flight back to Phoenix while Jack, glad to be back in the states, gets his bag and hails the first taxi he finds.

General Bishop Kincaid calls ahead and arranges for a meeting with the President. When he arrives the President's Chief of Staff accompanies him to the Oval office. In attendance are Vice President Granger, Secretary of Defense Hammond, and Secretary of State Lomax along with the President.

"General it's good to see you again" spouts the President "I'd like to congratulate you again for the splendid job you and your team did in stopping those drones. Having them fall into the ocean where they did we are able to suppress the story temporarily, explaining it as a joint Naval and Air Force exercise. I figured that with the Mideast ready to explode I did not want to further alarm our people. The truth will be made known once the tensions have subsided I hope. What else do you have for us?"

"Well sir since last we spoke a Navy salvage team is attempting to recover the enriched uranium canisters. When analyzed the decay signature will tell us the origin of the processed material. I have brought with me copies of most of the intercepted audio traffic plus email traffic between the perpetrators, for your review, which clearly implicates an Iranian involvement in the thwarted attack. We have identified the mastermind and financial backer of the group as Sayid Kamal of the Ministry of Intelligence and National Security of the Islamic Republic. We believe he was acting independently without the knowledge of the President and Supreme Council never the less we believe Iran's enriched uranium was added as a component to the deadly attack. If successful the impact to our ports would have been devastating. Sayid Kamal has since been silenced with extreme prejudice along with everyone having knowledge of the stealth drone construction per your instructions.

"Mr. President" asks Secretary Lomax "did the General just say he assassinated a senior member of the Iranian Government? an action that was banned by the signing of Executive Order 12333 by President Reagan in 1981."

"I don't know did he?" asks the President "I heard he was acting without the knowledge of the government therefore not a representative of the government. In addition his actions were, in my view, an act of war upon this nation and I took an oath to defend this nation and its national security interests. General, a grateful nation offers it's thanks to you and your team for a job well done. Bob, Ryan do you disagree?"

"No sir" both men meekly respond.

As the President shakes General Kincaid's hand and the other cabinet members beam with delight of a job well done there is a knock on the door. The Chief of Staff opens the door and announces "Mr. President there is a Mr. Hunter out here and says he has a package for General Kincaid."

Bishop excuses himself and steps into the hallway outside the Oval Office where Jack stands waiting.

Jack, looking a little bedraggled and tired from his ordeal holds out the pouch. "Here they are General. I think you will find them interesting. There resides a great weight upon the shoulders of the one possessing these documents. Good luck."

"Thanks Jack. Your country owes you a debt of gratitude. Go home get some rest you need it your assignment is over."

"Just use those wisely and we'll be good. As for the assignment being over all the members of the terrorist group are dead except for one, the chief financial backer in Macau all we have is a name for him and we don't know if its real or a code name. Also as I mentioned on the plane there is another very powerful and influential shadow group out there that was also looking for these documents and we may not have heard the last from these guys. I would not be surprised if the one name we heard was a part of this group.

"That's Ok Jack there will be another day. We'll keep our eye out for them. Go home. You've earned it."

The two men shake hands, Bishop returns to the President's Office while Jack, finally realizing he is done, stretches out on a sofa in the hallway of the White House and falls asleep.

"Mr. President" begins Bishop "I think you are going to want to see this. Do you remember the lost documents I told you about?"

The President seated at his desk opens the faded leather pouch and begins to reads with fascination the content of the documents before passing them to the other cabinet members.

"General I must congratulate you. You and your team really came through. I never expected you to secure something like this. It has been lost for almost 100 years how ever did you find it? This is amazing this just could be what we need to turn the tide and break the cycle in the Middle East."

Just then the Chief of Staff knocks on the door again and announces British Ambassador Timmons. The President turns and rises from behind his desk as two men enter the room "Jeffrey you old sea dog good to see you again."

"It is good to see you again too Mr. President."

The two men have been good friends for years ever since meeting during a joint US and British Naval training exercise in their early years. The President was a junior office on a destroyer and the Ambassador held a similar rank on a British frigate. The two collaborated in planning sessions and readiness drills.

"Thank you again Jeffrey" the President began "for getting our two men permission to utilize your Damascus embassy on such short notice."

"It's the least I could do after what you've told me has been happening. I was most alarmed to hear of this drone strike business. Nasty business that. But, you managed to get them in time. Good job 'ol boy. Glad to be of assistance."

I'm glad we can always count on the Brits when the chips are down. The big fish would have gotten away if you were not able to allow us access to your Embassy.

"Yes well you have some very talented people working for you. I'm told there are not many men that could have made that shot. So, what can I do for you today Mr. President?"

"Well, it's more of what can we do for each other. Something most unusual has crossed my desk and it just may be able to solve most of our problems in the Middle East."

The President briefs the Ambassador on the documents supplied by Jack and Bishop then allows him read and study them in detail.

When finished the Ambassador looks up "This is amazing. Are these for real?"

"You tell me" questions the President.

"Forgive me Mr. President. In the gayety of the moment I failed to introduce to you Mr. Hemfield from our National Archives. I asked him to join us, as you requested, to authenticate the documents. Mr. Hemfield if you would be so kind as to have a seat and review these documents."

The minutes pass as the historian examines the documents in detail. The President, his staff and Ambassador Timmons enjoy small talk as they wait. Finally the man stops, sits back in his chair and announces "the letter head is genuine, I've seen this period before and the water mark is visible and genuine. They are remarkably preserved for their age. The National Archives was helpful in providing copies of Abdulla ibn Hussein's and his father's signature pulled from old correspondence from the period which revealed a match to the sample you now provide and the notary identified on the document was an employee of the Cairo Embassy during the date in question. The investigation I conducted on these two individuals revealed they are who they said they were and they did have the authority to sign and commit to these documents. Gentlemen these are authentic legal documents."

The President and the British Ambassador look at each other in pleased astonishment.

The President stands erect to his full height of six feet and ponders to himself that the world is at a turning point, how is history going to record the next few moments, the beginning or the end? "Tony get me that little SOB of an Iranian Ambassador. The madness ends here."

"How do you want to play this Mr. President?" asks the British Ambassador.

"Just follow my lead Jeffrey."

An hour goes by. The President and the British Ambassador sit in quiet contemplation of what is about to take place realizing that the world will change very much in the next hour. But which way they could not say.

The Chief of Staff as before knocks and announces the Iranian Ambassador. The man enters but no one advances to shake hands or offer introductions. He stands solemnly and addresses the room in a flat tone of dismissal "I am confused as to your request to see me again so soon Mr. President there is little more I can add to offer any meaningful resolution to the current discourse in the Middle East" begins the arrogant Ambassador.

"Then perhaps I can help you" begins the president "I have documented proof that members of your government, initiated by a Mr. Sayid Kamal, are responsible for an attempted stealth drone attack on American soil. Here are copies of the emails, phone and voice data retrieved by our people. We can back trace the owners of the accounts through the internet provider's ISP. When we retrieve the uranium canisters from the stealth drones we intercepted that crashed into the Gulf of Mexico we will be able to match the decay signature to the material you are now producing. We have proof of everything. I intend to present all this before the United Nations so all can see the deceitful warring tyrants you people are."

"This is an outrage, this is nothing more than western propaganda of lies and fabricated evidence. No one will believe you."

"I can assure you that our proof is solid and not fabricated" responds the President coldly while locking eyes on the diminutive Iranian.

The Iranian Ambassador stands still for a moment thinking then adds "I have just received word that our intelligence minister, Mr. Sayid Kamal, was killed yesterday in Damascus."

The President smirks "how about that. I am very sorry about your minister and I am not aware of the details of his demise but accidents happen. We would not want to see other senior members of your government succumb to similar accidents. Would we?"

The Iranian Ambassador stands still staring into the Presidents eyes and drops his jaw slightly. "Did you just threaten members of our duly elected government Mr. President?"

The President grins widely and waves the Ambassador to follow him. "Come with me I have something to show you. Please sit here and review the documents I have set before you."

The Ambassador puts on his glasses and then for the next few minutes examines the documents closely even reading them over many times. "Is this some kind of joke?" he demands.

"I assure you they are quite real" replies the President. "They have been authenticated and duly signed by the empowered persons at the time. Since peace cannot be obtained thru peaceful diplomacy we will try another tact. Peace thru strength. Mr. Ambassador the US and Britain are going to construct our largest military base in the world on your doorstep plus take over the Arabian oil fields as we are now the owners. We will control the land and the oil. We will construct and direct our missile facilities and aim them directly at your heart, we will control all commerce thru the straits of Hormuz, and we will control what comes into and out of your country. You will be under our control from now on. We will also create a new Palestinian state in the northern most region of our new protectorate."

"You cannot do that."

"Oh yes I can I'm the new landlord remember?"

The Ambassador stands expressionless and says "you cannot do this, this will mean war."

The President puts on his best poker face, steps closely toward the Ambassador looks him directly in the eye and says "bring it. You petty childish people have played your hate game long enough. It ends here, now, because I have the power to make it so. The men who built copies of our stealth drone are all dead. I doubt if you can reproduce it any time soon. In the mean time I can rain down stealth drones, bombs and cruise missiles all day upon your head without one loss of American life, but you will not fare so well. If you want to continue your terrorist ideology and attacks I will step on you. It ends now. I'm in charge." The President steps back, takes a long breath, "Of course all this unpleasantness can be avoided by you if you wish."

"What do you mean" inquires the Ambassador.

"I mean if you dismantle your nuclear program and allow UN inspectors unrestricted access plus make a formal announcement that Israel is a welcome and trusted partner in the Middle East to which you intend to enter full diplomatic relations with plus cease sponsoring all terrorist operations then all this can be avoided. But we will be watching you closely and I will retain these documents and if you step back from this new understanding at any time I assure you we will take over.

The Ambassador stares at the President then Drops his head. "I will convey these latest developments to my people." The Iranian Ambassador collects his things turns and leaves.

"Mr. President you did it" applauds Secretary Lomax as the others all cheer and shake hands. "I think you finally got their attention" he says.

The President beaming with delight calmly remarks "I think their fear of us taking over may just be greater than their hate for each other and they may just rather have the Jews living there than us."

A round of laughter fills the room. "Either way" he adds "we may just have found peace in the region and it didn't cost us anything, no increase to the national debt and no loss of American life."

The President turns once again to General Kincaid "General I can't thank you enough for pulling a rabbit out of the hat. All I can say is this team of yours and the impossible are one and the same. They might be just the thing to keep in our back pocket. You never know when a situation may arise that requires the impossible. Let me get back to you on that."

"Yes sir Mr. President always here to help" responds the General.

"By the way" resumes the President "where is Jack I want to thank him myself on behalf of the country."

Bishop opens the door to the hallway and finding Jack gone returns and says "he was sleeping on the couch a moment ago but now he's gone."

"Where could he have gone?" the President wonders.

EPILOG
Wickenburg, Arizona

Anxious to get home and rest from his ordeal of the past few months Jack books a commercial flight back home from DC. Following an hour layover in Chicago he catches a connecting flight to Phoenix after calling Raul and Jennifer letting them know when he'll be back. Still strongly committed to the defense of his nation and content with his business, home life and his new relationship with Jennifer he wonders if he would ever get involved and do it all again. Finally arriving home Jack rents a car and drives out to his ranch home. Entering his driveway he notices a number of cars parked out back by the barn. As he pulls closer Raul, Sherry and all the tech people who helped the cause; Jason, Chester, Mitch including Jennifer White pour out of the house to greet Jack amid an abundance of cheers, hugs and slaps on the back.

They all walk Jack back to the house where Sherry has cookies, sandwiches and punch for everyone. A special cooler contains Pacifica Jack's favorite cold beer just waiting for him and Raul. They all gather around to toast Jack for pulling off the mission and to welcome him home. The celebration was just as much an excuse by the group to let loose finally of the tension that built up during the ordeal of the past few months as it was to welcome Jack and Raul home once again.

As the mariachi music blares and the laughter continues Jason pulls Jack aside "Hey Jack I've finished going through all of Sayid's and Azzir's emails dating back quite away and it appears Sayid WAS trying to plan an attack on either the Super Bowl, New Year' Eve in Times Square or the New York Stock Exchange. Evidently Azzir hijacked the operation for his own twisted desires."

Jack thinks for a moment. "That would explain the 10 extra dead men at the Tampico hanger, Azzir must have killed off security men loyal to Sayid so he would be free to wage his own war, one that would be blamed on Iran because of the uranium which would take much of the heat off of him. But I think more than that was hijacked. I think an entire religion has been hijacked by a shadow group destined for world domination."

With the gayety and warm comradery continuing Jack steps back to admire the group of talented dedicated men and women. Of all his years in the service never had he had a finer group to work with as these. Moved by their outpouring of dedication and affection for him, Jack is convinced they are the greatest collection of friends anyone can have. In a way he was sorry to see it all end.

Jack takes a moment to thank each one for their help and contribution to the task of bringing down a terrorist group and preventing a deadly attack on America and shares from his heart his admiration for each and every one.

As the party continues and drinks flow Jack finally corners Raul "I've been meaning to ask you what happened to all of Azzir's money?"

With a twinkle in his eye and a big grin Raul says "come I will show you. Everyone come outside I have a surprise for all of you."

With a dubious expression on his face Jack follows the rest of the team outside to where Raul has waiting a large van suitable to carrying everyone. Loading up the van with the happy crowd Raul drives 30 miles northwest of Wickenburg.

"Hey Raul if this is a surprise party I think you forgot the beer" comments Jack. "By the way where are we going there are no Mexican restaurants out this way."

Raul continues driving across the barren desert until he reaches a lone construction trailer up against the Harcuvar Mountains.

"Raul I know you've wanted to open a restaurant and if this is your restaurant it looks a little small and I doubt if clientele can see it from the road" Jack says kiddingly.

As they all pile out of the van Raul gathers them in a circle before explaining "With the money Azzir gratefully donated I purchased 1280 acres of land and I have architects and engineers working on designing and building your new security company complete with a 10,000 square foot main office building with conference rooms and a state of the art computer and communication center plus outbuildings for residences, motor pool, armory, indoor and outdoor shooting range, helicopter landing pad and landing strip with hangers. All purchased and constructed for Jack to start his private security company with me of course as second in command."

"But I thought you had your fill of shooting and looting besides what about that Mexican restaurant you always wanted to build?" queries Jack.

"Mon-Capitan, it is more important for the world to be made safe than for another Mexican restaurant" Raul answers.

They all laugh as Jack puts arm around his good friend of many years.

Jack steps back "but we can't do it all. We are going to need help from DOD, FBI, NSA, satellite surveillance, an outstanding tech staff, aircraft, ordinance and equipment civilians are not permitted to buy much less own plus much more".

Raul says "you already have the team. They are right here and all have agreed to sign on."

"But how are we going to acquiring the weapons and equipment?" asks Jack.

At that moment Bishop drives up and ambers over and says "Jack you just let me take care of that. The President was so impressed by you and our team he has granted funding to continue working on special assignments for him. What do you say?"

"I don't know" Jack says as he squints and turns his head slightly "you still owe me a car and my consultant's fee for the last job."

They all begin to laugh again and gather around Jack and Raul. Jennifer standing next to Jack takes his hand in hers and looks up at him and nods her head in full approval and says "yes."

Raul, lifting both hands into the air hollers "yahoo. So what are we going to call ourselves?"

As Jack gives Jennifer a hug and a kiss he says "we'll think of something we always do."

THE END